"**I**t's you," she whispered softly and beckoned him forward.

"I apologize, miss, but I didn't hear what you said." He leaned toward her. "Is there something I can do to assist you?"

She gestured for him to come closer still.

It was wicked, what she was about to do, but she had to be sure. She had to know he was the right man. And there was only one way to truly know.

He turned his head, so that his ear was just above her mouth. "Yes?"

"I assure you I am quite well, sir," she whispered into his ear, "but there is indeed something you can do for me."

She didn't wait for him to respond. Ivy shoved her fingers through his thick hair and turned his face to her. Peering deeply into his eyes, she pressed her mouth to his, startling him. She immediately felt his fingers curl firmly around her wrist, and yet he didn't pull away.

Instead, his lips moved over her, making her yield to his own kiss . . .

By Kathryn Caskie

THE MOST WICKED OF SINS
TO SIN WITH A STRANGER
HOW TO PROPOSE TO A PRINCE
HOW TO ENGAGE AN EARL
HOW TO SEDUCE A DUKE

Coming Soon

THE DUKE'S NIGHT OF SIN

KATHRYN CASKIE

THE MOST WICKED OF SINS

AVON

An Imprint of HarperCollinsPublishers

This is a work of fiction. Names, characters, places, and incidents are products of the author's imagination or are used fictitiously and are not to be construed as real. Any resemblance to actual events, locales, organizations, or persons, living or dead, is entirely coincidental.

AVON BOOKS
An Imprint of HarperCollins*Publishers*
10 East 53rd Street
New York, New York 10022-5299

Copyright © 2009 by Kathryn Caskie
Excerpt from *The Duke's Night of Sin* copyright © 2010 by Kathryn Caskie
Excerpts from *With Seduction in Mind* copyright © 2009 by Laura Lee Guhrke; *The Most Wicked of Sins* copyright © 2009 by Kathryn Caskie; *Captive of Sin* copyright © 2009 by Anna Campbell; *True Confessions* copyright © 2001 by Rachel Gibson
ISBN 978-0-06-149101-6
www.avonromance.com

First Avon Books paperback printing: October 2009

Avon Trademark Reg. U.S. Pat. Off. and in Other Countries, Marca Registrada, Hecho en U.S.A.
HarperCollins® is a registered trademark of HarperCollins Publishers.

Printed in the U.S.A.

10 9 8 7 6 5 4 3 2 1

For Dave,
my kilted hero.

Acknowledgments

My deepest thanks and appreciation to my wickedly smart agent, Jenny Bent; my wickedly insightful editor, Lucia Macro; my wickedly clever research assistant, Franzeca Drouin; and my wickedly organized personal assistant, Kim Castillo, whose wholehearted support and hard work allowed me to have wicked fun writing this book.

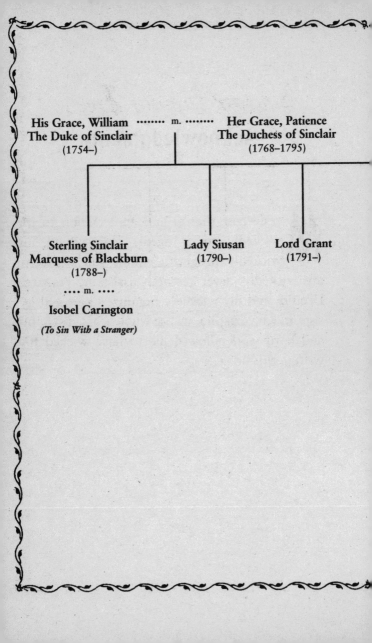

His Grace, William
The Duke of Sinclair
(1754–)

········ m. ········

Her Grace, Patience
The Duchess of Sinclair
(1768–1795)

Sterling Sinclair
Marquess of Blackburn
(1788–)

···· m. ····

Isobel Carington

(To Sin With a Stranger)

Lady Siusan
(1790–)

Lord Grant
(1791–)

Sinclair Family Tree

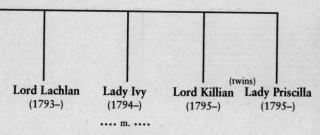

Lord Lachlan	Lady Ivy	Lord Killian	(twins) Lady Priscilla
(1793–)	(1794–)	(1795–)	(1795–)

···· m. ····

Dominic Sheridan
Marquess of Counterton
(The Most Wicked of Sins)

Prologue

July 30, 1816
The Sinclair residence
No. 1 Grosvenor Square, London

The day had begun like any other.

Lady Ivy Sinclair rose at noon for breakfast, still weary from a late-night gala at Covent Garden. She spread the *Times* out upon the dining table and giggled with her sisters, Siusan and Priscilla, over the outrageous and much-exaggerated Society gossip in the weekly *on dit* column.

And when Poplin, one of only two servants in the household, set a sterling salver before her, Ivy sorted through the disappointingly few invitations and letters their family had received. She sipped weak, twice-strained tea, setting the more interesting of the invitations to her right as she munched on a wedge of toasted stale bread dabbed with a lick of comb honey.

Aye, as far as Ivy was concerned, the day had been entirely unremarkable. Perhaps even a bit mundane.

Until, that is, she broke the crimson wax wafer and released from its folds a letter from Scotland—one that would change her life forever. Of course, she didn't know this for certain at the time, though the first sentence sent an unmistakable torrent of panic through her body.

"Of late, ye, Ivy, more so than any of my other children, have brought shame upon the Sinclair name."

Oh God. Her eyelids snapped high. Each word had very nearly been carved into the foolscap, and Ivy recognized the angry, heavily inked script as belonging to the Duke of Sinclair, her father.

Her vision blurred with a rush of tears, and her hands went cold as she raised the foolscap closer to her eyes.

"Will anything ever be enough for ye, or will ye continue to spend yer life peering hungrily over yer neighbor's fence, coveting her life, her possessions, wishing her ill?"

She lifted the cup of tea to her lips to stifle the whimper rising in her throat, but her hand began trembling fiercely, forcing her to return the cup clattering to its dish.

"I willna accept yer spoiled behavior any longer. Reform at once. Raise yerself up as a true example of decorum and respectability. Become a lady deserving of yer Lord Tinsdale's admiration and standards—worthy of his troth instead of merely his amusement. Earn the respect the Sinclair name deserves—or when I return to London next month, ye will be regret it."

Ivy's jaw fell open, and the whimper she had tried to contain suddenly slipped from her mouth. Even in his brevity, her father had made his expectations— and his harsh penalties for not meeting them— perfectly clear.

"Siusan." Ivy jerked her head up to her elder sister. Though she tried to school her voice, to sound nonchalant, Ivy's words sounded thick with alarm, and this frightened her.

Siusan's elbows were propped upon the table, her chin resting wearily in her palms. "I already told you. No, to the Cockburn tea. Aye, to the White-hall picnic." Her eyelids looked heavy, and she forcibly blinked her pale blue eyes. Her sigh made clear her boredom as she blew away a wisp of dark hair that had become ensnared in her thick lashes.

"N-not that." Ivy tucked a lock of copper hair

behind her ear and swallowed, hoping the extra moment would allow her to rein in her nerves. "*This.*" She started to pass the letter to Siusan, but Priscilla, the youngest of the Sinclair siblings, playfully snatched it from her hand and began to read.

"It's from Da!" Priscilla leaped to her feet the moment she made the realization. Her vivid blue eyes immediately began shifting wildly from left to right as she read the letter.

Siusan's eyes widened with worry, and she slowly straightened her spine. She reached out and took Ivy's hand and squeezed it. "What is it? The expression on your face is . . . well, positively ghastly." She squinted slightly. "Why, those are tears in your eyes!"

Ivy sucked her lips into the seam of her mouth for several seconds before speaking. Blood seemed to drain from the rest of her body and into her restless legs. She came to her feet, unable to sit for a moment longer. "Tell me true, Siusan. Do you think it possible to convince Lord Tinsdale to offer for me—within a month?" She paced nervously back and forth behind Siusan's chair.

"*A month?*" Siusan sat up straight in her chair and swiveled to look at her. "I was under the impression you had grown bored with him."

Ivy's feet stilled, and she stared at Siusan, astounded by the comment. "Bored? You could not be farther from the mark. He has my full attention and rightly so. He is a good man, titled and respectable. Why, Da commented upon Tinsdale's upstanding nature when he met the family at Sterling's wedding."

Siusan tilted her head and studied Ivy. "Hmm."

"You haven't answered me. Do you think it possible to secure an offer from him within a month?" Ivy asked, clutching at Siusan's hand. "*Please.* Answer me."

"All right," Siusan replied, wrenching her hand away from Ivy. "Tinsdale may be somewhat smitten with you, I'll concede that, but he's hardly at the point of getting leg-shackled. A month, Ivy? Are you completely mad?"

Priscilla slowly lifted her gaze from the letter. "No, Su, she's not." She rushed to Siusan and thrust the letter at her. "One month. It's all the time she has." She pointed at the letter. "I daresay there is no misunderstanding Da's meaning. Read it!"

Siusan lowered her gaze to the foolscap and quickly read down its length.

Ivy again resumed pacing the short distance behind Siusan's chair. "I have one month to change my life, Su. If I fail, Da will surely keep the promise he made the night he forced us from our home

for . . . this pauper's existence in London." Tears
welled up anew in Ivy's eyes, "And I'll be disin-
herited . . . and cast from this very house to the
workhouse."

Siusan dropped the letter on the table as she rose,
grabbing Ivy and hugging her tightly to her. "Dinna
fash, Ivy. It willna come to that. I promise."

Ivy took Siusan's shoulders and leaned away
from her. Through her tears, she peered at Siusan,
then at Priscilla too. "How can you make such a
promise?"

Her sisters exchanged meaningful glances, then
Siusan took Ivy's chin in her palm and tilted it
upward, not allowing her to look away. "Because
we will do whatever we must to prevent this, Ivy.
Anything we must to see Tinsdale's ring upon your
finger," Siusan said.

"Anything?" Ivy's voice broke.

Priscilla nodded in agreement. "Aye, Ivy—*anything*.
You have our promises."

Chapter 1

Of the seven deadly sins, only envy is no fun at all.
Joseph Epstein

August 1816
Almack's Assembly Rooms
London

ady Ivy Sinclair's moss-hued eyes were flecked with gold, and quite honestly closer to hazel in color, but she felt the green-eyed monster rising within her just the same.

Her gloved fingers nervously clenched around her fan's ivory handle as she narrowed her gaze at the Irish beauty who had just entered the assembly room and was now entirely surrounded by a rush of adoring gentlemen. The same doting cluster of men that had been lavishing admiration on *her* only a week before.

Blast! *She's not supposed to be here. Not tonight! She could ruin everything.*

Fretfully, Ivy's gaze tore through the ring of men encircling the ebony-haired miss before scanning the rest of the assembly room. She couldn't risk it. She had to find him before he saw Miss Fiona Feeney. *Och, where is he?*

And then she spied him emerging from the guests packed around a refreshment table. Her worry lifted away. There he was, her own Viscount Tinsdale . . . and he was headed back to her.

His thick golden eyebrows were drawn toward the bridge of his nose in a scowl. Struggling to balance the contents of two crystals of lemonade, he was attempting to squeeze his way between two hefty gentlemen who appeared to be in the midst of a heated discussion. She could see that Tinsdale's lips were moving as well, but the men clearly didn't notice him or realize his predicament.

Just then, a gourd-shaped woman with a feather-trimmed crimson turban backed straight into Tinsdale. He lurched forward a step. A flourish of liquid sprang up from one of the glasses and licked his face.

Ivy clapped her gloved hands to her mouth and concealed an amused grin as the viscount's left eyelid fluttered. His full, pale lips puckered as he frantically shook his head to rid himself of the drops coursing down his cheeks. He turned briefly and appeared to pardon himself to no one in particular before gauging his path anew.

Ivy giggled softly. He was so very polite. And completely ridiculous . . . no . . . *adorable* in his efforts to remain, at all times, the consummate gentleman. Why, she could learn a great deal from Tinsdale if she only allowed herself. And she would.

She had no other choice. After all, she had only twenty-seven days before her father returned to London. Her mouth became dry from nerves just thinking about it. Ivy focused again on Tinsdale.

Now raising both glasses high over his head, Tinsdale was taking advantage of a momentary gap between the two men. He edged his narrow hips between them, lest, Ivy decided, he was bumped and splashed again.

Ivy raised her chin proudly. She flashed a glance at Miss Feeney, who was idly tugging at one of the lace sleeves of her gown, seeming to ignore the three gentlemen who appeared to be speaking to her at the same time. The edges of Ivy's lips gave a little upward triumphant jerk. *Ha! Perhaps not every man is as enamored with you as you'd like to believe.*

Aye, Ivy realized that this week she might no longer be the undisputed toast of the *ton,* but Society's taste was as fickle as that of a miss just out for her first Season.

She was confident that the *ton* would soon become bored with Miss Fiona Feeney. They'd no longer find her quips quite so clever, or her delicate features so perfect. It was only a matter of time.

Ivy was being a goose, worrying about her own popularity at all. What did it matter?

Inevitably, London Society would return their favor to her. She broadened her smile and raised a single eyebrow. After all, she was always entertaining, witty, and pretty enough to draw male eyes—without eliciting even a modicum of jealousy from the women of London.

An abrupt shift in Lord Tinsdale's direction snared Ivy's attention. *Hmm.* Likely just lost sight of me. Nothing to fret over. His eyes are probably still stinging with lemonade.

But he was still moving in the wrong direction. An anxious ache started to build in her middle. She rose on her toes, ever so slightly.

It would not do for anyone to think she was even

the least bit concerned that Tinsdale would not return to her.

Och, he canna see me, that's all, she told herself. *Nothing more.*

Unlike the members of the Sinclair family, Tinsdale had not been blessed with commanding stature. But it hardly mattered. Everything else about him was absolutely perfect.

Aye, the viscount's impeccable bloodline, coupled with his most sensible, frugal, and agreeable nature, met every single requirement her father demanded in a potential husband for Ivy. Her father informed her of this within moments of meeting Tinsdale and his family during his first visit to London not long ago.

He had made sure that Ivy understood that her course was quite clear. And it was. Marry Viscount Tinsdale, and, for certain, her father would see how responsible and respectable she had at last become—and he would forgive her. He would welcome her back into the Sinclair family, just as he had done with her brother Sterling only two months ago.

It was only a matter of time until she saw their betrothal announcement published in the *Morning Post*.

Only, it had to be soon. She couldn't live like a

pauper scraping for tuppence while pretending she was a wealthy heiress for much longer. Neither she, nor her cast-out brothers and sisters, had the funds to carry on the ruse indefinitely. Time was fast running out.

No matter, though. Ivy was fairly certain that her increasingly pointed hints—that she would accept Tinsdale—had at last fallen on eager ears. She hadn't been so coy this eve about her wish to marry him, and this time she was sure he finally understood her, for the size of his eyes doubled by time she had finished speaking.

Aye, soon, he would request an interview with her older brother to ask for her hand in marriage. Perhaps . . . as soon as *tonight*.

Och, now where was he going?

Blast! I'm over here. A frustrated squeal slipped through her lips. Dozens of pale-hued fans, flapping in the hot air like butterfly wings, gradually stilled as ladies in heavy silks and gentlemen in dark coats turned to look at her.

Ivy didn't dare call out to Tinsdale, despite her worry, for she knew that would mark her as common. So she simply raised her chin higher so that her face might be visible to him over the heads of the other guests.

Her scheme seemed to work for he met her gaze

. . . for a moment. She was sure of it. But Tinsdale seemed to be trying to pretend that he had not seen her.

It was all quite confusing. Damned odd, actually—until she saw where his intended course had led him.

No. Oh, God, no. He cannot have chosen her company over mine. No. Please, no. We are meant to be married!

Ivy's chin dropped to her chest, and a hard lump fixed itself inside of her throat.

As if it was not humiliating enough to be stripped of her celebrity amongst the gentlemen of the *ton*—now her own Viscount Tinsdale was hovering at Miss Feeney's side. Lud, he was even giving the lass *her* lemonade. He was acting entirely besotted.

At that very moment, Ivy's older sister, who was wearing the most pitiful of expressions on her pretty face, came to stand beside her. "I wish to leave. Shall we locate Grant and away? I fear Lachlan isn't about to leave just yet. Not while he's ringed by a circle of infatuated misses."

A growl pressed between Ivy's clenched teeth. "Och, I can't bear it, Siusan. I simply can't." She swiped the corner of her eyes with her knuckles and desperately swallowed back her despair.

"Nor can I. The heat is unbearable this night."

Siusan futilely swiped her cutwork fan through the thick, humid air.

Ivy dragged in a deep breath and glared off in Miss Feeney's direction, not quite hearing what her sister had said—nor caring. Her situation was far more dire than whatever Siusan was whining about. "What say you, Su, do you think Lady Jersey would hear of it if I took Miss Feeney into the withdrawing room and throttled her?" She nodded toward the Irish lass, shifting her wilting sister's attention to the doorway. "I believe I have just cause—*theft*."

"What? Oh, lud, you mean *her*." Siusan's eyes rolled an exasperated circle in their sockets. "Ivy, if you are serious about accepting the viscount's offer—*should you actually convince him to make one*—then for god sakes do something about it instead of allowing the chit to steal him away. You haven't much time as it is."

"What do you suggest I do?" Ivy turned her body toward Siusan, but her head remained facing the doors leading to the staircase. She was not about to let Miss Feeney and Tinsdale stray from her sight.

"I haven't a notion. It is impossible to think in this infernal heat." A sprinkling of perspiration beaded along Siusan's brow, and she drew as deep a breath as she could. "Gads, my chemise is positively sticking to my skin." She gripped Ivy's wrist and tugged until she had her attention. "Let us away and think about it outside in the fresh air. Our thoughts will be much clearer."

Ivy glanced across the assembly room toward the refreshment table, where she immediately saw her brother Grant, who towered above the other men. As if he felt her notice, he turned and looked her way, allowing Ivy to capture his gaze.

She lifted her chin, silently summoning him, before returning her gaze to Siusan. "You go. Grant is coming now. I am sure he will happily leave the assembly room and escort you home. I will stay here with Lachlan. I cannot leave just yet anyway. Not until I know Lord Tinsdale's heart is still mine to claim."

Grant sidled up to his sisters. "I cannot tell you how relieved I am that you finally wish to leave. I have been basting in my waistcoat and coat for more than an hour, and I am certain I am tender through and through by now. Come, shall we away?"

Siusan waved her fan before Grant, urging a swish of heated air over his face. "Can't."

He grimaced and lowered his tone. "Why the hell not?" Grant batted Siusan's fan away.

Siusan fashioned an overwrought sigh. "Bec

Ivy will not leave until she is certain of the viscount's affections—and I promised to help her." She nodded toward the doorway, where Lord Tinsdale stood with the enchanting Miss Fiona Feeney.

"Of all the bleeding nonsense, Ivy," Grant huffed. "We shall be here *forever* because even I can see that Tinsdale's attentions have strayed from you. Why, he's entirely taken with *her*."

Ivy twisted a tendril of her copper hair in her agitation. Grant had the right of it. How could she possibly compete with Miss Feeney?

Her own hair was practically the color of a hothouse orange, while the Irish lass's was like the sky at midnight. Ivy was taller than most Englishmen, and though she possessed the sort of curves that drew gentlemen's eyes, she was not a fragile bird of a creature, like Miss Feeney, built to fit perfectly into a man's embrace.

She hadn't a chance.

"You're right." Ivy's eyes began to well with tears. "I can't compete with her for Tinsdale's affections. What will I do now?"

Grant offered up an arm to each of his sisters. "Och, dinna fret over it. You don't need to. All you need to do is find a gentleman to compete with Tinsdale . . . for *hers*."

"Compete . . . for *her* affections." Suddenly, a jolt

coursed throughout the entirety of Ivy's body and her eyes widened, the tears inside them instantly receding.

Siusan chuckled at Grant's joke, then took his proffered arm and turned to leave.

Ivy didn't budge. Her thoughts were moving too fast.

Her brother and sister stopped. Siusan sighed as if she already knew the answer to the question she was about to ask. "Aren't you coming?"

"No, I'm not." Ivy spun around, her flame-licked hair whirling around her like a cape as she turned this way and that, scanning the assembly room most earnestly.

"Ivy, what are you doing?" Grant lowered his head as if sensing defeat already. "Come, let us leave. *Please*."

"Please, I beg you both, go on ahead without me." Ivy rose onto the tips of her toes and surveyed the shifting sea of dark coats. "I think I would rather stay here for a little longer."

Siusan groaned. "Now you've done it, Grant."

"What are you going on about?" he protested. "I've done nothing."

"Aye, you have. You've given me the answer." Ivy set her hand on Grant's shoulder and leaned up to press a grateful kiss upon his cheek.

"What do you mean?" he asked.

Ivy grinned up at him. "If I can't compete with Miss Feeney, then I will simply find the perfect gentleman to compete with Lord Tinsdale—*for her.*"

Three days later
The Theater Royal Drury Lane

Lady Ivy Sinclair silently lowered the carriage window, then pressed back against the seat cushion, concealing herself from passersby in the inky shadows of the cab. Outside, the carriage lanterns glowed in the darkness, their soft halos of light just reaching the stage door of The Theater Royal Drury Lane.

Come now, I know you are in there. Show yourself. Ivy shifted anxiously.

The play had ended nearly an hour past, and, since tonight marked the final performance, the actors were only now beginning to quit the theater.

Small clusters of boisterous merrymakers exited through the stage door and passed by the carriage. Ivy leaned forward and studied each of the actors as they emerged, watching, waiting for *him* to appear.

She felt confident that she would know *her* Marquess of Counterton the moment her eyes fell upon him. She knew with the same surety that he would be found here tonight. Her sister, Siusan, had glimpsed the perfect man for the job onstage only two evenings past.

Siusan didn't manage to gather his name, but she'd said he would stand out from the others. His height would set him head and shoulders apart from the other men. And, though she hadn't given much else in the way of describing him, Ivy was sure that those shoulders would be impossibly broad and as hard-muscled as his chest and his capable arms.

She smiled at the handsome image pinned in her mind.

The marquess's hair would be whisky-hued and wavy, with rakish wisps fringing his entirely-too-handsome face. His eyes would be the color of a moonlit sea at night.

She sighed. He would be the sort that would make a woman's gloved hand tingle when he took it and guided her through a dance. And when he gazed down at her, she would feel completely under his masculine control. He need do nothing more than raise a single eyebrow or lift the edges of his lips seductively, and she would be utterly powerless to refuse him. How admired and complete she would feel with such a perfect escort.

Aye, Ivy would know him by sight though they'd never met, but it would be his kiss that would identify him beyond all doubt.

Ivy sighed inwardly. The touch of his lips would be firm, a claiming sort of kiss, one that would reduce a woman's knees to melted wax, making her collapse into his embrace. Making her want to never leave his arms.

She sighed again and eagerly leaned closer to the open window. Her driver was muttering to the team, but then an explosion of laughter drowned out the sounds from the street. Ivy's pulse quickened as the departure of actors and patrons grew steadily.

The stage door was flung open again and again. He was coming, she knew it . . . it was only a matter of moments now. She bit into the flesh of her lower lip and chewed it in anticipation.

Then the stage door closed and, to her dismay, remained that way for several minutes. She grew more and more impatient.

As the moments passed, Ivy's stomach muscles began to tense, and after a minute more, the backs of her eyes began to sting.

No, no. He has to be here. He must be. He must.

Lud, she didn't have time to look anywhere else! The play had closed tonight.

She had to find the perfect actor, the perfect foil, willing to accept her coin to woo the Irish beauty away from the man Ivy might still marry.

Precious time was slipping away. Her future was evaporating.

Ivy's heart double-thudded in her chest, and she felt faint. She set an unsteady hand on the latch and flung the carriage door open. Lifting her silk skirts to her knees, she leaped down to the pavers and ran toward the stage door.

She lunged for it just as it opened. Suddenly, her skull exploded with pain. Flashes of light blotted out her vision. And then everything became black.

"Damn it all, answer me!" A deep voice cut into her consciousness, rousing her from the cocoon of darkness blanketing her. She could feel herself being lifted, then someone was shouting something about finding a physician.

She managed to flutter her lids open just as her coachman opened the door and she felt her back skim the seat cushion inside the carriage.

Blinking, she peered up at the dark silhouette of a large man leaning over her. He was definitely not her coachman.

"Oh, thank God, you are awake. I thought I killed you when I crushed your head with the door." He leaned back then, just enough that a flicker of light touched his visage.

Ivy gasped at the sight of him.

He shoved his bronze hair back away from eyes that looked almost black in the dimness of the carriage light. A cleft marked the center of his chin, and his angular jaw was defined by a dark sprinkling of stubble. His full lips parted in a relieved smile.

There was a distinct fluttering in Ivy's middle.

It was *him*. The perfect man . . . for the position.

"It's *you*," she whispered softly.

"I apologize, miss, but I didn't hear what you said." He leaned toward her. "Is there something more I can do to assist you?"

Ivy nodded and feebly beckoned him forward. He moved fully back inside the cab and sat next to her as she lay across the bench.

She gestured for him to come closer still.

It was wicked, what she was about to do, but she had to be sure. She had to know he was the right man. And there was only one way to truly know.

He turned his head, so that his ear was just above her mouth. "Yes?"

"I assure you that I am quite well, sir," she whispered into his ear, "but there is indeed something you can do for me."

She didn't wait for him to respond. Ivy shoved her fingers through his thick hair and turned his face to her. Peering deeply into his eyes, she pressed her mouth to his, startling him. She immediately felt his fingers curl firmly around her wrist, and yet he didn't pull away.

Instead, his lips moved over hers, making her yield to his own kiss. His mouth was warm and tasted faintly of brandy, and his lips parted slightly as he masterfully claimed her with his kiss.

Her heart pounded, and her sudden breathlessness blocked out the sounds of carriages, whinnying horses, and theater patrons calling to their drivers on the street.

His tongue slid slowly along her top lip, somehow making her feel impossible things lower down. Then he nipped at her throbbing bottom lip before urging her mouth wider and exploring the soft flesh inside with his probing tongue.

Hesitantly, she moved her tongue forward until it slid along his. At the moment their tongues touched, a soft groan welled up from the back of his throat, and a surge of excitement shot through her.

Already she felt the tug of surrender. Of wanting to give herself over to the passion he tapped within her.

And then—as if he knew what he made her feel, made her want—he suddenly pulled back from her.

She peered up at him through drowsy eyes.

"I fear, my lady, that you mistake me for someone else," he said, not looking the least bit disappointed or astounded by what she had done.

"No," Ivy replied, "no mistake." She wriggled, pulling herself to sit upright. "You are exactly who I thought you were."

"I beg your pardon, but I know we have never met. I am quite certain I would remember meeting *you*."

Ivy smiled at him. How perfect he was. How absolutely perfect. "I am Lady Ivy Sinclair."

He peered back at her most casually, as if waiting for her to say something more.

How curious. He didn't react at all to the mention of the Sinclair name. Could it be he truly did not know she was one of the scandalous Seven Deadly Sins?

"I am—" he began, but Ivy raised her hand, abruptly silencing him. He raised a quizzical eyebrow.

Ivy straightened her back and looked quite earnestly into his eyes. "You are the Marquess of Counterton . . . or rather you will be, if you accept my offer."

Chapter 2

Those who are most distrustful of themselves are most envious of others.

William Hazlitt

Very late that same evening
Mr. Felix Dupré's residence
23 Davies Street

Nick leaned back into the terribly worn yet surprisingly comfortable armchair, and tipped a thick glass of brandy to his lips. Even through the earthy peaty notes of the spirits, he could still taste the flame-locked beauty's honeyed kiss. He ran his tongue across his lower lip and savored the sweetness.

His lips still throbbed, and Nick amusedly wondered if in the morning he would awake to find them mottled blue from the bruising force of her yanking his mouth down to hers.

What an astonishing evening it had been. He scratched his temple and ran his fingers through his thick hair. He honestly didn't know what to make of what had happened, for the events had been so entirely unexpected. He'd left the calm of Lincolnshire, and after only one night in Town, he'd been passionately kissed by a woman he'd never met— and offered an acting role—impersonating the Marquess of Counterton, no less.

Damn. If she was not entirely mad, which he hadn't quite ruled out yet, she was at the very least completely audacious. Though, as he thought about it a little longer, Nick realized he wasn't entirely convinced of that either. How could he be? This was London, after all, not Averly.

He had to consider the possibility that what would be labeled insolent and reckless behavior in the sleepy hamlet where he'd lived nearly his entire life might pass for usual outside The Theater Royal Drury Lane in London. It was possible.

But that kiss, well, that he was sure about. That kiss sent both his body and mind spinning like never before. It had been bloody wonderful. Perhaps it was the surprise of it. Or, that for the first time in his life a woman had taken the initiative in seduction instead of him.

Whatever the reason for his very visceral reaction to the kiss, even the slightest chance of repeating it had been enough for him to agree to meet the Scottish vixen again to discuss her outrageous and certainly highly illegal *business arrangement*.

A jingling of keys outside the front door, then a thud followed by a ribbon of colorful curses, prompted Nick begrudgingly to his feet and from the comfort of the library for the entryway. Reaching out his hand, he twisted the lock and pressed down the tarnished brass latch.

His cousin, Mr. Felix Dupré, who had obviously been leaning against the door to better aim his key, fell inside.

"Oh, there you are, Nicky," Felix slurred. The smell of rum punch saturated his cousin's breath and wafted through the entry hall. "You never showed at the closing gala. Missed a damned good party, you know. I wanted to introduce you around. Everyone would be so impressed to learn we are . . ." Felix clapped his hand to his forehead. "What are we to each other again?"

"Our mothers were sisters."

Felix stared blankly at him, his eyes glazed over from drink. "So, we are . . . remind me, will you?"

"We're cousins." Nick leaned back against the wall and eyed Felix. In truth, Felix really was more of a brother to Nick. His mother had very nearly raised Felix when her sister had taken ill.

Felix was by far the youngest and certainly most unconventional of the three Dupré sons. While his older brothers, Frederick and Phillip, made their father infinitely proud—one managing the tenants and the estate, the other expanding the Dupré imports business (with each somehow finding the time to marry and sire sons of his own)—Felix possessed a more colorful nature. As a child, he had never excelled at ciphers like Phillip or displayed a talent for sports like Frederick. And though his mother clapped her hands, and from her sickbed, encouraged Felix's singing, dancing, poetry, and flair for the dramatic, his father was openly disgusted and humiliated by it.

In fact, had Felix not escaped on a mail coach for London when he had, word within the family was that he would have been forcefully packed off to his aged uncle's remote parish outside Inverness to be trained for a life in the Church.

"I apologize for not meeting you after the performance," Nick admitted, "but I had . . . a superior offer. Sorry, coz."

Felix eyed Nick quizzically for some moments,

then sighed and walked to the dust-streaked table beneath the entry-hall mirror, where he deposited his hat, gloves, and key. "A better offer. Oh, I see." He whisked a handkerchief with an exasperated flourish, strode purposively up to Nick, and dabbed his mouth before he could protest. "You still have a bit of lip paint on your mouth." He pressed the rose-smudged linen into Nick's hand.

He glanced to Felix, and the edge of his lips twitched upward. He reached out for the hand-kerchief and swiped it over Felix's thin lips. "So do you." He arched an eyebrow and grinned as he shoved the cloth back at his cousin.

"Really?" Felix hurried to the wall mirror and, given the dimness of the room, moved close enough to touch his narrow nose to the mirror's glass to see the offending smear. "Hardly what you think, cousin. It's only stage paint."

Nick chuckled and cocked an eyebrow. "Oh, I had an inkling it might be just that."

Felix leaned back from the mirror and whirled around. "I cannot believe that my friends let me walk out on the street like this—and attend the gala as well."

"I am sure they simply didn't notice. Hardly vis-ible." Nick rolled off the wall drowsily, banging his shoulder on the doorjamb as he headed back into the library—or what might have been one had there been any books instead of a litter of newspapers and empty wine bottles on the dust-frosted shelves.

Felix surveyed his face, then wiped away a smudge of white from beneath his ear, tossed the crumpled linen onto the tabletop, and hurried in behind his cousin.

Nick eased his head back against the solid-backed armchair and sighed. "You know, I was sure I would dislike London."

Felix's hand hovered indecisively over the open decanter of brandy before snatching up the dark bottle beside it and pouring himself some port. He sat on the edge of the chair directly across from Nick, carefully resting the foot of his glass atop his yellow Cossack trousers.

Not surprisingly, while the house was nearly devoid of comforts, Felix was dressed impeccably, if rather flamboyantly, in keeping with his exuberant nature.

"I know you have your reservations about Town." Felix exhaled, expelling a cloud of port wine fumes into the library now as well. "You've said so as much twenty-two times since you arrived yesterday. You prefer the moors. The chalk hills are your world—but London is mine."

As something seemed to occur to him, Felix quieted suddenly. then drew his lips into his mouth as if he was trying to stave off a sob. His chin wobbled. "Nicky, I cannot possibly tell you how it touched my heart to have you come all the distance to London for my performance in 'Fortune's Frolic.' I know the journey was a long one. But thank you, dear cousin. Thank you." He sniffled.

"Oh, come now, man. You needn't thank me for anything. It was not a difficult thing at all. Had to come to London sooner or later anyway. Instead of stirring up the staff, I just came alone by coach so I could stay with you. Less bother. I still haven't gotten used to servants buzzing about me nowadays." Nick gave his sotted cousin a warm smile. "Besides, you know I would not have missed seeing your first performance in a leading role."

Felix swallowed deeply. "I do know, Nicky. I do. You have always been at my side when I needed you." His large dark eyes seemed to well and shimmer in the low candlelight of the library. "It was only for a night . . . the last night of a special summer performance series, but I was the lead—*the lead*—and I was brilliant. Everyone at the gala afterward told me so, everyone, and I would never be so rag-mannered as to disagree."

"Your performance was exceptionally memorable, Felix. The applause was deafening." A smile lifted Nick's lips. "Your mother would have been so proud."

"I know," Felix replied softly. "God rest her."

"And . . . I am sure had your father been witness to your talent, he would have—"

The light in Felix's eyes dissolved in that moment, and Nick realized he had erred by saying something that both of them might wish to, but never would, happen. Felix's father had made it abundantly clear that he would never condone his son's involvement in the theater.

Felix sipped his port in silence for a brief time before donning a mask of nonchalance. "Well, I am abundantly grateful that my favorite cousin was in the audience tonight. Though I believe you are my only cousin. Still, meant everything."

At the reminder of his own brother's passing, the draught of brandy Nick had just taken suddenly misdirected in his throat, the sting bringing on a hail of coughs.

"Oh God, Nick, I apologize. I-I didn't mean . . ." His mouth remained open, for once emptied of words.

Nick cleared his throat and swallowed deeply. He peered up at his cousin. He could see the distress in Felix's eyes. "It's been more than a year. There is no need to apologize."

"Yes, well"—Felix reached across and tapped Nick's knee—"at least let me express how dreadfully sorry I am that your portmanteau didn't make the journey. I tell you, I do not know how I would exist sans my clothing."

"I daresay, I cannot honestly understand how the mistake occurred. I had it with me at the White Hart Inn in Ware. I was sure the driver carried my bag inside when I arrived here, but it seems all I have now are the documents I had tucked in my coat pocket."

Felix shrugged his shoulders and sighed sympathetically.

"I suppose my portmanteau was left at the inn." He waved off any visible concern. "I sent word and am confident that my clothing will be returned to me within a day or two."

Felix excitedly lifted a hand and quieted Nick. "I will share my own wardrobe until you depart Monday next. Not a problem at all. Besides, you'd look like a Captain Queernabs in your country-squire garb. Hardly appropriate for Town. I tell you, not a woman in London would so much as glance your way dressed in your manner, Nicky."

Nick ran his finger across his lips, then glanced down at it. It still came away with the slightest smear of waxy color. "Really? Hmm. No, you may be correct. For I detected a lilting northern tone to Lady Ivy's words. She's certainly a Scot, not from London at all, which must be why she saw fit to overlook my rustic ensemble this night."

Felix shot to his feet, managing to level his glass just in time to prevent the port from showering the carpet. "Lady Ivy?" His eyes went impossibly wide. "*Sinclair?* You do not speak of Lady Ivy—of the Sinclair family. No, it's i-impossible."

"Sinclair. Yes. I do believe she mentioned that. I admit, however, I am not acquainted with the family, which oddly enough seemed to surprise her." Absently, Nick swirled his brandy around in his glass, peering down its vortex.

Felix stared at him, a racing whirl of thoughts plain in his wild eyes. "Wait right *here*," he said abruptly as one of those thoughts propelled him from his chair. "Do not move even the slightest." He rushed from the library, then returned with the mussed-up handkerchief. "Do not tell me that this lip rogue belonged to Lady Ivy." His hand shot out and dangled the linen before Nick's eyes.

He raised his eyebrows and gazed at the wrinkled cloth. "Well, some of this is yours . . ."

Felix groaned in frustration. His index finger jabbed at the mark on the lowermost corner of the linen. "This—the rose smudge."

Nick looked down his nose at it. "Well, the interior of the carriage was quite dark, making it impossible to identify the color for certain." He paused for a moment and made a closer assessment. "Yes, it must be the color that was upon Lady Ivy's lips. After all, I only kissed one woman this eve."

Felix flung himself backward into his chair. His eyes remained wide and fixed on Nick. "Good God, you really kissed her . . . in a carriage . . . in the dark."

"Actually, she kissed *me*. I only happily reciprocated."

Felix gasped at that.

Damn me. Why is he getting so stirred by this? "Didn't want to be rude, being new to Town and all." He grinned at Felix.

"Blast it, this isn't folly, Nicky. It's quite serious, you realize. You are as good as dead," Felix announced, quite matter-of-factly. "*Dead*, I tell you."

Nick arched his eyebrow disbelievingly. As always, his cousin was merely being overly dramatic. "What do you mean?"

"W-what do I mean? Only that she is a Sinclair—one of the *Seven Deadly Sins*, that is all."

Nick lifted his eyebrows and shook his head.

"Gads, Nick, have you not heard of them? Do

you not read any newspapers at all? London is ripe with gossip about the harum-scarum family—has been since the day they arrived. Seven brothers and sisters, so wayward and wild that they were cast out of Scotland . . . by their own father, a duke, no less, and told not to return until they mended their wicked ways."

"Is that so?" Amused, Nick raised his chin and awaited the Banbury tale.

Distracted by a thought, Felix stood and crossed to a pile of newspapers on one of the shelves. "Got to be here somewhere. They only arrived in the spring." He thumbed through the papers, opening each to the second page before passing his gaze over the inked columns. After another protracted minute he raised a copy of *Bell's Weekly Messenger*. "Here it is, the first mention of the Sinclairs, darlings of the *on dit* columns." Angling the newspaper to the candlelight he began to read.

Though little is known of the S. family, recently arrived in London, the seven are notorious within the ranks of Edinburgh Society and have been so since childhood. After the sudden death of their mother, it is reported that their grieving father allowed the children to run amok, earning the terrors the befitting label, the Seven Deadly Sins.

Pray, which sins might each of the seven Scots embody? Only time will tell, for the Season has just begun.

"Lady Ivy is one of the Seven Deadly Sins?" Nick fashioned a grin. "Which sin is assigned to the chit? Do tell me it's lust."

Suddenly, Felix appeared quite sober. "It doesn't matter at all. She's one of their lot, and that is all that should concern you."

"Oh, please, Felix. Stop this nonsense." Nick couldn't help but chuckle. Felix was acting completely thunderstruck.

"Please, please, do not make light of this," Felix implored. "I do not exaggerate when I tell you that she is not a woman to trifle with."

He hated to admit it to himself, but the more Felix warned him about Lady Ivy, the more intrigued Nick became. Just what was she about?

Felix looked increasingly alarmed. "Hear me well. Lady Ivy is not like any other women you've known, Nick. The Sinclairs do not think or act in the way anyone would expect."

"Ah, but she is beautiful." Nick closed his eyes for a moment, remembering the intensity in her eyes just before she pulled him tight and kissed him hard.

"Yes, yes, I am sure she is beautiful . . . all seven of them are said to be, but you must stay clear of her. If for no other reason than her brothers are huge—and bulging with muscles—and one, Lord Killian, I believe, is rumored to have killed a man who simply winked at his twin sister."

Nick laughed. He didn't believe any of this tara-diddle, though he was sure Felix did. His cousin had always been as gullible as he was eager to share any tasty morsel of scandal with anyone who would listen.

"Felix, I assure you, Lady Ivy is no threat and this is no Cheltenham tragedy." He exhaled, frustrated. "Still, I swear I shall take your advice into consideration—just not yet."

"But you must—"

Nick interrupted. "Lady Ivy and I have an engagement tomorrow evening to discuss a very *unusual* business proposition. And, this, dear cousin, is a discussion I would not miss for all the world."

Felix crinkled his nose. "A-a business arrangement? What sort?"

Nick exhaled slowly, and in his breath rode his refusal to answer.

"So, this business arrangement you must discuss with Lady Ivy . . . is it of a nature that will require you to extend your stay in London?"

He knew Felix was only casting a baited line for more information. It wasn't going to work. "No, no, Felix. My travel plans have not changed in the least. I will just ensure that my man has everything in order here in Town, then I will leave on Monday." He reached out his long arms and clapped Felix's shoulder. "Until then, I will reside with you, dear cousin." He rose and stretched. "But I will take you up on your offer to borrow some clothes until my portmanteau arrives. Our forms are close enough, eh?"

With a critical eye, Felix surveyed Nick. "Close, but you are a little broader in the shoulders. And then, your hands and feet are considerably larger." Felix wrinkled his nose. "Certainly you will agree that at the very least we will need to fill in any temporary gaps in your wardrobe. Gloves and shoes, perhaps. Tomorrow morning?" Felix waited until Nick hesitantly nodded, then rubbed his hands together gleefully. "I cannot wait to dress you . . . as a man of your stature should be dressed—instead of as a farmer."

Nick cringed slightly. "I will need something appropriate for dinner tomorrow night. Do you have anything that might suit . . . and fit?"

"Oh, yes, yes. Certainly." Felix bounced on his heels. "Where are we going?"

"Not *we*, Felix. Lady Ivy and I."

"If you refuse to avoid her, then at least introduce me. I know all about the Sinclairs." A smile curled Felix's lips, and his attention drifted. "Imagine, Mr. Felix Dupré meeting a real Sinclair." His eyes swerved to Nick. "My chums will be completely apple green with envy."

It was very late, and Felix would chatter on about the Sinclairs for the rest of the night if indulged in the slightest. Nick wasn't about to do that. He turned and lifted a candle to light a small chamber lamp. "I am afraid not, Felix," Nick said as he started up the stairs. "Not this time."

Felix came to stand at the bottom of the staircase and cupped the newel post. "That must have been quite a kiss."

Nick smiled to himself as he ascended the treads. "It was quite an offer."

Felix tossed the remaining port into the back of his throat. "Last chance. Care to share the details?"

Nick turned into the darkness of the first landing. "A gentleman never kisses and tells."

Chapter 3

*A human being, at the sight of another's pleasure
and possessions, would feel deficiency with more
bitterness.*

Schopenhauer

*Dawn, the next morning
Berkeley Square*

Ivy peered out of the carriage door at the regal
town house on the most-sought-after corner
of Berkeley Square. Lavender flowers jutted
through the wrought-iron fence that framed the
front of the house, their faint, sweet scent wafting
through the open window into the carriage.

Ivy wrinkled her nose. She didn't need to utter a
word to the family's manservant to let him know

she was disappointed. Aye, it was lovely, truth to tell, but . . . well, she had just expected more.

"Are you sure this is the one, Poplin?" She leaned her head a little farther out the window for a better look. "I daresay, 'tis only that I am paying a hundred pounds for one short month." She turned her head and looked at Poplin, awaiting his answer.

The elderly manservant, whose dubious services were included with the rent paid by the Duke of Sinclair for his children's temporary lodgings in Grosvenor Square, nodded his head warily. "When I inquired, the carpenter . . . umm . . . butler, Mr. Cheatlin, informed me that renovations are being undertaken both inside and out in preparation for the new marquess's arrival just before Christmastide. As long as your pretender, should you actually acquire one," he added in a barely audible tone, "has quit the residence within thirty days, you've naught to fear. After that, the house's interior will be entirely stripped and re-dressed for the new marquess. *Thirty days.* That's all the time you have. Not a day more."

Ivy grimaced. Actually, with her father's visit just shy of that, she had *less* than thirty days. Her temples throbbed at that thought. Still, she knew she could do it. In less than a month. She could.

She had to.

Ivy raised her chin, hoping that by looking more confident, she would be so. "You needn't fash so, Poplin. I have everything in hand. In truth, I've already engaged my man." Ivy smiled proudly. "Last night, outside The Theater Royal Drury Lane."

Even Ivy had to admit that securing Counterton House was pure serendipity.

And, though she hadn't known it at the time, it was also the linchpin of her brilliant plan.

To lure Miss Feeney from Viscount Tinsdale, Ivy needed two things: a peer unknown in London and a home in Mayfair. Counterton House had supplied both—a smart Berkeley Square address owned by a deceased marquess whose heir, the new Lord Counterton, was not to arrive in London until Christmastide. What could be more perfect?

Except the actor she'd found for the role.

"I beg your pardon, Lady Ivy. Did you say that you engaged an actor . . . *last eve*?" Poplin's mouth dropped open before he remembered himself and snapped his lips closed again.

"Aye, I did." The manservant didn't utter another word but instead stared back at Ivy. "Oh, good heavens. I told you my plans, so you ought not appear so flabbergasted."

"I—I was only surprised that you had managed to engage a gentlemen willing to—I beg your

pardon, my lady, but I must say it—risk imprisonment for impersonating a peer."

*Imprisonment. Hmm . . . I probably should
have thought of that.* But the worrisome thought
remained in her head for only a moment before it
evaporated. "Well, believe me, I plan to offer whatever coin I must to convince the actor to take on
this role. I suppose the risk of arrest *might* increase
the fee somewhat, but my sisters promised to help
me. I have no doubt they will lend me whatever
I need of their portions of Sterling's winnings to
see my plan through." Ivy sucked the edge of her
bottom lip into her mouth pensively, trying to
make herself believe her sisters' help would extend
to parting with a few guineas.

Worry seemed to creep in around her suddenly.
She peered across the carriage at Poplin. Since the
day they had arrived in London, the old man had
always spoken his mind directly to her and her
brothers and sisters as well. The sage advice he
regularly offered, though not always wholeheart-
edly welcomed, often turned out to be a blessing.
Time after time, he prevented several, if not all, of
the Sinclairs from stepping into the muck caused
by their rash heedlessness. For this reason, the
brothers and sisters tolerated his comments rather
than chastised him for speaking out of place. For

though Poplin's serving skills were lacking, they all trusted his counsel. Ivy had to believe that this time was no different.

"Oh, dear Poplin, you've said it yourself, again and again—I only have a month before I no longer have use of the house. So why, pray, would I tarry?" Ivy raised her copper eyebrows and waited for him to reply, but he didn't. "Still, I shouldn't think it should take that long," she added confidently. "I have a plan, and even Siusan agrees it is brilliant." She gazed through the window toward the house again. "So, shall we have a look inside and meet the staff?"

Poplin suddenly appeared worried. "The staff . . . well, Lady Ivy, they'll be costing you a bit extra."

Ivy was incensed. "Their services were to be included! I was very clear on that point. I may be a Sinclair, but my purse is nearly empty."

When the hackney wobbled to a complete halt before the house, Poplin did not wait for the driver to open the door. Instead, he shakily descended to the pavers, then stepped in front of the footman and reached his own gloved hand up to Ivy. He held his voice low. "Their . . . services, cooking, cleaning, gardening . . . yes, those are all included—God help you—but keeping their mouths closed about your pretender . . . allow me to rephrase . . . *your*

Marquess of Counterton, and supporting your efforts when they can—well, that will cost you a clean guinea for each staff member . . . five total."

Ivy was aghast at this new development. She had only just identified the perfect gentleman to lure Miss Feeney away from Tinsdale, which, as Poplin noted, would likely cost her more than she'd planned—and already she was out two hundred and five pounds and five shillings for dressings—a house and a full staff. Robbery.

Poplin led her up the walk and rapped upon the door with his knobby knuckles.

"Will you be sure the door knocker is replaced?" Ivy asked, leaning down to polish the door latch with the edge of her skirt. "All appearances must establish that the Marquess of Counterton is unexpectedly at home. He is unknown in London, so there should be no problem."

"Lady Ivy," Poplin asked quietly as they waited for the door to be answered, "dare I inquire as to what happens if your *Lord Counterfeit* is exposed as a fraud?"

"Oh, I am sure he will be exposed . . . eventually. It will be my prime task to delay that eventuality for as long as possible." Ivy shared a conspiratorial wink with the worried little manservant. "By then, if all goes well, Miss Feeney will have jilted

Tinsdale, and I will have a ring upon my finger. It will be too late for anyone to do anything about it by then, won't it? My plan is a feat of social *tour de force*. It will succeed. I believe I have planned every last detail. How could anything possibly go wrong now?"

Poplin groaned softly.

The latch depressed, and Ivy could hear grunting noises on the other side, but a moment later the door came unstuck and swung wide. A tall, burly man in sooty breeches and shirt topped with a kidskin work vest stood before them, blocking entry. "So, is this her, the lady, Poplin?" He peered down at Ivy.

Lud, Ivy thought, *he didn't look the least like a butler.* She tensed, and doubt in her plan suddenly clouded her thoughts.

" 'Tis." Poplin, seeming unnerved by the man, took a step backward.

"Has she got the coin?" The man did not remove his hard gaze from Ivy.

She studied Mr. Cheatlin narrowly. Perhaps if he never spoke, he could carry off the role of a butler to a peer. She'd have to talk to Poplin about that.

"She does—" Poplin began.

Ivy broke in. "I do, so if you do not mind, the sun has nearly risen, and I must come inside so I am not spied from the street." Ivy charged toward Cheatlin, and, when he did not move, she squeezed between him and the door, then beckoned for Poplin to follow. "You don't look at all like a butler, you know. Have you any skills at all?"

"Plenty." He waggled his thick eyebrows at her and chuckled nastily before truly answering her. "My da was a manservant, so I have some notion about what is required. Officially, though, in case you're wonderin', I'm the master carpenter, hired to oversee the renovation on the new Lord Counterton's town house. But don't you worry none, your ladyship, me and my crew have the *skills* you're looking for—and then some you probably ain't realized you'll be needin'—we can do anything that's needed as long as your guineas gleam."

Ivy dug inside her reticule, counted out five guineas, then pressed them into Mister Cheatlin's huge, outstretched hand. Next, she whisked off her bonnet and thrust it at him. "Well, then, shall we begin? I have some very specific requirements." She flashed a mischievous smile. "But then, you did assure me that you and your staff can do *anything,* no?"

Cheatlin took her hat from her, chuckling as he set it on a hook beside the door. "You can sure tell she's a Scot," he said to Poplin. "But I think we'll all get along just fine." Pressing the door firmly closed behind them, he bade Ivy follow him on a tour of the house.

"God help us all," Poplin muttered, as he turned to follow his mistress down the passage.

Mr. Felix Dupré's residence
That evening

Lady Ivy didn't step down from the carriage. From what Nick could see, she didn't even condescend to look through the window toward the door.

But she was waiting for him. He grinned at that. Then again, he hadn't really left her any choice but to wait if she wished him to take part in her *plan*.

Nick made sure of that, even though Felix was practically writhing in agony on the floor at the very idea of the daughter of a duke being forced to wait on the street for his cousin.

"Bloody hell, Nick." Felix gingerly inserted two fingers between the thick curtains drawn across the parlor windows and peered through. "Can't you just go to her? You said that this offer must be kept secret. She can't very well walk up the steps and rap on the door, now can she?"

"No, but she could send the footman on the perch to advise me that she has arrived."

"But you know she has arrived." Felix inched the curtains closed, slow enough that no sway of fabric could be detected from the street.

"How would she know that?"

"We could send a footman down to let Her Ladyship know that you have been advised of her arrival and that you will be joining her directly."

"Excellent idea, Felix." Nick tied his starched neckcloth in the reflection of the hazy mirror in the entryway. Felix darted past him and around the corner. He paid his cousin's frenetic movement no mind. "Only there is no footman to send to her—in fact, this house hasn't a single staff member . . . at my last count anyway." Nick paused when Felix didn't reply. "I said—"

"I heard you quite clearly, but you are mistaken, cousin." It was Felix's voice he heard, but it was an old man with a wild gray duster of hair who was suddenly reflected in the mirror.

Nick whirled around and stared. "Damn it all, Felix, you startled the breath right out of me!"

"Brilliant, eh?" Felix exhaled onto his knuckles, then polished them on the heavy black coat he wore. "I wore this in a play less than a sennight past. Had it in one of my costume trunks. I played a butler two seasons past. I was fabulous." Felix spun around, flung the door open, and darted from the house before Nick realized what he was about to do.

Nick hurried into the parlor and peeked through the curtains as his cousin had done minutes before. The carriage door was open wide, and Felix was gesticulating wildly toward the house. A slim hand grasped the half-open window glass and pulled the carriage door closed.

As Felix turned to the house and started up the steps, Nick raced into the entry, stopping so abruptly that he nearly slid into Felix as he shot through the front door.

"I cannot believe you approached her dressed like that." Nick scowled at Felix. "I only wanted to teach her a lesson. That even as a noblewoman, she is no better than anyone else and cannot expect everyone to leap simply because she has arrived."

Felix looked back at him quizzically. "Gads, what did she do—besides kiss you—that made you decide she needed to be taught such a lesson?"

Nick straightened his shoulders and tugged on the slightly-too-short sleeves of the blue kerseymere coat Felix had lent him for the evening. Truth to tell, he didn't know why he decided her behavior needed correction. He just . . . did, and now, being made to consider his possible prejudice made him damned uncomfortable. "It was the way she kissed me. Didn't ask permission, or even give me a hint she was going to do it. She just grabbed me and kissed me."

"What a positively hangable offense. Well, I can see why you would task yourself with educating the wild Scot. It's a matter of public safety, isn't it?" Felix feigned a most-serious expression, but then, unable to contain himself any longer, he doubled over and burst out laughing, clutching Nick's arm to keep from collapsing straight to the floor. When he finally caught his breath a moment later, he pointed to the door. "I told her you would join her presently."

"Thank you, Felix." Annoyed, Nick brushed his cousin's arm from his sleeve and started across the entryway floor. "No need for the . . . um . . . footman to wait up for me. I suspect I will return quite late in the evening."

Felix was resting his hands on his knees, waiting until his breathing returned completely to normal. "Oh, I have no doubt. I saw her, up close. She's very beautiful, Nick, and she spoke directly to me even though I had addressed her footman. And evidently, she's an excellent kisser too." Felix snorted a laugh, and in a tick of the second hand, couldn't catch his breath again.

Nick peered into the mirror and gave his neckcloth one last departing tug before opening the door and striding down the steps to the carriage.

The door latch pressed down from inside, and Lady Ivy beckoned him into the carriage. "Come on now. Please hurry. I do not wish to be observed with you. Not yet, anyway."

"Good evening, Lady Ivy." Nick flashed a bright smile, then bent and ducked inside the carriage. The driver closed the door behind Nick, then the carriage tilted as the driver leaped to his perch.

Though he could have quickly seated himself on the bench directly opposite her, a mischievous thought broached his mind—one that might allow him to steal a kiss from her, just as she had stolen one from him the night before.

He told himself it would serve her right, but in the back of his mind he knew that wasn't the truth of it. He simply wanted to kiss her again.

Nick took a shaky step in her direction, then pretending to lose his balance, he teetered on one foot, then the other, his arms waving. He bent at the waist, so as not to bump his head on the cab's roof, then suddenly lurched toward her in a dead fall. "Oh dear—"

Lady Ivy's eyes rounded. Gasping in surprise, she flattened her back against the leather squab a scant instant before Nick slapped his hands on the seat back on either side of her shoulders, catching himself.

The carriage shook and began to move, its momentum knocking him over her. His mouth hovered just above hers, so close that he could feel her warm breath on his face.

Dare he take his prize?

Perhaps he should. He lifted the edges of his mouth, smiling down at her as he tilted his head as if to kiss her. Then, something astonishing happened. As if without a thought, she closed her eyes and angled her mouth upward, nearer to his.

Waiting.

Wanting.

He could take her kiss if he wished. But he didn't. He only wanted her to know he could. "I do beg your pardon, Lady Ivy. I should have seated myself sooner."

Her eyelids snapped open, and even in the gray dimness of the cab, he could see the rosy flush of her cheeks.

"Well, do sit now, *please*." Even embarrassed as she obviously was, his mouth still hovering above hers, she managed to instill an air of authority into her words. "Our journey will not be lengthy. I have arranged for a very private dining room nearby. My brother Grant will meet us before we enter, for propriety's sake, but you needn't worry about concealing our arrangement with him. He knows all about it. We will discuss your . . . role while we dine, if you do not mind." Her throat worked hard, and she swallowed deeply.

He peered into her eyes as she spoke, not retreating, not giving her even an inch more. Just then, the carriage wheel dropped deep into a hole in the road, driving Nick's mouth down hard upon hers.

She wedged her hands between them and pushed him back, skewering him a distinct glare.

"I beg your pardon, Your Ladyship. The road, you know."

She was not amused. That was clear enough. But from the narrowing of her eyes and the soft crinkle of her brow, he also knew that she wasn't certain if he was toying with her or telling the truth.

He stepped back then and collapsed onto the bench behind him, fighting back a grin. She snapped open her fan, concealing her flushed cheeks as she waved it before her face. She swayed slightly from side to side but did not say another word as the carriage barreled through the streets.

Yes, Nick decided, tonight would be most fascinating indeed.

Chapter 4

*Envy is the art of counting the other fellow's blessings
instead of your own.*

Harold Coffin

Only a clutch of minutes later, they arrived at their destination. The carriage door opened, and Ivy and her Lord Counterton stepped out on the pavers before the grand St. James's Royal Hotel, where, as promised, her dear brother Grant was waiting.

"I do so appreciate your support, Grant," Ivy whispered.

Grant leaned close as if to peck her cheek, but whispered into her ear instead, "So long as I am not hauled before a magistrate, I am at your disposal, Ivy." He straightened and smile overbrightly at her.

"Always the jester." Ivy turned to her actor, who tipped his head to Grant.

A well-dressed couple, thankfully unknown to her, cast curious glances at the three of them as they passed by. Her actor's eyes nervously sought out Ivy's.

Lud, there were others milling about, and she hadn't thought about a plausible story about how Lord Counterton had come to know the Sinclairs.

Ivy opened her mouth to speak, but Grant nodded in greeting. "Lord Counterton, how good to see you again."

"Good evening, Lord Grant," her pretender replied instantly. "Yes, it has been far too long."

Oh, Siusan had been ever so brilliant in suggesting that she engage an actor. He was perfect. So natural. She exhaled, and felt her nerves begin to untangle.

Ivy looped her left arm through Grant's, then her right through her actor's and started them all toward the doorway, whispering as they walked. "Unfortunately, *Lord Counterton,* we shall be required to pass through the main dining room to reach the private saloon I have arranged for us." Of course, that was the entire point of discussing her plan there. It was his first test—to be sure he could move comfortably and naturally within elevated Society. She simply could not hire him, no matter how lovely he looked, if he could not blend with his betters.

Ivy slowed her step to a crawl as it suddenly occurred to her that this outing was actually his second test, not his first. The first had been his kiss. She smiled as she rapidly increased her pace again, pulling the men along with her. *The kiss*. Well, he'd passed that challenge most admirably.

Grant shot Ivy a sidelong glance, then tugged gently on her arm, making her realize she'd nearly broken into a trot. "From what I have heard, London is usually deserted during the month of August for grouse season, if you can imagine such a thing, but the ridiculous amount of rain has chased nearly everyone back from the country. Nothing to do in the country when you can't leave the house, I suppose."

"With the right company, there is actually quite a variety of diversions in the country," her Lord Counterton replied.

"Good heavens, do you truly believe that?" Ivy replied. She was sure he didn't, or perhaps he just didn't know better. He was not, she assumed, raised with the best of everything available to him, as she had been.

"I do. I find the country far superior to Town

in every"—he broke off for a moment and peered intently at her before amending his position—"in *most* every way."

It was queer the way he had looked at her. Unsettling, because she didn't know what to make of it.

"Well, you may be correct," Grant said as they approached the hotel entrance. "Perhaps our experience differs from yours. Sitting in a huge old stack of stone never compared to dining and dancing in the finest establishments in Edinburgh."

Liveried footmen in pale blue opened the doors for them, and they went inside the St. James's Royal Hotel.

Ivy lifted her eyes to peer up at her actor as they walked, needing to make sure that he understood the great importance of her next words. But when he turned his head, and his deep blue eyes met hers, she couldn't for the life of her remember what those words were.

My heavens, he was so beautiful, so knee-weakeningly handsome, that her mind had emptied of every single thought.

"Yes, Lady Ivy?" He paused them both on the starburst centered on the marble floor of the reception hall, and turned her to face him, waiting.

"I . . . I—" No other word made it through her lips. The clink of cutlery and the murmur of voices from the public dining room beyond drifted into the hall, but Ivy couldn't manage a sound. She simply stood there, her lips moving silently like an old woman praying as her withered fingers moved over the beads of her rosary.

"Lady Ivy!" came a female voice from the direction of the dining room. Ivy turned away from her actor and saw Lord and Lady Winthrop hastening toward them. Suddenly she remembered those all-too-important words.

Do not speak to anyone!

But it was too late to impart her warning. All she could possibly do was fill the gaps of the introduction with the very loose history she had created for her impostor.

The men bowed, reminding Ivy to curtsy. Her heart pounded against her corset. "Lady Winthrop, how wonderful to see you and Lord Winthrop." Lady Winthrop's aging features were as sharp and overpronounced as her temperament. Though she had managed to marry a title, Ivy was certain it had nothing to do with comeliness and everything to do with her family's money.

Ivy offered her hand to Lord Winthrop, a short, squat earl, who cupped it in his own and raised it to his lips.

"Lady Ivy." He paused to assess her attributes,

in the same veiled manner of so many gentlemen of the *ton,* one that balanced precariously on the sharp edge of propriety. "You are positively radiant this evening."

Her Lord Counterton saw the comment for the rude leer that it was, and stepped forward protectively.

Ivy panicked.

Grant moved smoothly into the breach. "Lord Counterman, having just arrived in town, I do not believe you have met our dear friends Lady Winthrop and Lord Winthrop."

"Indeed I have not," the actor replied, smiling at them both.

Lady Winthrop extended her hand. "We have not met, Lord Counterton, it is true, but you are not entirely unknown to us. Your uncle was a frequent visitor to our home." She looked at her husband, then nodded to the younger man again. "Darling, this is Dominic Sheridan, old Lord Counterton's heir."

Lord Winthrop clapped him on the back as he took his hand. "The new Marquess of Counterton, is it?" Then, he added under his breath, "My, my. The misses and their mamas will be thrilled to meet you."

"Wilber!" Lady Winthrop cast a scathing glare

at her husband, then edged between Ivy and her actor. "Lord Counterton, we had not expected you in London so soon. I believe the rumor about Town settled you in Berkeley Square at the end of the year."

"My plans changed somewhat recently." The new Lord Counterton graced the gray-haired woman with a beguiling smile. "Had I known the Town was home to so many beautiful and charming women, I would not have delayed my arrival by a single minute."

Grant turned slightly and covertly rolled his eyes in Ivy's direction.

Lady Winthrop giggled girlishly, quieting only when Ivy circled back around the woman's wide hips and reminded Lady Winthrop of her presence. Then, with a suspicious glance at Ivy, the countess returned her attention to Lord Counterton. "My lord, if you do not mind my asking, how did you come to make the acquaintance of Lady Ivy and Lord Grant so soon? The Sinclairs only arrived this spring."

Ivy opened her mouth, but her impostor spoke first. "Our fathers were acquainted."

"Your fathers?" Lord Winthrop glanced at Ivy.

"Yes, indeed. Sadly, my father passed away when I was a child." Lord Counterton raised his arm, offering it to Ivy as if they were about to depart.

She looped it through the crook of his arm again. "I knew no one else in Town, even remotely, so begged the honor of the Sinclair family to properly introduce me into Society."

At this response, Grant nodded approvingly. Aye, her actor was brilliant, wasn't he?

An excited wiggle shot through Lady Winthrop. "Oh, please do allow me to assist you with introductions as well, my lord. Ours is one of the oldest families in Town. Our connections are numerous. You shan't ever spend an evening at home unless by choice, I promise you." She glanced at her husband beside her. "I would consider it an honor to host a rout to allow you to know the finest families in London. Will you allow it?"

Even through his coat sleeve, Ivy felt his arm tense. She leaped into the verbal gap. "How very kind of you, Lady Winthrop, but you see, my family has already requested that particular honor—and Lord Counterton has agreed."

The older woman grimaced, then looked back to the new Lord Counterton. "Then . . . a musicale perhaps, my lord?"

"Go on, give it up, Counterton," Lord Winthrop insisted, a laugh riding astride his words. "You must, for she never will stop until you have agreed to something."

The actor's arm relaxed then, and Ivy knew he would accept. "Very well, Lady Winthrop. I would most enjoy another opportunity to converse with *you* . . . and your friends, certainly."

Ivy knew this was it. The moment of their escape.

"Well, then, it is settled," Ivy said, enthusiastically. "But, please, do excuse us this night. We are expected for dinner, and I fear we are already late."

She turned her gaze to Lady Winthrop and smiled as pleasantly as she could manage. "I look forward to your invitation."

"As well do I, Lady Ivy." The corners of the older woman's lips suddenly drooped, and for a moment, Ivy could not tell if Lady Winthrop was scowling at her or, like her family's cook, simply smiled upside down.

It didn't really matter anyway, for the Winthrops graciously allowed them to depart and Ivy, her brother, and her actor strode across the main dining room, where they were promptly ushered into one of the hotel's three private saloons.

Grant produced a flask from each pocket and quickly filled their glasses with fine whisky from Scotland. "The room is private, so do enjoy the whisky, Ivy. Can't have my sister sipping the lemon swill served to ladies." Once Ivy approved the listing of courses, the serving staff quit the room to allow their party the privacy they had paid for this night.

Grant rose, taking his glass of whisky along with him, thoughtfully leaving the flasks on the table. "Do excuse me. I saw a few friends in the dining room, and I would be remiss if I did not notice them."

The actor came to his feet.

"Ivy, send for me when your discussion has concluded." Grant grinned. "Before the second remove, preferably." He cuffed her actor's biceps, then quickly excused himself from the saloon.

The moment Grant departed, Ivy lifted her diminutive glass and, searching for her courage, swallowed nearly half in one draught. The actor's eyebrows arched in his surprise.

"You take your whisky well . . . for a woman," he said with no hesitation. He smiled then, tilted back his somewhat larger glass and matched her measure.

Ivy's lips twitched. "And might I say that you take your whisky well . . . for a Sassenach?" With no footmen in the saloon, as was her request, Ivy rose and fetched one of Grant's flasks of whisky from the table and, as if she were taking the role of mother at tea, topped off both their glasses with the amber spirit.

"You were entirely convincing," Ivy told her actor as she returned to her chair. "And incredibly charming."

"I take my role as Lord Counterton very seriously."

She tilted her head and smiled beguilingly across the table at him until she felt the coquettish flutter of her eyelashes and remembered the purpose of his company. A quick frown found her lips and she straightened in her chair. "My only concern is that you mentioned the passing of your father. We do not know the details of Lord Counterton's inheritance, and since the Winthrops are acquainted with the family—"

He lowered his chin toward his chest, then gazed up at her from beneath his brow. "His father died when he was a child, and his uncle only met with him occasionally. Lord and Lady Winthrop have no cause to doubt my identity."

Ivy leaned back a bit in her chair and folded her arms over her chest. "And how are you so sure of this?"

He raised his head and lifted his glass of whisky from the table and took a long sip. Instead of answering her directly, he ran his tongue lightly over his perfectly chiseled lips, as if savoring the taste of the whisky upon them.

Ivy realized she was sucking her own lips into her mouth, and for the second time in as many moments, she reminded herself that this man was merely a means to winning back Viscount Tinsdale, the one she sought to marry, nothing more.

"If I am to be Lord Counterton, should I not know everything about him?" He peered at her across the linen-draped table. "His father died when Dominic was a boy in school. Of this, I am certain. His older brother, last year at Waterloo. His uncle, the Marquess of Counterton never married, making Dominic Sheridan the Counterton heir presumptive. When the marquess passed on, Dominic became the Marquess of Counterton."

As he spoke, Ivy removed her gloves and absently ran her fingertip around the lip of her glass. When he paused, she reached out and patted his hand. "You are a professional. You clearly have researched the role of Lord Counterton quite well. And so quickly. Did you consult Debrett?"

"That is, Lady Ivy, what you are going to pay me for, to *be* Lord Counterton, is it not? Or is it something more?" His tone was low and somehow sounded to her the smallest bit mocking; she wondered for an instant whether his reason for considering accepting her position was truly only for the coin this work would bring.

He raised a single eyebrow, and the expression on his handsome face changed, as if he'd somehow detected her sudden doubt.

Heat rushed through Ivy, and she felt a blush rising from her chest toward her cheeks. She swallowed deeply, resting her hand upon her throat, hoping, foolishly, that she might conceal the rising color.

Lud, how nonsensical it was to react to him this way! Aye, he was arguably one of the most—very well, he was *the* most beautiful man she'd ever seen—but that was no reason for her to suddenly lose all hold on her mind and body.

She had brought him here for an important reason. To detail his role in her plan to win back Lord Tinsdale's affections.

He'd obviously passed his suitability test, so it was best to start now.

As she drew a deep breath in preparation of delivering her daring, but quite logical, plan, her gaze fell to the table, and at once her eyes focused on the whisky. She slid her hand forward and wrapped her fingers around the glass, holding it tightly in her grip.

He reached for her wrist and curled his fingers around it. "Lady Ivy, what is wrong? We are here to discuss the role you offered me in the carriage outside the theater, nothing more. Your conviction was so strong then, but now, you hesitate. Have you reconsidered your plan?" He pinned her with his gaze then. "Have you suddenly realized that conspiracy to impersonate a peer is quite illegal?"

Lifting her chin, she met his gaze. "Nay, I have not reconsidered my plan. Do you not understand—I have no other choice?"

He released his hold on her wrist, and she immediately brought the glass to her lips and drank it down. The whisky stung her throat, and, embarrassedly, being a Scot, she coughed until her eyes welled with tears. "I beg your pardon." She schooled her features, set the empty glass on the table, and folded her hands primly in her lap. "There is nothing in this world that could change my mind. I mean to marry Viscount Tinsdale, and I will do whatever it takes to win him back."

"Including the use of an impostor." A small laugh rode his exhalation.

"Exactly . . . *Dominic*. You don't mind if I address you as such when we are alone?" Ivy lifted the corners of her mouth. Her head was spinning a little. If she did not have the confidence she needed, she could at least pretend she did.

"Why, certainly . . . *Ivy*." He flashed a perfect

smile. "Dominic is my Christian name, after all, is it not?"

She laughed softly. "Why, yes, Lord Counterton, it is. Besides, if I learn your true name. I might accidentally use it when we are together in public."

"Well, we can't have you exposing my true identity, now can we?"

Ivy raised her hands from her lap, rested them on the edge of the table, and leaned forward. "Neither of us can, which is why it is imperative that you always remain in character. You must always be Lord Counterton."

He shook his head almost resignedly. "You and I both know that engaging me to pose as the marquess will be not nearly enough to convince Society that I am he."

"You are correct. Which is precisely the reason why you will move into Counterton's home on Berkeley Square." Ivy felt her nose wrinkle as she grinned.

How clever Poplin was to have managed that feat for her. How could anyone in Society possibly doubt her man's identity when he was living in the true Marquess of Counterton's own house?

"I beg your pardon?" Dominic—how that name suited him so nicely—stared wide-eyed back at her.

She waved a dismissive hand in the air. "Oh, dinna fash. I have arranged everything. Cost me good coin, too. You will have a full staff . . . though I wouldn't expect too much from them when you do not have callers. Their . . . um . . . skills, shall we agree, lie more fully in other areas."

"W-what folly is this?" The flickering light from the chandelier above made Dominic's blue eyes glow as hot and vibrant as the heart of a flame. "You have appropriated not only the Marquess of Counterton's identity—but his home as well?"

He was very nearly sputtering.

Good heavens.

"Dear sir, you need not worry in the least. My *temporary* claim on Lord Counterton and his home in Town will be relinquished within thirty days. I promise you, you will not be arrested. I assure you. I have *rented* the house for you."

Och, it is not as if she were asking him to break his way into the house. He would have a key. Why, she had *paid* for everything. It was all quite legal—as far as she was concerned, anyway. Mr. Cheatlin, on the other hand, well . . . there was no need to concern Dominic with such trivial things. He had an important job to do. "Within a month, if you perform well, and I know you shall, Tinsdale will have already asked me to marry him.

Who knows, I might even have a ring upon my finger. It all depends on you. But I have no doubt you will succeed. Then you may take your money and, oh I don't know, invest it in a play or something grand."

Dominic still appeared wholly bowled over. He stared at her, mouth agape.

Blast! Was it possible he was going to refuse the role after all?

"Please, allow me to explain my plan more fully. Then you will understand that there is no need for concern. None at all."

Dominic raised his index finger in the air, signaling her to wait, and in that moment he drained the whisky from his glass completely.

Startled, for he was an Englishman, Ivy peered down at his empty glass. A bit more whisky might help lift his thoughts from the risks of the plan and allow him to concentrate on details more fully. "Please allow me to refresh your crystal, Lord Counterton."

"*Dominic.*"

"*Dominic.*" The way she spoke his name sounded queerly low and husky to her ears, seductive. *'Tis the whisky. Nothing more.*

Lifting the second flask again, Ivy circled around behind his back and bent, inadvertently brushing against him as she allowed the whisky to trickle leisurely into his glass.

Again, she hadn't meant to touch him at all. Truly. She'd just slipped a bit.

'Tis the whisky. That's all.

Nick rubbed his temple with his thumb and ring finger. It was beyond all imagination. Even for a Sinclair, if Felix's stories of the family's audacity were to be believed.

Not only had she stolen the identity of Lord Counterton (borrowed, was that how she put it?), but she had taken over his house on Berkeley Square as well. And she didn't seem the least concerned about either of them getting caught.

Nick was foundering in a shifting current between outrage . . . and amusement. He couldn't decide whether he should do exactly as Felix bade him—get as far away from the lady as he possibly could—or at least hear the details of her plan.

He had just set his hand on the arm of his chair to stand, and he thought his decision had been made to put an end to the charade, when the door opened and a flurry of footmen swept in with several steaming dishes and serving bowls.

"Everything smells delicious," Lady Ivy announced, as the footmen began to serve her soup. "Do you not agree, Lord Counterton?"

He lowered his hand and replaced it upon his knee. "I do."

"Please leave everything else," she told one of the footmen. "We will serve ourselves."

"But my lady—" He looked genuinely offended, but Lady Ivy was determined to have her request met.

The ruddy slash of her left eyebrow snapped upward, and her lips pinched, ending all discussion. The footman signaled for the other servers, who settled their dishes on the table between Lady Ivy and Nick and hurriedly quit the room.

She tilted her head slightly to the side and raised the edges of her lips. "I believe a bit of privacy is required for our discussion. I am certain you agree."

"Yours must be quite a plan."

"Brilliant, actually." Lady Ivy sipped some consommé from her spoon and gestured for Nick to do the same. She seemed to take an inordinate amount of time to swallow and lower her spoon before speaking, but then, it might just have been that the pause was intended to increase his interest in her ruse.

"Do share." He lifted a spoonful of soup to his

mouth, since drinking . . . or eating seemed to put her more fully at ease—and more forthcoming.

"The plan is simple," she explained between mouthfuls. "I am sure Viscount Tinsdale was on the verge of asking me to marry him—a union my father has indicated he would agree to—when Miss Fiona Feeney, who is new to Society, set her cap at him and promptly stole his affections from me."

"No one can steal affections, Lady Ivy," he told her gravely. "Affections can only be given away."

Ivy's grip tightened on the silver handle of her spoon, but her face betrayed no hint of agitation. "Be that as it may, my goal is to steal . . . *win* back his attentions. My dilemma is that I cannot compete on any level with Miss Feeney. She is startlingly beautiful, charming, and witty."

"But *Ivy,* you hold all of those qualities in abundance." Nick leaned forward and pinned her with his gaze. He was being completely honest, and he hoped she would believe him and call off her nefarious machinations.

Ivy's eyes suddenly grew bright, and her earlier smile flattened. "Obviously, I do not. I cannot compete with her, else I would not have needed your assistance."

His urge was to argue the point, but her emotion was growing steadily. She was becoming upset, and he knew it was better not to say anything more about it. And in this moment of weakness, the words he did not wish to say fell from his lips. "How can I assist?"

Excitedly, Ivy pushed her bowl aside and leaned toward him. "I cannot compete with Miss Feeney for Tinsdale's affections—so you will compete with Tinsdale for hers!" Her eyes were bright and wide. "You will steal Miss Feeney's affections from Lord Tinsdale. Woo her, charm her, do whatever must be done to make her fall in love with you and set Tinsdale aside."

An uneasy chuckle fell from Nick's mouth. "Your belief in my abilities is unfounded, Ivy."

"Do you not recall our kiss?"

Nick smiled. "Oh, indeed I do."

"Then you should also know it was a test—a test that proved to me that I am not overestimating you or your abilities at all. One kiss from you, and had I not been sitting on the carriage bench, my knees would have given out from beneath me." She drew a fortifying breath. "You are everything Lord Tinsdale is not. You lack nothing, except a title, smart address, and a few accoutrements. I have provided these things."

Steam curled up from the bowl before him, prompting Nick, while he considered his next words, to dip his spoon into the consommé and swallow the broth. "Even if I do what you ask, there is no guarantee that Lord Tinsdale will return his affections to you."

"Well, you will assist me with that as well."

Nick looked up from his bowl, balancing his next spoonful of broth in the air. "Pray, do tell me how." He put the spoon into his mouth, then removed it, leaving a smile on his lips.

"By pretending to fall in love with me."

Nick choked on the hot soup still inside his mouth. He dragged a linen napkin to his lips. "So, your plan is that I woo Miss Feeney, make her fall in love with me—but at the same time, I pretend that I am in love with you, in order to make Tinsdale resume his courtship of you?"

"Exactly." Ivy laughed. "Though the key piece you are missing in your understanding . . . is *envy*."

"Envy." Nick shook his head. She was right; he didn't understand this at all.

"Miss Feeney, my rival in London Society, set her cap for Lord Tinsdale because I possessed his heart. If I thought him worthy, then clearly he must be the most desirable and eligible unmarried gentleman in London."

"And is he?"

"Aye. He is wealthy, titled, from a good family, and very, very steadfast." She folded her arms at her chest and leaned back in her chair, looking somewhat frustrated with him. "In short, he is everything my father wishes for me in a husband."

"Everything *your father* wishes."

"Did you not hear me?" She was growing more agitated by the moment. "Aye."

Nick still was not satisfied with her explanation. "Allow me to see if I am following your logic correctly. So when Miss Feeney sees us together at Society events—"

"And learns that the incredibly handsome, charming gentleman courting me is none other than the new Marquess of Counterton, she will be dreadfully envious of me. Within no time at all, she will shift her attentions and affections from Tinsdale, a mere viscount, to you."

Nick chuckled softly at her convoluted reasoning. Not that he thought her wrong. He had no idea how the female mind worked—and a Sinclair female . . . well, he daren't even attempt to begin to figure her out. "And Lord Tinsdale, seeing your radiance in the reflected glow of another gentleman's love, will understand how wrong he was to leave you in favor of another."

"My, you don't have a solid comprehension of

human nature, and yet you must understand this. Lord Tinsdale must *feel* Miss Feeney's affections slipping away. This makes him vulnerable. It is at that time that I show him the smallest amount of favor while you make love to me."

Nick's eyebrows inched toward his hairline. "Make love to you? Lady Ivy, that is something we have not discussed." A grin tugged at his lips. "There would be an additional guinea for that, of course."

"What?" Ivy's eyes rounded. "Oh, good Lord! You know I was not speaking of *that*. I only meant that you make it appear that you are madly in love with me . . . in public."

"To make him jealous. To make him feel that he must have you back with him again. To make him envious of what I have."

"Aye. Oh, you do understand." Ivy laughed aloud but then embarrassedly clapped her hands over her mouth to stifle the sound. "As I said, the plan is brilliant. Is it not?"

"Absolutely brilliant." Nick appeased her with a smile. Her thinking possessed great originality, he'd give her that—but it was ripe with peril for all involved. "When do we begin?"

"Why, tonight, of course." Ivy slowly dragged her soup before her once again and started to consume what was left. "After our meal, I will take you to your new home on Berkeley Square."

"Berkeley Square. Tonight?"

"Och, aye. Tonight. So hurry yourself with your soup. We have several other dishes before us still—including the beef course."

Dear God. Just what the hell have I agreed to?

Chapter 5

Nothing sharpens the sight like envy.
Thomas Fuller

Nick exhaled a sigh of relief when the Sinclair town carriage drew up before Felix's narrow house on Davies Street. She had taken him home—not to Berkeley Square.

He felt the bounce of the vehicle on its springs as the driver leaped down from his perch and heard the ring click on the hitching post. Sliding to the edge of the bench, Nick waited for the door to be opened. "It has been an . . . enlightening evening, Lady Ivy."

In the flickering light of the small brass carriage lamp, he saw a veil of confusion whisk over her face. "Aye, but I daresay, it is about to grow more interesting." She scooted to the edge of her seat as well and leaned forward.

A kiss? Blood charged into Nick's heart and pumped through him in anticipation of a re-enactment of the night he first met her in the carriage. When she pulled him down to her and passionately kissed him as he'd never been kissed before.

But then the carriage door opened.

Damn it all. The driver had opened the door before she could lean just a little closer and—

"My lady," the driver interrupted. His eyes were cast downward, as if not to breach his lady's privacy inside the cab. "His . . . err . . . *man* will deliver everything on the morrow."

"His *man?*" Ivy scrunched her nose. "Oh! I see. Can he not accommodate us by doing it now?"

My man? Just who was he speaking of—Felix? Then it dawned on him. Of course, Felix. Good God, ever the actor, he must be playing the footman again for the sake of Lady Ivy. Or maybe a valet.

"I . . . err . . . no, my lady. He claims he cannot collect everything with so little notice." The driver brought his fist to his mouth and cleared his throat. "Shall I drive on?"

"Please do." As the driver pressed the door shut,

Nick shot his hand out and caught it before it could be closed. "Shouldn't I be getting out?"

Ivy paid his question no mind but slid back against the seat rest and exhaled a frustrated sigh. "I hope you do not mind sleeping without a nightshirt."

Nick's eyes widened and his hand fell to his side. The driver took his perch. "The night is mild." He tapped his finger agitatedly atop his knee. "Besides which, I never wear nightshirts anyway." The carriage lurched forward.

"Oh." Ivy's expression looked a bit startled though Nick doubted it was the sudden movement of the carriage as it started down Davies Street but rather his confession. "Well then, I-I suppose tomorrow will do." She peeled off her gloves and, without seeming to think about it, fanned herself with them.

"Berkeley Square?" he asked, but he already knew the answer.

"Aye," she replied. "Was I not clear about our plan at supper?"

"Your plan . . . oh yes." Nick leaned back, having given up on that kiss he had expected. "Quite."

Only he hadn't expected he would begin impersonating himself, the new Marquess of Counterton, that night.

Berkeley Square

Nick stood beside Lady Ivy, staring up at the towering house before him. It was much larger than he had imagined. The white house sat at the corner and was at least twice as wide as the other elegant town houses on the west side of the square. He peered up and counted four levels above ground, and then down past the black wrought-iron fence to a set of stairs leading from street level to what he guessed would be an entrance to a kitchen.

"Grand, isn't it?" Ivy said. She was beaming proudly as she gazed upon it, almost as if the house were her own.

But it wasn't. From what he'd learned, she'd rented the house illegally from some sly-booted fellow who had about as much right to the house as she—none.

Before he responded, the front door opened. A tall, burly man stood in the doorway, beckoning to them.

Ivy grasped Nick's arm. "Please hurry. It is late, but the moon is bright. Let's go inside before one of your neighbors sees the new Lord Counterton and Lady Ivy coming up the steps and alerts everyone so that they might come and greet you—and seek to ruin me. I cannot be seen alone here with you."

Nick allowed himself to be pulled up the steps but only because he was curious about what he might find inside—and more interestingly, whom.

The man at the door, dressed in an ill-fitting dark butler's coat and smudged breeches, stepped aside and let them pass into the house. The light of a four-armed candelabra cast a golden glow over the entryway.

Nick started forward to peer through the doorway of the room to his right when Ivy pulled his arm and spun him around.

"Lord Counterton," she said quite formally, "your butler."

"Cheatlin, my lord," the butler snickered.

Cheatlin? Bloody hell.

Nick studied the butler. The man's coat was too snug for his enormous biceps. His hands were rough, scabbed on the knuckles and chafed. "You're a carpenter by trade." Nick extended his hand, but Cheatlin did not take it.

"She weren't supposed to mention that to the likes of you." Mr. Cheatlin glared at Lady Ivy. "I was supposed to decide when and *if* I told the chap."

"She didn't tell me anything." Nick protectively angled his shoulder between Cheatlin and Ivy.

"I noticed your hands. My good man, I am no stranger to physical labor."

"I know you ain't really Lord Counterton, just like I ain't really a butler." Cheatlin's voice was low and gruff. "But we might as well start acting our parts now so we get into the habit." He took an awkward heavy step backward, then bent at the waist, and bowed at Nick.

"Oh, of course, you are right." Nick turned a bit and glanced at Ivy, who gave him a little prod, before facing Cheatlin and tipping his head in acknowledgment, as a marquess would do. "Cheatlin."

"Well, that's better." Cheatlin clapped his hands tightly and rubbed his palms together. "In truth, you are correct. I am Counterton's master carpenter. I'll be tellin' you this only because when you ain't got visitors, I will be working on some needed repairs on the upper levels."

Ivy nodded, agreeing with the carpenter's message. "Before you leave the house, always inform Cheatlin when you are to return or send a message to him if you are to return unexpectedly with . . . a guest."

"You won't want me hammerin' or hollerin' at my men, not when I should be in my blacks answerin' the door or serving you tea and little cakes,"

Cheatlin added. "You'll have a cook, a sixpounder . . . um . . . a maid, and a footman. They'll get their domestic duties done, but I will tell you now, like me own, their skills lie elsewhere. Get my meaning?"

"I do." Nick looked down at Ivy. "Interesting house staff you've assembled." He lifted one corner of his mouth and flashed her a cocky smile.

"They are only for appearances." Ivy grimaced, then slid her arm from Nick's and started for the door. "I did my best with the money I had."

"Wait, where are you going?" Nick felt dumb-struck. Was he actually supposed to stay here—tonight?

Ivy stopped and turned around. "Cheatlin will show you to your bedchamber. Your . . . man will come with your personal effects in the morning. I shall arrive at noon to begin your training. Good eve, Lord Counterton."

Cheatlin jogged past her and swung the door open. "My lady." He bowed his head.

Training? Dear God. What else did she have planned for him? Nick reached the door just as she stepped outside onto the stoop. "Please, Lady Ivy, do allow me to escort you to your carriage." He offered his arm to her.

She gave a furtive glance around the west end of the square.

"I am supposed to be courting you, after all," Nick added, raising his elbow higher.

"You are correct, of course. But as a maid, it is not permissible for me to call upon a bachelor—especially in the dead of night."

"The carriage is only a few steps from the door. Please."

Sighing with resignation, Ivy looped her arm around his, and together they descended the stairs to the carriage.

Nick did not hesitate, but opened the door for her and hurriedly handed her up the stairs and inside. She had just seated herself, when he leaned into dimly moonlit interior of the cab. "Allow me just one more moment of your time, Lady Ivy, if you do not mind."

"Of course not." She scooted forward on the bench toward him to listen.

Sliding his hand around the back of her neck, he drew her forward so quickly that she had no time to resist and pressed his lips to her warm mouth, drawing her soft body against his chest as he kissed her firmly.

When their lips parted, he felt the flutter of her breath on his face as she gave a pleased sigh. She lifted her lids lazily and straightened herself on the seat, sitting there as if dazed.

"It is important to rehearse," he whispered to her. "I am a professional after all."

"Oh, my." Ivy lifted her fingers to her lips. "I admit, you are a very, very good actor, sir."

Nearly noon, the next day
Berkeley Square

"Damn you, Felix, what the hell did you pack in this trunk—or by the weight of it, should I be asking whom did you pack?" Nick balanced most of the weight of the boulder-heavy trunk as they climbed the stair treads to the third floor.

"Your clothing is still missing," his cousin replied, panting from the exertion of carrying the trunk up the long staircase. "So I had to pack *everything*— of mine." Felix set his end of the trunk down as they reached the passage that led to the room designated as Nick's, the master's, bedchamber. Grimacing, Felix whisked his hands behind him and kneaded his lower back. "Had to pack it all. I have no notion what might fit you properly. If you recall, we are not exactly the same measure, Nicky."

It took another moment before Nick, who was still holding his end of the trunk by a brass handle, realized his cousin was not going to offer a moment's more assistance. "You were supposed to be at the house by first light," he huffed as he dragged the trunk down the passage to the first door on the right. "Lady Ivy might arrive at any moment . . . to begin my training, whatever that means."

He kicked open the bedchamber door and pulled the trunk inside.

"She plans to *train* you this morning? How, pray, was I to know that? Suddenly a man claiming to be in the Sinclair family's employ raps upon the door and shoves a note in my hand, bidding me to bring your clothing to him at once." Felix followed him into the room and immediately began his perusal. "I laughed, thinking you were having me on, until I saw the Sinclair carriage in front of the house. Since you had no clothing, I proposed delivering them to you, wherever you were, at first light this morning. Thankfully, the man agreed." He walked to one of four large windows and drew back the curtain to peer out at the square. "So tell me, Nick. Why the hell are you here at the Berkeley Square house? I thought you were going to stay with me until you left."

"You wouldn't believe me. I am certain this isn't wise, but somehow, I know I will regret it if I don't play along. Besides, you will allow that I have never been one to walk away from a beautiful woman."

"Allow me a moment, cousin." Felix opened

one palm. "Lady Ivy, believing you to be an actor, offers to pay you quite a lot of blunt to impersonate the new Marquess of Counterton—having no idea that you *are* the true marquess himself."

"You've got the right of it. Five hundred pounds."

"But five hundred pounds is nothing to you. And yet you accepted her offer?"

"I did. Thought it wise to play myself instead of some other chap she might engage outside the theater."

Felix shook his head. "Why not just tell her who you are and put a quick end to her nonsensical plan? Doing so would be far easier."

Nick looked up at him. "Yes, you may be right there, but it would hardly be as amusing. As it is, I am able to oversee the renovation of my house—and make sure Cheatlin isn't exaggerating costs. And, as long as I am the one impersonating myself, what harm is there in spending a little time with a most beautiful and entertaining—and did I say passionate?—woman." He waggled his eyebrows rakishly for effect.

Felix clapped a hand to his forehead. "Oh, Nicky, I fear, in this instance, you will regret having not walked—no, having not *run* away from this particular beautiful woman."

Nick shrugged a shoulder, ignoring Felix's concern, as he flung open the trunk and began tossing the coats, neckcloths and waistcoats of every color of a summer flower garden, gloves and a single beaver hat onto the carved mahogany tester bed. "Were you in complete darkness when you assembled this collection for me?"

Nothing suited. Nothing. It was all too . . . dramatic.

Annoyed, he jerked his head around to ask for assistance in assembling morning wear.

Felix was now bent over the copper hipbath, humming as he washed his hands. "Ah, the life of the lord. The water is still warm."

"Yes, it is." Because it had taken Nick so bloody long to light the kitchen fire, heat the water, and carry it pail after pail, up the stairs—himself. It had taken him more than an hour to complete the task, causing him to wonder where the phantom maids and footmen were. For, despite what Cheatlin had told him, they were not present in the house at all. Not even on the fourth floor . . . working.

With pinched fingers, Nick reached deep into the bottom of the trunk and withdrew a hothouse-lemon-hued neckcloth and waved it at his cousin. "And you thought I would wear this—this *thing*?"

Felix straightened, pausing only briefly at the washstand to dry his hands, before crossing the chamber and snatching the neckcloth from Nick's fingers. "Don't be such a goose, of course not." He paused for moment, then glanced up coyly. "I brought this treasure for me."

Nick came to his feet, realizing where the conversation was headed and the request Felix would make. "Oh, no. No. You are *not* staying here!"

Snorting, Felix waved off the reply. "Come now, why ever not? You obviously could use a little help around here. There has not been a footman or maid in sight since I arrived." He flipped up the tails of his coat and sat down on the edge of the tester bed. "Now that the theater is closed, I haven't anything to do. Have some consideration."

"No."

"You have not been informed about the structure of London Society or its key players. I can assist you. I know all of the Society gossip. I never miss an *on dit* column." When Nick remained silent, Felix became persistent. "Nicky, you've established some sort of intimate connection with a Sinclair— a bloody Sinclair. I cannot exist another day if you do not tell me how this came about. Please confess. I can help you."

"*No!*" Just then the pounding of the brass knocker

on the front door echoed through the house. Nick looked up at Felix. "Dear God, it's Ivy." His gaze shot to the mound of clothes on the bed.

The knocker sounded again. No one was answering.

Felix leaped to his feet and began tearing through the clothes. "This, and this too." He threw a coat and waistcoat at Nick. "White neckcloth, and . . . the breeches you are wearing. They will have to do." Then his cousin shed his own bottle green kerseymere coat and slipped a black broadcloth coat over his shoulders. Nick immediately recognized it as Felix's butler costume. "I shall admit Lady Ivy and settle her in the parlor . . . assuming I can find it."

Nick thought to argue, but Felix pointed at the waistcoat.

"Hurry now. If you don't, I would not be surprised if she came right up the stairs to see you. You know she would do it," Felix said, with a bit of playful warning in his voice. "Besides, you don't want to leave me alone with her for too long . . ." Felix laughed at his reflection in the mirror as he quickly removed a wisp of lint from his waistcoat and straightened his coat. Then, turning on the ball of his foot, he disappeared through the doorway and rushed down the stairs.

Grabbing up a wrinkled but still serviceable white

neckcloth, Nick hurried before the standing cheval mirror and fumbled his way through fashioning a simple mail coach tie. It took three attempts, due to his lack of focus.

But how could he concentrate on anything at all? Felix was right. Nick didn't want his mischievous cousin alone with Ivy.

Not even for a tick of the clock's minute hand.

Ivy's gaze flitted around the crimson parlor, while she, her brother Grant, and the two tailors he had engaged waited for Dominic to join them. Why the room was called the crimson parlor, Ivy hadn't a clue. The parlor walls were buff and the wooden trim a muted green. Dusty damask swags were tacked above two large windows, but they were so old and faded that she couldn't quite discern what color they had once been.

The tall footman hovering just outside the parlor door was no help in solving the mystery, but, as one of Cheatlin's new members of the house staff, she supposed he couldn't be expected to. La, he even had trouble finding the parlor once he'd ushered her and the gentlemen accompanying her inside.

She'd have to speak to Cheatlin about the staff's familiarity with the house. It was essential that they all play their roles flawlessly. This morning might have been a disaster. What if Lady Winthrop had come to the house this day, instead of her? What then?

When Dominic (it was amazing how easily Ivy had come to think of him by that name) entered the crimson parlor, which was not red at all, she was immediately reassured that she had done absolutely the right thing in spending the coin so that Grant could engage two of London's most prominent tailors, Mr. Schweitzer and Mr. Davidson to craft Lord Counterton a basic wardrobe.

"Good morning, Lady Ivy"—Dominic crossed the room in less than three strides, lifted her hand, and pressed a chaste kiss atop it—"Lord Grant. Gentlemen."

Ivy felt her cheeks color, which was ridiculous. How had she actually allowed herself to misread those subtle signals that told her that he might truly be a little attracted to her—despite the fact that she was his employer. Gads, how blind had she been? Why just looking at the man's tight-waisted, plum-colored coat and flamboyant waistcoat made it blatantly evident to everyone in the room that he was . . . an actor. And, all of the ladies in London could tell you that all of the most handsome actors in London, the sort that made the women swoon, preferred the company of . . . other actors. Which was a terrible shame for all the misses in Town. Ivy sighed inwardly as she gazed upon Dominic's perfectly handsome face and silently added herself to the number of the disappointed misses.

"Lord Counterton," Grant was saying, "may I introduce two of the finest tailors in London, Mr. Schweitzer and Mr. Davidson of 12 Cork Street."

"I am afraid I do not understand . . ." Dominic said, glancing quizzically at the tailors.

"They are here to take measurements for a new wardrobe. I mentioned their shop because you will need to go there on the morrow to have your evening coat fitted. We all will be attending the ball at the Argyle Rooms that evening. Mr. Schweitzer and Mr. Davidson have assigned their entire staff to complete your wardrobe."

"They understand how important it is"—she pinned Dominic with her gaze—"that the new Marquess of Counterton is appropriately dressed to assume his elevated station in Society."

The two tailors graciously tipped their heads to Dominic.

The footman left his post at the doorway and charged forward. "I see nothing wrong with his ensemble! Every piece, except the breeches perhaps, is of the highest quality."

"Felix, please." Dominic caught the footman's

arm and drew him away from Ivy. "Of course I agree with you. I believe Lord Grant only means that a more formal ensemble is required for this event. Is that not so, Lord Grant?"

Ivy blinked. *Did he just call the footman "Felix"?* Suddenly the footman's lack of knowledge of the layout of the house made sense to her. The footman was not one of Cheatlin's staff who had been working in this house for two months—he was Dominic's man . . . from Davies Street. Though, he looked much younger. It must have only been a trick of evening light that had made his hair appear gray before.

"Lord Counterton is correct. The waistcoat he is wearing is especially quite fine, but something . . . er . . . less splendid is required for this particular ball," Grant replied, as if trying placate this Felix fellow.

But Ivy decided not to waste a moment longer thinking about who Felix truly was, not when there was so much still to do to prepare Dominic to take on his role as Lord Counterton *tomorrow*!

Grant turned his attention away from the overstepping footman and to the tailors. "Dear sirs, you are very gracious in coming to Berkeley Square to take Lord Counterton's essential measures, so let us not delay your ministrations any longer." He widened his eyes meaningfully at Ivy. Only she didn't quite understand. She stood there glancing from one gentleman to the next until Dominic suddenly crystallized Grant's hint for her.

"No, indeed." Dominic did not look at her but addressed the tailors directly. "Shall I remove my clothing?" There was a slight grin upon his lips as he shrugged the coat from his shoulders and dropped it upon a chair beside the hearth. He turned and held her gaze as his fingers slid down upon the mother-of-pearl buttons of his waistcoat and released them one by one.

Ivy gasped as she unintentionally imagined Dominic removing his clothes. The heat in her cheeks doubled in intensity.

"I-I . . . will leave you to your work, kind sirs." She was stammering like a fool. "I would greatly enjoy a view of the rear. The garden. What I meant was the garden in the rear of the house."

Oh, good God. Leave now, Ivy. Just go.

"I will return shortly to discuss . . ." The two tailors, one on his knees before Dominic and other stretching a measuring tape across his broad shoulders, paused and looked up at her expectantly. Ivy could not seem raise her eyes and meet Dominic's gaze. "To discuss . . . things."

Oh that was brilliant. In her humiliation, she was sure her face glowed like a hot coal.

Ivy spun around, and, as she retreated from the room, she thought she heard a chuckle from Dominic's direction.

Clapping her hands upon her cheeks to cool them, Ivy raced from the room. How humiliating. She had made an utter fool of herself, gawking at him and fiercely blushing like a bride on her wedding night.

Suddenly, she had quite a fanciful notion as to why the parlor, without a hint of red, was called the crimson parlor.

Chapter 6

Envy is like a fly that passes all the body's sounder parts and dwells upon the sores.
Arthur Chapman

Two hours later
Berkeley Square

A hired hackney rolled up before the Counterton house on Berkeley Square, drawing Ivy to the parlor windows. "Thank heaven, Lachlan is here."

Her brother Lachlan, like all of the other Sinclair brothers, was an exceptionally tall and well-muscled man, and he had to bend slightly at the waist to step down from the cab. He reached and offered his hand to someone still inside as the driver removed a leather bag from the perch and set it down beside him. Ivy leaned closer to the window, squinting her eyes against the golden afternoon light until she recognized the tall, slender woman lifting the hem of her blue silk gown to step down to the street. It was her sister, Siusan.

As her two siblings climbed the steps to the pavers before the house, Ivy spun around to Dominic, who was sitting across from the useless footman, Felix, in a lyre-back chair. The most bored expression dressed his far-too-handsome face.

"Before we left this morn," Grant said, "it occurred to me that Lord Counterton might wish to borrow a few Town suits until the tailors have completed his. I asked Poplin to stir up a few of my own clothes for him. Lachlan said he'd deliver them. Seems he's brought Siusan along with the clothes."

Dominic came to his feet. "Forgive me, but I do not understand what is deficient about what I am wearing if we are only going to take tea in the garden."

"Nothing at all if you are a performer at the Bartholomew Fair," Ivy murmured to herself. Since the footman made no effort to stand to answer the door, Ivy gave an exasperated huff and started for the passage herself. She opened the door before

Lachlan could slam down the brass knocker and, clasping their arms, hurried her two siblings inside.

"I cannot thank you enough for coming to help us. He's in the parlor."

Grant spied the portmanteau in Lachlan's hand. "Bring that too, Lach. When you see our friend, you'll know why I asked Poplin to send something appropriate for day."

"His clothing cannot be as bad as all that. You have always been one to exaggerate, Ivy," Siusan was whispering, as they strode into the parlor and beheld Dominic. She stopped the moment she saw Dominic and Felix and gave her head a shake. "A dark coat? Yes, I can see why you are so concerned," she said, sarcasm licking her words.

"What?" Ivy realized then that Lachlan and Siusan were looking at Felix. "No, no, no. *He* is the footman, *supposedly*." She stepped forward, took Dominic's arm, and drew him to her sister. "*This* is my Lord Counterton."

Siusan covered her mouth to stifle a laugh as she noticed the brightly hued, somewhat-too-tight apparel.

If Dominic bristled, his countenance did not show it.

Grant stepped up beside them and claimed the

honor of introduction. "Allow me to introduce you both to Dominic Sheridan, the Marquess of Counterton. Lord Counterton, my sister, Lady Siusan, and brother, Lord Lachlan."

"Lady Siusan, it is an honor to meet you," Dominic said in that low, resonant voice of his. He took her hand gently in his, bent over it, and placed a kiss atop her glove.

Siusan's eyes grew lazy, and she brought her hand up and laid it atop her collarbone and curtsied. "The honor is entirely mine, Lord Counterton."

"And you, Lord Lachlan." Dominic stepped toward Lachlan and reached out for his hand.

"I shall pass on the hand kissing, if you do not mind." With an cheeky grin, he tipped his head in greeting.

Ivy, who watched the introduction of her sister with a blend of fascination, and maybe a wee bit of jealously too, broke in. "Dears, he is not truly Lord Counterton, Su. Don't you recognize him? He is the actor you recommended."

Su became instantly confused. "No, no, no." She gestured to the footman. "*He* is the actor I saw at the Drury Lane—the lead—and recommended to you." She looked at Dominic, and a slow flirtatious smile eased across her mouth. "But, oh my, Ivy, magnificent casting, I must say."

"The footman . . . this footman . . . is the actor you saw?" Ivy jerked her head around and studied Felix. Now that she looked at him, really saw him, she could see how Su might have thought he was ideal for the role of Counterton. He was tall, like Dominic, had dark, wavy hair and a lean, athletic build. They actually looked similar in many ways. But Dominic was the superior selection for the role. He was so much more . . . well, everything.

"I admit, I am not privy to the details of these goings-on"—Felix's eyebrows shot upward and several lines dug into his forehead—"but am I to understand that I-I was being considered for this role?" He skewered Dominic with his gaze. A flicker of a smile crossed his lips before he returned his attention to the women, "The role of Lord Counterton? Truly" He looked excitedly from Siusan to Ivy, waiting for a confirmation.

Ivy struggled to come up with words. "Err . . . I suppose my sister's description could have fit you both," she said. "But it is my opinion that 'Dominic' is perhaps better suited for the role."

Surprisingly, Felix nodded. "I must agree with you, Lady Ivy, but I think I would have carried the role splendidly."

"Aye, be that as it may . . ." Grant, who had been observing the entire exchange, took his portmanteau from Lachlan and set it down beside Dominic. "Lord Counterton," he said, with a hint of laughter in his voice. "Inside there should be two sets of clothing, both suitable for day." Grant drew closer to Dominic and tugged at his sleeve, which even Ivy could see was too short, then circled around him. "I think you'll find that my wardrobe will fit you well enough. The only differences in our measure might be an inch in height."

"An inch is not so great that I cannot hide the difference in my boots," Dominic said, gesturing to his feet.

"Hoby?" Grant asked, glancing down at Dominic's footwear with sudden interest.

"Yes, they are!" Felix was beaming. "They are new."

Grant grinned, and Ivy could see the amusement in his eyes. "You know quality then. Felix, is it?"

"Thank you, Lord Grant," he chirped, "and, yes, Mister Felix Dupré, late of The Theater Royal Drury Lane." He gave Grant a sweeping bow.

Dominic, who clearly felt uneasy with this whole borrowing of clothing, took the portmanteau. "I shall return in a moment or two since I know Lady Ivy has been looking forward to taking tea all morning."

"I shall assist you with your neckcloth, Your

Lordship," Felix announced and, for an instant, Ivy could actually imagine him as a true valet.

The moment the two men ascended the stairs, Siusan and Ivy rushed together, grasped each other's hands, and squealed like little girls.

"Ivy, he is absolutely gorgeous—and la, I don't think I have ever said those words about a man!"

Ivy bounced on the balls of her feet in excitement. "I know. He is perfect, exactly the sort of gentleman I need to woo Miss Feeney away from Tinsdale. But in truth, I cannot refrain from staring at him, which is highly embarrassing. La, my cheeks have been burning since the first moment I saw him, which is quite nonsensical. Not only did I engage him for the sole purpose of winning back Tinsdale—but he is also . . . well, an *actor*."

"Och, so he is an actor. Dinna fash about the way he sets your toes tingling. He is handsome; there is no denying that. Your reaction is completely natural," Su told her. "I felt a little warm myself when he kissed my hand. Besides, the more infatuated you appear with him, the more Miss Feeney will want to steal him away from you."

Ivy hugged Siusan to her. "My dear sister, you are completely right."

Grant shook his head. "No, you are *both* completely mad."

The Garden of Eden Tea Garden
Marylebone

Dominic looked up and saw both Lady Ivy and Lady Siusan intently watching him as he took a bit of cake into his mouth from his fork. He froze, fork still in the air, then hurried to swallow his cake down. "Is something amiss?"

Ivy shook her head. "Not at all." She turned and whispered to Siusan. "He eats so very well, does he not?"

"Almost as if he has been doing it all of his life," Grant said beneath his breath.

Lachlan snared Ivy in his gaze. "This is absurd, Ivy. The man clearly does not need training in table manners."

"Lachlan is quite right, Ivy," Siusan supported. "Why, it is not as if he grew up in a hovel in Cheapside."

"I am well aware of that," Ivy snapped at her sister. She smiled at him. "Your manners are impeccable."

"Thank you kindly, Lady Ivy." Dominic set his fork on the edge of plate and folded his hands in his lap. "I do try. Really, I do." Once his point was made, he lifted his fork and broke off another bite of cake.

Ivy forced a chuckle at the ridiculousness of her thought to bring him to the tea garden for a lesson in table etiquette. It was only that she desperately wanted her plan to succeed, and she did not wish to leave anything to chance. But then, Siusan's passing comment about his upbringing began to nip, and her curiosity got the better of her. She felt compelled to ask. "Actually, I do not believe I know where your family is from, Dominic . . . I mean, Lord Counterton."

He lifted a single eyebrow but took his time chewing the bite he had just taken before swallowing to reply. Dominic smiled, a lift of his lips in which Ivy thought she might detect a bit of mischievousness. "I was born and raised in the hamlet of Averly, near Lincolnshire—until I was packed off to school."

"Lincolnshire, eh?" Grant seemed surprised. "Imagine that. I have a fine ear, but I do not detect the dialect at all."

Siusan waved her hands to quiet her brother. "Probably worked it off of him at school. Shrewsbury, I would wager. The school's known for sanding down the rough edges of its students."

Dominic leaned back in his chair and folded his arms across his chest. "Very good, Lady Siusan. I am quite impressed."

Ivy huffed at that and leaned in over the edge of the table. "As am I," she whispered. "That you were taken in by his story. The true Lord Counterton hailed from Averly near Lincolnshire and was schooled at Shrewsbury—not *him*."

Dominic laughed. "But I am Lord Counterton, Lady Ivy." He uncrossed his arms and leaned across the tiny tea table until his nose nearly touched Ivy's, and whispered to her, "Is not that what we agreed?"

Ivy's mouth dropped open for an instant before she had the wit to snap it shut again. "Touché, my lord."

This all struck Grant as being very amusing, and he laughed a little too loudly. Siusan burst forth giggling like a besotted miss, clapping her hands enthusiastically.

"Well done," Lachlan exclaimed, before adding, in a confidential tone, "I honestly believed you, man."

"And so you should." Dominic came to his feet, and, placing one hand atop his stomach and the other behind his back, he bowed to each of them, exactly like the stage actor he was, in truth, before resuming to eat.

Siusan, Lachlan, and Grant laughed even louder. Ivy did not. Dominic was not being the least bit diverting. In all honesty, he was on the verge of destroying any chance of her plan working—because everyone around them was now looking at him! He, and her brothers and sister, had drawn the attention of nearly everyone at the tea garden.

Suddenly, she saw an older woman rise from her table and lift a quizzing glass to her eye.

Oh dear. Lady Winthrop. And she was not alone.

"Dominic," she tried to whisper, but her warning came out more like a hiss. "Behind you. It's—"

It was too late. Ivy clamped her mouth shut and felt the blood rushing from her head.

Dominic stared at Ivy, his eyes wide. She didn't know if it was because of the ghostly pallor she was sure her face must be taking on or because, somehow, he'd taken her warning. He set his fork down and slowly rose from his chair, just as Lady Winthrop and three other matrons arrived at the table. He reached for Lady Winthrop's hand and raised it, pressing a quick kiss atop her gloved knuckles. "Lady Winthrop, how good it is to see you again. Lovely day for tea out-of-doors, is it not?" To her astonishment, despite the look of shock upon his face only seconds ago, he now presented himself with poise and charm in abundance, as if meeting Lady Winthrop was the most delightful event in his day.

Siusan was looking at Ivy in a most startled manner, even if Dominic was not, and whisked up her cutwork fan and began to wave it madly before Ivy's face. "You are so pale. Are you ill?" she whispered.

"No," Ivy hissed, and pushed the fan away so that she could see what was happening. She was relieved that, owing to Dominic's sinfully handsome appearance, not one of the ladies seemed to observe Siusan's expression. Their eyes were fastened to the new Marquess of Counterton, as if they'd been secured with a hatpin.

Lachlan reluctantly rose but stared longingly at his cake, unwilling to waste his rakish charms on women he would not wish to bed.

Grant, however, was standing on the other end of the broad line of elderly ladies, charming them completely. Ivy doubted if they were aware that she and Siusan were present at all. With all the female sighing and gushing over every word the handsome men were saying, the women must have thought they'd transcended the Garden of Eden and were now in heaven.

She felt a hand on her arm then, and Siusan moved her mouth closer to Ivy's ear. "You see, little sister, you have nothing to fash about. Lord Counterton is perfect. There is not a woman in all of London who will be able to resist him."

Ivy peered up at Dominic as he charmed the ladies, transforming them into giggling misses of far fewer years.

"Not a one," Siusan repeated.

Unfortunately, Ivy already knew how true that was.

Later that evening
Berkeley Square

"For the last time, no! You have not been invited and will not be attending, Felix." Nick's nerves were twisted at the prospect of beginning the ruse—meeting Miss Feeney and wooing her away from Tinsdale. At another time the game of capturing a young lady's attention would have had its allure. The delight of charming a beautiful woman would have been reason enough to attend a dreary ball. But not tonight. The sole appeal of the ball this night was Ivy's presence. Damn, but she was as lovely as she was entertaining.

"Certainly you will find a waltz on the official program this night." Though trying to project a preoccupation with a water spot on the rim of a crystal glass, Felix was unsuccessful in veiling his interest.

Nick's cheek muscles twitched, tugging the

edges of his lips upward. He consciously flattened the expression to conceal his amusement. "The waltz—that indecent foreign romp? I daresay not."

"Indecent? Surely you jest—"

Nick raised a hand to silence Felix, knowing full well it would tie his cousin in knots of frustration. With an air of disinterest, Nick walked to the windows and drew the curtains closed. "English-women are far too genteel and refined, their morals too high to allow themselves to entwine their limbs and compress their bodies most obscenely with a man while on the dance floor. Women in Averly—"

Felix could withhold his opinion no longer. He clanked the glass down upon the table. "Must I continually remind you that you are no longer in Averly. This is London and, I tell you, here the waltz is *à la mode*." Felix scurried into the library, from which he returned moments later with a newspaper in his hand. "Thankfully I brought my collection of columns for the last month in the event we needed them for Society research. Here it is. The waltz is entirely proper." He opened the newspaper to the second page and thrust it at Nick. "See here. The *Times* reported it just two weeks past. The waltz was introduced at the English court Friday last. Entirely respectable. His Highness, the Prince Regent was in attendance."

Nick accepted the pages from Felix and read over the column. "Oh, yes, entirely supported." He chuckled, then cleared his throat and read a phrase from the *Times* directly.

> . . . So long as this obscene display was confined to prostitutes and adulteresses, we did not think it deserving of notice; but now that it is attempted to be forced on the respectable classes of society by the evil example of their superiors, we feel it a duty to warn every parent against exposing his daughter to so fatal a contagion.

"I tell you, Nicky, the waltz is all the crack. Now that the Regent has given his blessing, dancing masters are being summoned to all the houses in Mayfair to teach the steps. They haven't enough hours in the day to instruct so many students."

"Then you will allow that I shall be forgiven for not being trained this evening." Nick had never been one for dancing. Though he possessed passable technique for country dances, which was helpful in wooing the ladies, Nick never quite mastered anything more complicated than a reel. No, he'd realized early in his years that convincing a pretty maid to take a turn about the ballroom was more in keeping with his skills and more likely to result in seduction—rather than giggles of amusement if he dared to dance. "I daresay the uninformed shall outnumber the fashionable if what you claim is true."

Felix bowed in Nick's direction, then, when he straightened his back, extended his hand to his cousin. "But you need to stand among the fashionable."

Oh dear God.

Felix strode forward and snatched up Nick's hand before he could step away. "Fortune smiles upon you, Nick, for I have received the requisite training in the waltz." He smiled proudly, tightening his grip lest Nick pull away. "In fact, I will teach the most fashionable of waltzes—the Quick *Sauteuse*. Leap, hop, close. It's very simple actually."

Nick groaned. Allowing Ivy to put him through his paces was one thing. Enduring a dance lesson from Felix was quite another.

"Come now, we haven't much time." Felix nudged Nick's foot with his own. "Commence by bringing your left foot from the fourth position behind into the second position with a turn of the body, like this. Then, follow with a pirouette. Oh, very good, Nicky . . ."

Ten of the clock, that evening
Berkeley Square

"Wait, please, Your Ladyship," Felix, the footman, called out to Ivy as he pursued her up the staircase to Dominic's bedchamber.

Ivy held the tied parcel tightly against her chest as she raced up the treads. "I cannot delay. We are already late as it is!"

"But, Lady Ivy," he persisted, "you cannot enter!"

Just as her hand pressed down on the latch to the bedchamber Cheatlin had pointed out as the one Lord Counterton would occupy during her first and only tour of the house, Ivy cast a look of exasperation over her shoulder at the footman. "Why ever not?"

"Because he's not decent," the footman managed to utter just at the moment the bedchamber door slowly swung open.

Ivy snorted back an indelicate laugh. "I know that, else he would not have—."

The footman beside her was blanching now. "I am dreadfully sorry, my lord," he whispered. "Couldn't stop her."

"Oh, I do not doubt that all," she heard Dominic say in that low, wholly seductive way of his, the words followed by the sound of splashing water.

Ivy whipped her head around, only to find herself rendered speechless. Dominic was stepping from the hipbath. Rivulets of water raced down his naked body, dripping onto the floor as he reached for a bath linen draped across a nearby spoon-back chair.

She couldn't help but stare at the hard mounds of his chest, the scores between the muscles of his lean abdomen, and lower to . . . God above.

The water must not have been cold.

Oh, good heavens. Since yesterday, when he nearly disrobed before her, she had been envisioning, most sinfully, Dominic completely naked. And now he was, and his form was even more amazing than she had imagined.

He rubbed the linen towel through his hair. "Go on, have a look, Ivy. After all, you're paying good coin for this." Flashing her a cocky grin, he began drying his arms. Bare arms she would so like to feel wrapped around her.

My God. She was staring at his naked body. Her fingers felt for her lips. She hadn't been smiling too, had she? The edges of her lips were tipped up. *Oh perdition. How mortifying.*

Whirling around, she faced Felix. She knew she looked like a veritable numbskull with her eyes wide as tea saucers, and her mouth agape, but there was no helping that. She had to catch the breath she'd lost from the race up the stairs a moment. Not because of—*oh my word*.

"Come in, Lady Ivy," Dominic said. "I assure you, though I am not decent, as you pointed out, my naughty bits are covered."

Hesitantly, Ivy turned around. *Those weren't bits at all.* The bath linen was wrapped around his hips, but his broad chest was exposed. Not that he minded, for it was clear he didn't in the least.

It was then she realized that he was gazing appreciatively at her. "I have never seen a more beautiful woman, than you, Lady Ivy, tonight," he said to her, in such a tone that . . . la, had she not known he was an actor, she would have believed him.

But even though she knew he was only charming her, truth to tell, she did feel a little beautiful this evening. She glanced down at her newly fashioned blue silk gown with tiny pearls lining a daring French neckline. It had been an extravagance, one she and her family could ill afford. But still, it was essential to her plan to win back Tinsdale. For it was all well and good for Dominic to steal Miss Feeney's affections, but there would still be the task of bringing Lord Tinsdale to heel.

She raised her eyes and saw that Dominic was still peering intently at her. "The gown . . . it's new," she stammered.

"I hadn't noticed the gown." Dominic gazed deeply into her eyes. "It is lovely, as well. It suits you."

She tossed the parcel on the tester bed. "Late, but your evening ensemble is finally finished. Please dress immediately. The ball began nearly an hour past."

"Absolutely, my lady." His fingers released the linen and, as it fell to the floor, he kicked it out of his way as he came to the bed, completely naked, and his fingers began working to open the package.

Lord above. Her eyes fixed on the leanness of his thighs and muscled curve of his buttocks. "I-I shall . . . leave you to it." Ivy felt heat bursting up from her bodice. "I will await you in the crimson parlor."

Dominic turned his head and winked at her, causing her flush to flood to her cheeks. She tried to quit the room in a slow, calm stride, but she ended up trotting to the door instead.

"Five minutes," he promised. "Less if Felix assists me with tying my neckcloth."

Felix passed her on her way out. "Five minutes,

then," she said, stealing a sinful peek at tight buttocks as she turned down the passage.

She paused at the banister for a moment, then forced her chin up. "Miss Fiona Feeney," she said aloud. "You haven't a chance."

"Nor does Tinsdale," came Dominic's deep, rich voice.

Ivy whirled around to see him standing in the doorway, wearing naught but the buff-colored breeches. "I beg your pardon. W-hat did you say?"

"Tinsdale doesn't stand a chance."

Ivy nodded dumbly, then watched him turn slowly and disappear back into the bedchamber.

The unexpected compliment sent a stew of emotions bubbling up inside Ivy, and for the life of her, she didn't know if she was going to laugh or cry. Her emotions were just a seething jumble.

So, she simply turned away and hurried down the stairs, wondering if this night would be the best, or worst, of her life.

Chapter 7

*A woman has two smiles that an angel might envy;
the smile that accepts a lover before words are
uttered, and the smile that lights on the first born
babe and assures it of a mother's love.*

Thomas C. Haliburton

*The Argyle Rooms
Regent Street*

Lady Ivy was clenching Nick's arm so tightly
as he escorted her up the grand staircase that
his hand was beginning to tingle from lack of
blood. He pumped his fist, trying to urge some life
back into it before he would be required to shake
some gentleman's hand or use it to lift a lady's in
greeting.

In the light of the Grecian lamps illuminating their upward path, the streaks of summer gold in Ivy's long copper locks gleamed. Had he any feeling in his hand, he might have forgotten himself and run his fingers through her lustrous hair.

"Three of my brothers and my two sisters are meeting us in the Turkish Room just ahead." As they reached the top of the staircase and passed an exquisite lounge supported with Ionic columns, Ivy released his arm and paused. "Since you told the Winthrops that our fathers were old friends, I feel it imperative that you learn each of my five siblings' names and a bit about them. You will only have moments to do so, so please focus."

"I thought there were seven of you." While Nick waited for her to answer, he looked ahead and saw a room swathed with blue draperies and luxurious carpeting on the floor. Several ottoman sofas ringed the room. Upon one sat Lady Siusan beside another woman possessing the same delicate features as Ivy.

Lord Grant was sipping from a glass of what looked to be claret with Lord Lachlan, as he pointed out to another dark-haired giant of a man something on the ceiling that Nick could not yet see. The Sinclairs.

"There are," Ivy said quite softly, as she took his

arm and started him walking toward the Turkish room again. "My brother Sterling and his wife, Isobel, have been welcomed back into the family. They are currently in Scotland with our father." Then he thought he heard her add something under her breath. "The rest of us hope to be so lucky someday."

Nick looked quizzically at Ivy, waiting for her to explain what she meant, but she didn't. She looked straight ahead and guided him into the Turkish Room.

Immediately, they were surrounded by beings of such physical perfection that Nick wondered if the room was bewitched and the Greek statues of the Argyle Rooms had come to life here.

Ivy did not tarry; at once she began a hurried series of whispered introductions. "Lord Counterton, we haven't much time before we are noticed, and you are supposed to be acquainted with us all. These are my brothers and sisters, also known in Edinburgh and London Society as the Seven Deadly Sins. I tell you this only because you may hear of us referred to this way."

He fought any expression that might betray that he had indeed heard the horrid term . . . from his cousin, no less.

"Of course, you have met Siusan." Ivy gestured

to her sable-haired sister, who stepped forward and extended her hand to him to kiss. "Her sin, because you should know, is sloth." Ivy lifted her eyebrows and her chin and peered down her nose at her sister, who had now raised her other hand for him to kiss too. "We just refer to her as lazy Siusan."

Siusan flashed a glare Ivy's way, then lowered her hand and stepped back. She pushed Grant forward. "And, you also know Grant," she said taking charge. She smiled wickedly back at Ivy.

"My sin is gluttony," Grant admitted, "but I prefer to being known as a connoisseur of the finer things in life." He put his hand on one of his brother's shoulders. "You've met Lachlan, who endeavors to become the most notorious rake in all of London."

Lachlan grinned and shook Nick's hand. "Lord Lust, at your service, Counterton."

Ivy shook her head disgustedly at her brother before moving along with her rushed and informal introductions. She caught the arm of the young woman whose features most resembled her own, though her hair was ebony black and her eyes blue as a clear summer sky. Her vibrant coloring was simply stunning. "This is Priscilla."

Priscilla pulled away from Ivy and approached

Nick for a closer look. "Such beautiful children we could have, Lord Counterton. So, so beautiful." The dark slash of her left eyebrow lifted for an instant before she spun around to her sister and spoke to her as though Nick wasn't even there. "May I have him when you're through, Ivy? I vow I have never seen a man so handsome. Imagine the two of us together. Beautiful."

"Her sin is pride," Ivy interjected. "I know," she added with a prick of sarcasm in her voice, "surprising, eh? Had I not told you, I wager you would never have guessed."

A huge young man, with hair as dark as a raven's wing extended his hand. "I am Killian, Priscilla's twin."

Then Ivy leaned her mouth to Nick's ear. "Word over scandal broth is that he killed a man for simply showing disrespect to Priscilla. But I shouldn't believe it were I you. His sin is wrath, but more for his talent in inspiring the sin in others than embodying it himself.

"Whom have I missed?" Ivy spun around in a circle. "Oh, Sterling. He is the eldest and is visiting our father in Scotland. You might have heard about the largest wager in White's history earlier this Season? My brother arranged an anonymous bet that he would marry Miss Isobel Carington before the end of the season—that was after she publicly spurned him, no less. His sin is greed . . . or rather *was*. According to our father, he has reformed. And, I suppose it's true, because he and Isobel are now married." She clapped her hands together. "So, there you have it. Do you have any questions before we enter the saloon to steal Tinsdale back from Miss Feeney?"

He really only did have just one question. "What is your sin, Lady Ivy?"

A scarlet poppy suddenly bloomed on each of her cheeks.

"Oh that." She glanced at her sisters, as if waiting for one of them to reply for her, but when neither did, she raised her golden green eyes and without the least bit of shame told him. "*Envy.*"

Even before they entered the Saloon Theatre, Nick's ears were buzzing with the chatter and laughter of the crowd. Lady Ivy had certainly been correct about the rains driving Londoners back into the city like cattle home from the pasture.

With Ivy on his arm, he followed the other Sinclairs into the massive saloon. Within a blink, a ripple of silence swept from where they emerged through the entire assembly.

Lady Siusan leaned close and, being nearly as tall

as Nick, whispered into his ear. "Do not take their reaction personally, my dear lord. This is quite usual behavior whenever the Sinclairs appear any-where *en masse*."

"Conversation will begin again once they've had a chance to gawk," Priscilla added, as she blatantly tried to press between Siusan and Nick. "Why, you would think we were carnival novelties with snakeskin, a third arm, or inappropriate female facial hair by the way they stare, wouldn't you?"

"Your family is a sight to behold," Nick told them. "Were I not standing amongst you, I, myself, would have stopped and stared at such a stunningly beautiful group."

He did not know if he was imagining that the crowd seemed to be staring at Ivy particularly, or if, like him, they simply could not take their eyes from such a beguiling creature.

It might have been her gown, a celestial blue crape frock over white satin, embroidered with shaded blue silks. Or perhaps the vibrancy of her golden copper hair, prettily accented with tiny blue and ivory flowers. It might even have been the way a small necklace of pearls drew his eyes to the long pale column of her throat.

Yes, it could have been any of these things that inspired his admiration for her.

As he stared at her, though, he knew the truth of the answer. Just as anyone who might have observed him as he looked at her.

It was not admiration he was feeling for Ivy. It was an attraction so much deeper than that. The realization was startling, and he tugged at his neckcloth, which suddenly felt too tight.

"Ivy, I am the eldest sister," Siusan suddenly said in a hushed voice, "so Dominic should be mine, not Priscilla's when . . . his work is finished." She chuckled then, but by the way Ivy glared back at her, Nick wasn't completely sure that she believed her sister's statement was simply in jest.

"Well, I, for one, have had enough of this rude staring." Lord Grant broke from the Sinclair column and strode purposefully across the marble floor. He signaled up to the orchestra's conductor, who stood before the musicians on a wirework dais.

Though it was impossible to hear what the huge Scot said to the man, the conductor seemed almost to shudder, and he hurriedly raised his baton. The musicians lifted their instruments, and before Grant had even managed to return to the Sinclair fold, a flurry of notes filled the air.

The Sinclair clan divided themselves into two groups and moved off toward opposite ends of the grand saloon.

Ivy, clutching Nick's arm, didn't move. Instead, her eyes flashed this way and that, searching for someone.

He didn't need to ask whom.

But even had he thought to, it would not have been necessary because suddenly she tugged excitedly on his arm and trotted in place like a nervous filly. "There they are—Tinsdale and Miss Feeney. Do you see them near the screen of columns?"

"You really must possess extraordinary eyesight, Lady Ivy." Nick looked up toward the ceiling painted like an afternoon sky and counted six balloon-cut chandeliers, each supporting twelve candles. "I fear I cannot see more than five yards ahead."

"What, no spectacles?" Ivy wrinkled her nose. "Then I will bring you closer, my dear old man."

"I'll have you know I am only thirty years of age."

Ivy snapped her head around and grinned up at him. "*Really?* Thirty is the ideal age for a man to marry." She stopped walking. "You will mention your age to Miss Feeney, won't you? Maybe twice. Aye, at least twice. I think your age is just one more factor to recommend you." She laughed softly. "As if you needed anything more to increase your perfection."

With a slight tug, Ivy urged Nick to the center of the floor. Instinctively, he turned her into place.

Ivy's pink lips parted, and she smiled at him like a proud mother. "Very good, Dominic. You begin very well. Very well, indeed."

He opened his mouth to reply, to tell her that he was not a stable boy, and one country dance is not so different from another (he'd omit the bit about a Scottish reel being one of the three dances he knew passing well), but suddenly an ebony-haired goddess in the arms of a narrow-nosed, pale-haired gentleman came into view beside them. There was little question in his mind that the couple was none other than Miss Fiona Feeney and Viscount Tinsdale.

Ivy tensed as the steps of the dance drew them even closer to the pair. Nick ran his fingers over the back of her hand, hoping to soothe her. But her gaze nervously bounced again and again in the direction of Tinsdale and Miss Feeney.

"Do not dare to look at them, Ivy," he whispered to her as they crossed. "Focus on me. Look into my eyes."

She did as he asked and lifted her head upward so that her golden green eyes met his dark blue ones. He held her gaze captive.

"You are so beautiful," he said softly. "No woman in this room can compare."

He heard her breath catch in her throat, and her eyes glistened suddenly. She shook her head the smallest amount and gazed downward just as the last notes of the reel played out.

Within moments of being in the proximity of Miss Feeney and Lord Tinsdale, Ivy's supreme confidence had flagged and faded away into nothingness.

Settling his fingers under her chin, he made her look up at him. "I swear to you, I am telling you the truth. No other woman can compare to you, Ivy."

She blinked up at him, traces of moisture lighting up her lashes in the light of the chandeliers.

He leaned his face close to hers so she, and no one else, could hear him. His lips paused a finger's width from hers. "Believe me, for it is true."

Ivy stared back at him, wordless. And he knew she did believe him, even if only just a little.

The other couple moved beside them just then. "Lady Ivy, I was not aware you were to attend the ball this night." Miss Feeney spread her lips and smiled brightly. A little too enthusiastically. She wrapped her arm around Tinsdale's and pulled herself a little closer than propriety would dictate at a public event. "Did you know she would be here, Sweeting?"

Before Tinsdale could answer, Nick caringly brushed a lock of Ivy's red hair from her face and spoke. "I do not doubt that you were surprised. Who would have guessed that of all of the invitations, Lady Ivy would have chosen *this* event." He seared Miss Feeney with his most seductive of gazes, paying absolutely no mind to Lord Tinsdale. "But I confess, it is my doing. I wanted to dance with her, so what is a man to do but beg this beautiful lady to condescend to attend the ball?"

He felt Ivy straightening her back and coming to her full height beside him. She gazed up at him and feigned a missish giggle.

"How could I refuse an invitation that would put me in the arms of such a handsome gentleman?" She peered up into his eyes, blinking, and sighed sweetly.

Nick nudged her. "My dear . . ."

"Oh, do forgive me, Miss Feeney, Lord Tinsdale," Ivy said abruptly, "but when we are together I sometimes forget others are even in the room." She summoned her brother Grant, who did the honors of presenting Miss Feeney and Lord Tinsdale to the esteemed Marquess of Counterton.

"Lord Counterton," Grant said, "Miss Fiona Feeney of . . . oh, someplace in Ireland isn't that right, Miss Feeney? And of course, my sister's dear acquaintance, Viscount Tinsdale. Miss Feeney, Lord Tinsdale, Dominic Sheridan, the new Marquess of Counterton." He bowed slightly to Counterton, which Nick thought a bit too much on his part, but the gesture seemed to catch Miss Feeney's notice.

Her eyes widened, and it was not until Lord Tinsdale nudged her that she even attempted to rein in her awe.

Ivy, too, was doing her best to restrain her emotions. Her glee at seeing Miss Feeney take the bait was clear.

Nick reluctantly released Ivy's arm, caught up Miss Feeney's gloved hand, and slowly raised it to his mouth. He prolonged the delivery of the smallest kiss, holding her hand just below his lips for some seconds. Miss Feeney's breathing became faster, her breasts visibly straining with each inhalation against her daring neckline.

Nick knew he had snared her interest. His uncle had told him he'd been born with that talent, just as his father had been. And it was a skill he'd made use of too many times to count, with too many women of no importance in his life.

He ran his fingers lightly over the underside of her wrist, feeling her pulse become more rapid, as he transfixed her with a smoldering gaze that promised everything. Then, at last, Nick touched his lips to her glove and kissed it.

Miss Feeney audibly sighed as Nick straightened. He turned and offered a gracious nod to Lord Tinsdale as he stepped back beside Ivy. "My lord."

Miss Feeney dropped her hold on Tinsdale's arm and stepped toward Nick, opening her mouth as if beginning to say something. Just then, the music recommenced.

"I beg your pardon," Nick interjected before turning to look at Ivy, "but you did promise me another dance, and I intend to hold you to your word." He cupped her hand in both of his, and she laughed a little embarrassedly.

"So I did." Ivy looked at Tinsdale. "Do forgive us for not staying to converse longer, but I did promise . . . and I find it exceedingly difficult to refuse Dominic—Lord Counterton—anything."

Miss Feeney and Lord Tinsdale stood at the perimeter and stared at them. As did at least half of the assembly, a number that was growing by the moment.

Nick supposed it could have been nothing more than the Sinclair effect. Until, that is, he noticed that the Sinclair brothers and sisters were intently watching them as well.

And then he wondered whether he was completely obvious. If everyone could see what Ivy could not.

That he was already smitten with her.

Dominic looked up from the program, his eyes bright and excited. "A waltz. Do you know it, Lady Ivy?" He enthusiastically offered her his arm before she could reply.

"Indeed I do." Dancers were already scurrying to claim their positions upon the floor. "Do you waltz? Truly?"

Dominic raised his eyebrows and smiled at her.

"Well, then, let us dance." She took his proffered arm and allowed him to lead her into place. Such a brilliant choice he was to portray the Marquess of Counterton. Why, the waltz had just been deemed proper, having been danced in court only days ago and already he had mastered the steps.

Or it seemed for a brief instant.

While Ivy had no doubts about his prowess with the ladies, with the first steps (he leaped then hopped before returning to close) Ivy had her doubts about his abilities in the dance line. She held tight and used all her muscle to get him off, but the other dancers were already moving.

He smiled at her as he leaped in place like a fish fighting the line. "The *Sauteuse*. I learned it just

today. Very fashionable, I was told." Dominic suddenly began to move in ¼ time instead of the ¾
tempo the sedate waltz required. He enthusiastically galloped her across the floor, managing three
exaggerated turns directly into the path of two
dancers who were gracefully turning in time with
the music.

"Lord Counterton!" Ivy shrieked. Her warning
came too late. Dominic backed straight into them
like a ramrod, sending all four tumbling into a
mass of crumpled skirts and lost wigs on the floorboards.

The music stopped. The crowd gasped.

Dominic scrambled to his feet, splitting one knee
of his new breeches in the process. "Dear God, are
you injured, Lady Ivy? I am so dreadfully sorry."

Ivy sat on her bottom in the middle of the floor.
And a laugh barreled up inside her throat and rang
out into the otherwise-silent room.

Dominic offered a hesitant smile as he assisted
Ivy to her feet, and then the couple he'd barreled
into as well.

When he returned, Ivy was waiting for him with
a raised eyebrow. "So I assume the answer to my
question 'do you waltz' is *no*."

Chapter 8

Envy eats nothing but its own heart.
German proverb

ake this." Grant pressed a glass of lemonade into Ivy's hand the minute she approached him at the refreshment table. "You look exhausted—and you must be aching from your waltz with Counterton."

Ivy laughed. "Well, if he did not have the attention of all of Society before, he certainly does now. Thankfully, our accident happened so quickly I do not believe it will be attributed to a lack of skill." She gratefully accepted the lemonade and drank it down, but her gaze trailed after Lord Counterton, who had, at her direction, set out to find and greet Lady Winthrop—to verify that he was still in her good graces after the fall. Of course, according to Ivy's plan, his path would take him in the vicinity of Miss Feeney—his true destination.

It was evident that Miss Feeney had been watching Dominic all evening, for as he began to cross the ballroom in her direction, she gestured to the refreshment table and stepped away from Lord Tinsdale. Then she set out on what Ivy knew would be a purposeful course that would lead her into Dominic's path.

"You know, Ivy, I like Counterton quite a lot," Grant admitted.

"Well, you also know," she leaned close and whispered, "that he is not truly Lord Counterton."

"Still, I enjoy his company, so much more than dreary Tinsdale's," Grant added. "Counterton is the proper size for a man. No need for padding in his coat or anywhere else. Probably a Scot on his mother's side. You should inquire about that."

"Why, pray, should I do such a thing? I do not wish to know anything about him that I might accidentally blurt out in conversation," she snapped, "and risk ruining everything."

Grant snatched a glass of wine from a passing footman's tray. "I just thought if he was a Scot—and gads, look at the size of him, he must have some plaid in him somewhere—Da might be more accepting of him."

Ivy looked up at her brother, fully confused. "Why, pray, would I ever mention his possibly being a Scot to Da?"

"Well, Counterton is quite taken with you." He chuckled. "Ivy, everyone in this room can see that."

Ivy chortled. "Believe me, Grant, one thing I do know for certain is that you are entirely wrong on that point. He is simply a very talented actor. His lovelorn appearance is part of our plan. I assure you."

Ivy could not help but watch Dominic's progress with Miss Feeney. His back was to her, so she couldn't see his face, but judging from the dreamy expression on Miss Feeney's, he was doing quite an admirable job of charming her.

"He is perfect," Ivy muttered to herself.

"Still," Grant said in a most matter-of-fact manner, "I fear Da will never see you marrying a stage actor as *reforming*."

"*Marrying Dominic?*" Ivy yanked her head around, astounded. "Gads, who mentioned anything about that?"

A slow grin spread across Grant's face. "No one needed to say anything. One needs only see the way the two of you look at each other when you do not realize you are being watched."

Ivy's mouth fell agape, and she stood staring in disbelief at her brother. Was he insane? "I mean to marry Tinsdale," she said flatly. "That is the only reason I have established an association with this so-called Dominic Sheridan."

"Perhaps it commenced that way"—Grant exchanged Ivy's empty glass with a crystal of wine—"but I know, with all certainty, that the two of you are falling in love. Your feelings for one another are as transparent as the air."

"You are as mad as . . . our father," she ground out beneath her breath. Whirling around, she started across the saloon. She did not wish to hear any more of Grant's nonsensical—and completely erroneous—ramblings.

Because he was wrong. Oh, so very wrong.

Ivy was fully halfway across the length of the grand saloon when she heard a gentleman speak her name just behind her.

"*Lady Ivy*," he said again. Louder this time.

Tiny wisps of hair on the back of her neck rose up as she recognized the voice. Oh dear. She wasn't ready. She hadn't seen him coming.

Ivy slowed her step and halted, then drew in a

fortifying breath and affixed a pleasant smile to
her lips. Then she turned. "Tinsdale?" She looked
around him.

*Miss Feeney is not with him. That is something
to be thankful for just now.*

"Ivy." His tone was honeyed, not chilly, the way
it had been when she had Grant present him to
Dominic earlier this night.

*Hmm. Could it be my plan is working so soon?
Hardly likely, but then . . .*

"Have you misplaced Miss Feeney?" Ivy
laughed, hoping she sounded jovial, not desperate.
"Alas, I have not seen her since the two of you
were presented to Lord Counterton." She glanced
around the saloon again. "She might have quit
the saloon and gone outside for a breath. It is
terribly warm this night, do you not agree, Lord
Tinsdale?"

"*Ivy,*" he said yet again, while peering at her in
the queerest manner.

"Lord Tinsdale, what is it?" She gently laid her
hand on his coat sleeve. "Is something the matter?
You have spoken naught but my name four times
within the past minute."

He paused, as if thinking about whether or not
anything was wrong, but then he shook his head.
"No, nothing. I only wished to . . . apologize.

There, I have said it. I have been meaning to, and now I have."

"Apologize?" Aye, he *did* owe her an apology for discarding her like a wedge of moldy bread. Well, she wasn't going to let it go with him voicing just *a wish* to apologize. He was going to have to have to truly say the words. *I apologize. I was a complete pompous fool. I want you to forgive me. I want you to marry me.*

"Yes, dear Ivy. I know that you heard me, even over the drone of the guests."

Ivy eyed him most seriously. "Did you spill something on my gown?"

"No."

"No? Well, if you passed wind, you could have foregone an apology. The saloon is so crowded, no one would have guessed it was you."

"No, I didn't. *Ivy,* please, stop these games."

She had to concede that perhaps that was a bit much. But he deserved it after the way he humiliated her before all Society. "Well then, what do you wish to apologize for, my dear lord?" Ivy batted her eyes innocently, as if she did not know exactly why he *needed* to apologize. "Do tell me."

Tinsdale was having a dickens of a time forming the words. Why he was very nearly sputtering.

"Ivy, I—I must beg your forgiveness for appearing to cast you off in favor of Miss Feeney."

"Oh, you are apologizing for *the appearance* of doing so? So, you in truth, you did not actually cast me off in favor of her then."

"No, I mean, yes, I did. Damn it, Ivy, you are not making this easy for me." He rubbed his jaw, almost as though speaking of this pained his mouth.

"And should I make this easy for you? I do not believe you gave me the same consideration when you tossed me aside for Miss Feeney."

He lifted her hand from his sleeve. "I admit my wrongdoing. I slighted you, but not intentionally. She stole my heart. I was helpless, I tell you." Tinsdale shoved his fingers through his yellow hair in frustration, then looked deep into her eyes. In his gaze, Ivy saw sincerity. "I apologize for hurting you, Ivy. Doing so was never my intention."

It was as though someone were squeezing her heart. She feared at any moment tears would bud in her eyes. She had to leave before she embarrassed herself and revealed her continued vulnerability to him.

"Och, Lord Tinsdale, dinna fret. You did not hurt me in the least," she exclaimed, lifting her false smile into place once more. "In fact, I should thank you, for had you not pursued Miss Feeney so passionately, I might still have believed there was a chance for us for to be together—and not allowed myself to come to know Lord Counterton's heart."

"So, you are not upset with me?" Tinsdale swallowed the truth she had provided like a bitter pill.

"Och, no. Not in the least." She struggled to hold the tears inside her eyes. "In truth, my dear friend, I wish to thank you."

"*Ivy,* you do not need to do this." He reached out for her, but she stepped back. Her mask was crumbling. She could feel it breaking into pieces.

"No, you are wrong. I must thank you, Tinsdale. Do you not understand? Without your setting me aside for Miss Feeney, I might never have realized that Lord Counterton and I are truly meant to be together. And we are. Even you must see that. Everyone else does."

It wasn't true, of course, despite their contrived appearances, but still, she had to thank Grant for the idea of it.

"But Ivy, you and I—" Tinsdale began, but then he stopped trying to explain himself and closed his thin lips tightly.

Ivy didn't know if he was having second thoughts about setting her aside or not, but she did know that it was not the time to wait to find out.

She raised her hand and waved at some invisible acquaintance behind him on the far side of the grand saloon. "Must be off now. Good evening, dear Tinsdale."

She was shaking a little, and her heart was pounding so loudly that she was sure he heard the rhythm as she dashed past him. From the periphery of her vision, she saw Tinsdale turn and drop his head as she ducked into the churning crowd.

She hurried through the throngs of ladies and gentlemen until she reached the Turkish Room. No one else was there, and so she allowed herself to collapse upon the nearest ottoman. She sucked a draught of air into her burning lungs.

Had she done it—had she both communicated that she cared enough to be hurt by being jilted and made him envious of Lord Counterton? Or, had she ruined everything?

She cupped her hand over her mouth to stifle a sob. Lud, she wished she knew.

"I told you I saw her come in here!"

"Oh, there she is, Letitia. Such eyes you have, sister."

Ivy lifted her head from her hands and looked up to see two elderly matrons dressed in identical gowns of pale purple.

"What luck, Viola," exclaimed the heavier of the old women. "Now we will have all of the details before anyone else."

"Good evening, Lady Ivy," said the bonier of the two. "I do not know if you recall meeting us at the Haver-Smythes' musicale last month, but we certainly remember you."

As Ivy's eyes refocused, she recognized the women as two of the London Society's most notorious matchmakers, the Ladies Letitia and Viola Featherton of Hanover Square.

Ivy came to her feet and curtsied, meaning to leave as quickly as she could. The two old women were known particularly for cleverly converting military rules of engagement into stratagems for snaring husbands for their charges.

She could not have them interfering for their own amusement with her own strategy to win back Tinsdale's affections.

"Good evening, ladies," Ivy said, searching her mind for any viable excuse for quitting the Turkish Room. "Certainly I remember meeting you both. How are you enjoying the ball?"

Lady Letitia snickered at that, sending both of her chins wobbling. "Not half as much as you are, dear, judging from the smile on your face while you danced with young Lord Counterton."

Oh God, the heat was already headed into her cheeks.

"How blessed you are to have so quickly hooked the most eligible bachelor in all of London," Lady Viola added.

They were both studying her intently, as if waiting for a reaction. Unnerving her.

"H-his father was a school chum of my father's," Ivy stammered. "I suppose I was fortunate that he sought out our family to request an introduction into Society."

"Oh, very fortunate, indeed," Lady Letitia said, but the old woman's expression told her she did not truly care in the least. There was something more she wanted to know.

And then it came.

"The way he looked at you, he is in love," Lady Viola said.

"Which I am happy to see. It only proves that the rumors that preceded his arrival are just drivel." Lady Letitia's head shot forward in her expectation of a reply, startling Ivy.

"W-what rumors might those be?" Ivy looked at the thin woman, who didn't seem as tricky as her sister Lady Letitia.

"Oh, I am sure they are nothing," Lady Viola

replied softly, "now that I have seen the man for myself."

Hesitantly, Ivy redirected her gaze to Lady Letitia, who seemed to have her answer waiting on her tongue. "Please, what have you heard?"

"Well, I will tell you only because you may jeopardize your reputation and that of your family if you are not made aware of a possible risk." Lady Letitia came closer and set her hand on Ivy's shoulder. "Word is that the new Lord Counterton is a wicked scoundrel, adept at charming women, never once giving his heart in return for theirs. Instead he pitchforks them aside when it suits."

A bubble of laughter welled up inside Ivy and burst from her lips. "I assure you, ladies, the rumor is quite unfounded. Lord Counterton is a very kind and thoughtful gentleman, though I must admit, he is very charming."

The two old women bobbled their heads in agreement with her.

"Oh, we are well aware of that," Lady Viola exclaimed enthusiastically, "for we met him just minutes ago. He is most amiable, so very handsome, and when he spoke to me, it was as—" She sighed dreamily. "Well, if I were only . . . a few years younger—"

Lady Letitia rolled her eyes and interjected. "He could be your grandson."

"Oh, Letitia, how wicked you are!" Lady Viola playfully pretended to elbow her sister in the ribs.

Lady Letitia chuckled. "Yes, we agree he is charming, Viola." Then she grew quiet for a prolonged moment and pinned Ivy with her pale blue eyes. "But do be careful, dear gel. It is so easy to lose one's heart to a gentleman like that. So easy to have it broken too."

Just then, Ivy saw Dominic enter the Turkish Room.

The Feathertons did not seem to be aware of his sudden presence, for Lady Viola offered one last piece of advice. "Unless she has already claimed his. For to win a rake's heart is a great prize, indeed. Remember that, dear gel."

With that, the two lavender-clad ladies, smiled at her, then turned and gave Dominic nods of greeting. "Good evening, Lady Ivy, Lord Counterton," they said quite naturally, as if they had known he was there all the while. Then they waddled from the Turkish Room in the direction of the grand saloon theater.

Ivy plopped back down onto the ottoman and looked up at Dominic.

"Pray, what was that all about?" He knelt before Ivy to face her.

"I honestly don't know." And she didn't. She could not determine whether they were warning her about Lord Counterton or congratulating her.

No matter. The faults of the true Lord Counterton didn't warrant a moment of worry. After all, it was clear that the Feathertons, and indeed everyone else they'd met this night, believed her actor to be the true Lord Counterton.

All that mattered was whether or not her marquess was being successful in attracting Miss Feeney. "Dominic, did your discussion with *Miss Feeney*—"

Her eyes threatened to pop from their sockets when, to her horror, she saw Miss Feeney and Lord Tinsdale pause near the doorway, their mouths fully agape. "Tinsdale!" She leaped up, nearly toppling Dominic over.

Dominic came to his feet and stood beside Ivy.

A horrified expression pinched Lord Tinsdale's face.

Oh, dear. With Dominic down on his knee before her . . . it must have appeared that—

Tinsdale hauled Miss Feeney into the room. His brow was furrowed, and his gaze was worriedly focused on Dominic's clenched hand. "I daresay, I hope we have not interrupted a private moment."

Ivy was already shaking her head, but Dominic replied to Tinsdale. "Actually, yes, you have indeed." He turned to Ivy and lifted her hand, caressing it through her glove. "But it will wait—*for now*."

Ivy realized she hadn't blinked since Tinsdale and Miss Feeney had appeared, and now her widened eyes burned.

What in the blazes are you doing, Dominic? This is not part of our plan!

Chapter 9

You can't be envious and happy at the same time.
Frank Tyger

The Sinclair residence
No. 1 Grosvenor Square, London

The Morning Post
The waltz, introduced most recently at court, has made the leap into respectability. Just Friday evening, the waltz was included in the program at the Argyle Rooms and danced most enthusiastically by such esteemed members of Society as Lord C. and Lady I. S. After witnessing the pair together on the floor, it was speculated by some that dancing the waltz together is nothing less than a prelude to a march down the aisle.

Ivy twisted the newspaper and thrust it into the coal basket inside the hearth. She did not wish her siblings to read the column and resume trying to convince her that she and her Lord Counterton were truly meant to be together.

Though *The Morning Post* columnist was entirely mistaken, Ivy was more than a little pleased with what was reported. Tinsdale would surely read the column this morn, and after espying her alone with Dominic last night, in all likelihood, his jealousy would be piqued. One could hope.

She paced the parlor, glancing each time she passed the large windows looking out onto Grosvenor Square. She felt so foolish allowing herself to feel so discomposed.

I have dominion over my life. The plan will be successful. It will!

And it was already working. Perhaps not exactly as she would have preferred, but it was working. Dominic would arrive at any moment, driving the gleaming phaeton she had hired for the day, to collect her for a delightful and strategic afternoon in Hyde Park.

But it wasn't the fact that she and Dominic would be spending the afternoon together that set her nerves to fraying. It was the fact that they were going to join Miss Feeney and Lord Tinsdale for a picnic under the trees bordering the Serpentine.

At Miss Feeney's invitation.

There was no possible way she could refuse, though, lud, how she wished she could! Ivy had no desire to sit on a coverlet beside the most beautiful woman in London—and be woefully compared and found wanting.

Until now, Ivy had consciously kept at least one person standing between her and Miss Feeney whenever they met, so that the stark differences between them would not be so glaring. She, however, doubted this tactic would be effective during the coming outing.

Unless . . . unless Dominic's wooing of Miss Feeney became so visible that Tinsdale would be forced to keep his eyes trained on Lord Counterton—instead of bouncing between the fragile, ebony-haired beauty and the fire-headed Amazon.

The clopping of hooves outside on the square heralded Dominic's arrival. "Mrs. Wimpole, is the picnic hamper packed?"

"It's coming, Lady Ivy," came a female voice from the other end of the passageway. Mrs. Wimpole hurried to the door as best she could given the size and apparent weight of the hamper she carried with both hands like a huge iron kettle of water. "I went out to buy a few hothouse oranges from young Nellie. Such a treat, eh?"

"Oh, lovely. Thank you so much, Mrs. Wimpole, but you oughtn't to have gone to the trouble. *Really,* you oughtn't to have."

"No problem, my lady," Mrs. Wimpole replied. "None at all."

There was a problem, however. Now, there would be no question as to whether or not Ivy's hair was exactly the shade of an orange, as Miss Feeney had once rudely noted. All she need do that afternoon was to hold one up to Ivy's and compare.

Mrs. Wimpole, whose somewhat questionable services, like Mr. Poplin's, were included with the rent of their Grosvenor Square home, squatted and opened the wicker basket, pointing out the contents. "There's sliced beef, bread, a loaf of cheese, peas from my sister's garden—"

"Sounds wonderful . . . um . . . anything *new*, a new experiment, perhaps?" Ivy asked, peering into the basket for anything of suspicious origins—or unnaturally green.

Mrs. Wimpole stood and set her hands on her wide hips. "Why, you know me too well, Lady Ivy. What do you reckon it might be? Go on, Lady

Ivy, have a guess." She poked her tongue into the inside of her cheek and rocked back and forth as she waited for Ivy's answer.

Ivy nudged the side of the hamper with her slipper, shaking the contents inside a little. "Tarts?"

"Oh, you saw them, did you?" Mrs. Wimpole chuckled. "My mother's receipt. Apple, but with a *special* gelatin glaze."

Ivy tensed. "Special glaze?" Gads, she daren't even dream what unlikely ingredient she might have used. Something horrid, Ivy was sure. Mrs. Wimpole's heirloom receipts were regarded, at least by the Sinclair brothers and sisters, to be the vilest of concoctions. Though the dear old woman did try her hardest. She just didn't have a flair for cooking, and well, given what little money their father provided them, the Sinclairs could not afford to engage a proper cook.

Why, had their brother Sterling not earned a small fortune placing wagers and fighting, Ivy could have never financed her plan to win back Tinsdale. But that money would run out just about the same time that her father returned to London. Lud, Dominic just had to steal Miss Feeney from Tinsdale and quickly!

"Fish gelatin," Mrs. Wimpole finally blurted,

unable to contain her secret ingredient any longer. "You would have never guessed. It adds a savory flavor to the tart without tasting like fish at all."

Oh, good God.

The door knocker sounded. *Dominic is here.* A little thrill cut through her middle.

Ivy kicked the hamper lid closed and fastened the buckle. She sighed softly. There would be no opportunity to remove the tarts from the basket now. She'd have to slip them out without anyone seeing at Hyde Park . . . else risk poisoning everyone.

Mr. Poplin scurried past Ivy and opened the door.

"Such a beautiful day." One side of Dominic's lips lifted, as his gaze swept past Poplin to her. "But not half so lovely as you, Lady Ivy."

Oh, good heavens. He never stepped out of his character. Why, if she hadn't met his companion, Felix, she would swear the actor she'd hired was truly a rake of the first order—and she still hadn't discounted the notion. "Good afternoon, my dear Lord Counterton." She curtsied most properly.

She heard Poplin, who'd made it very clear that he thought her plan mad from the very beginning, sigh ruefully from behind the door.

"Poplin? Would you please assist me by bringing the hamper to the phaeton?"

"No, my lady." The little man didn't even bother to step out from behind the door.

"I beg your pardon?" Ivy exclaimed. "*Please,* Poplin."

"Oh, he ain't being disrespectful or nothin', Lady Ivy," Mrs. Wimpole broke in. "Poplin can't lift it. Already tried to help me tote the picnic hamper up from the kitchen. Too heavy. Here, I can do it." She bent for the basket's handle.

Dominic brushed past Ivy and easily lifted the hamper out of Mrs. Wimpole's ruddy hands. "Allow me, my dear lady."

Mrs. Wimpole blushed. "Oh, my." Beaming, she dipped into an unsteady curtsy and honored him. "Why, thank you, Your Lordship." She leaned close to Ivy and whispered into her ear. "Handsome and strong. Can't do wrong with a man like that, eh?" She set an elbow playfully into Ivy's side.

Amazing. Within a blink, he had already charmed Mrs. Wimpole. Was there anyone the man could not reduce to jelly?

Besides herself, of course.

She'd firmly set her cap for Lord Tinsdale.

And well, she knew his flirtations were naught but an act. Nothing more.

"Shall we be off?" she asked, walking through the front doorway without waiting for an answer.

"Absolutely, Your Ladyship." There was something in his voice that didn't sound quite right. A bitterness. And instantly Ivy regretted her rudeness.

Ivy stopped and spun around so quickly that Dominic, who was closer behind than she realized, walked straight into her. She teetered backward, and might have fallen, had his free arm not looped around her lower back in a flash and held her in place against him.

"I beg your pardon, Dominic. I didn't mean to be rude." Ivy peered up into his blue eyes. "I-I admit that I am overcome with nerves over the prospect of our day with Miss Feeney and Lord Tinsdale. So much depends on our . . . performances. As an actor you know how to quell a bout of nerves, but I admit that I do not. This is all completely new to me."

Dominic smiled down at her. "It is not so difficult, really. Do not consider our outing as a performance. Just enjoy the day in the park . . . and my company." He winked at her, then lowered his hand from her back. "Any reaction you force, any emotion you manufacture, will appear false to everyone."

"Very well then, I shall leave the acting to the professional." Ivy straightened her gown, then cupped her hand and peered up at the sun.

"Just enjoy the day, my sweet." He passed her by and hoisted the heavy hamper into the phaeton, stowing it behind the seat.

Ivy walked to the pavers and extended her hand for him to assist her into the phaeton's high perch. Instead, he grasped her waist in his large hands and easily lifted her and deposited her into the phaeton.

Ivy sat down and fumbled for her cutwork fan. My, she must have misjudged the heat of the day, for she was suddenly feeling rather warm.

A high-perch phaeton, though quite fashionable according to Felix, who would know, was probably not the wisest choice of a hired vehicle for one, such as Dominic, who was raised in the country.

Such a speedy, precarious carriage required some skill, and when coupled with pair of spirited young horses, even more so.

"I fear we are going to be late." There was a hint of blame in Ivy's words. "I do hope Tinsdale and Miss Feeney do not think we've abandoned them."

Dominic grimaced. "Regretfully, it took me longer to drive from Berkeley Square to your residence than I had anticipated."

"When did you leave?" Ivy wasn't going to let it go.

"Noon." He tightened his fingers around the ribbons and prayed the pair remained at a walk as the carriage turned out of the square and onto Upper Brook Street toward Park Lane.

Ivy thumped his arm. "*Noon?* I could have walked the distance faster!"

"Right then." Dominic pulled back on the ribbons, and the horses halted. Maintaining the tension, he handed the reins over to Ivy. "Here you go. You may drive."

The sound that came from her mouth resembled a cough, but he knew it for the mocking laugh that it truly was.

"You can't handle a phaeton?" Ivy was fighting back a grin. "You, the perfect gentleman?"

He gritted his teeth. "You might have asked if I have driven such a vehicle before sending it around. I know it must have cost you a pile of coin. Not all of us had the privilege of being raised in a family where being a fine whip was something to aspire to."

"Careful, sirrah, your polish is losing its sheen." Ivy slipped her fingers around the reins. "And there is quite a bit about my upbringing that you are not aware of and would certainly not envy."

"I do not doubt it, Ivy. Something in your past made your need for approval more important than your own happiness." He regretted the words the moment they left his lips.

Ivy's back stiffened, and she sat very still.

"Ivy, I am very sorry. I should not have said such a thing."

"But, for some reason, you did." Ivy angrily jerked her head around to face straight ahead. "And you are quite correct, which only adds to the sting of your assertion." With a growl, she snapped the reins, and the horses jolted forward. Ivy focused on the road ahead of them.

"Ivy, I apologize." Dominic grasped the seat as Ivy urged the horses into a trot and did not slow in the least when they cornered onto Park Lane. She did not utter another word until they wheeled through the gates of Hyde Park.

The team clopped down Rotten Row, flinging up clotted bits of soft, sandy earth in the air as Ivy and Nick glanced out, searching the Serpentine's shore for Miss Feeney and Viscount Tinsdale.

Honestly, Nick didn't care in the least if they ever met up with the other couple, and found himself looking at trees and flowers and splashes from fish on the water's surface.

Ivy, did not, of course, realize this, and she too was really only pretending to maintain a crow's-nest lookout for Miss Feeney and Tinsdale.

And even though their meeting this day was not as amiable as she might have wished, Ivy actually quite liked their heated exchange—and learning both last evening and this afternoon that Nick was not quite as perfect as he seemed to be.

Somehow, silly as it sounded when she voiced the notion in her head, it made her feel calmer around the handsome actor.

In some small way, it removed her need to shine so brightly. Ivy tightened the reins and slowed the horses back to a trot. "What say you, Dominic?" she said, finally looking back at him. "Do you think we ought stop and set up in the shade of the oak tree, just there, by the water?"

"I am glad you are no longer perturbed with me." He peered back at her, relief flooding his beautiful face. Waiting for her response.

"I never was. Your observation was correct." Ivy sighed and transferred the ribbons into her left hand and gestured with her right. "Aye, what you said is true, but out of necessity, I assure you. If I do not regain my father's approval, I will soon be destitute and without a family." Her voice broke as she admitted this.

Blast. Heat itched at the backs of her eyes. "Do you agree that we should lay our picnic here or not?"

"Ivy, we're already tardy thanks to my inadequate phaeton-driving skills." Nick looked down, but she could see a slight creasing of his lips. "They will be looking for us."

"We've been looking for *them* and have not seen them. Perhaps they have been delayed as well." She separated the ribbons into each hand and pulled the horses to a halt. "Besides, we will be far easier to locate sitting still instead of driving along the Serpentine, don't you agree?"

"I expect you are right. Here will do." Nick leaped down from the perch. He reached up and took the ribbons from Ivy, then led the horses to a hitching post not more than a yard away and tied them off.

Hoisting the hamper with both hands, Ivy swung it down to Nick, who set it on the ground, then took her hand and guided her down the steps.

The sky was vibrant blue and the sun warm on their backs as they walked together through the cool grass, then beneath the leafy shade canopy of the great oak beside the water.

Ivy hummed as she spread the coverlet she had borrowed from Lachlan's bed so that it abutted the ancient tree's wide trunk. When it was smooth, she gestured for Nick to position the hamper nearby, and she sat down and bade him to sit beside her, resting his back against the trunk.

For comfort.

Not to be near her.

And certainly *not* for the purpose of obscuring the sight of them from anyone who happened to peer toward the Serpentine from Rotten Row.

But if they were unintentionally hidden, so much the better.

For despite her plan, a day without Miss Feeney would be a perfect one indeed.

Ivy peeled off her gloves and tossed them atop the picnic hamper. Her skin was as smooth and white as fine porcelain, save the two tiny pink bumps on her arm she was scratching madly. "We've not been in the country for two minutes, and already I've been bitten. Look there, do you see it?" She angled her forearm toward him.

"This is hardly the country, Ivy. We're in the center of London." He took her wrist and pulled her closer to peer at the bite. "Oh dear," he murmured.

"What is it?" Her eyes were growing wider with each passing second. "What is the matter? Do you know what bit me? Was it a—*spider*?"

"Possibly. I can't quite tell if there are two separate bites or one two-fanged spider bite." He squinted. "My aging eyes, you know."

"Fangs?" Her gaze raked her skirts and the coverlet for any sign of an eight-legged marauder. Seeing nothing, she started scratching at imaginary insects on her ankle, then her throat.

Finally, she jumped to her feet and frantically began shaking her skirts and brushing at her sleeves. Yanking up the coverlet, she started shaking it furiously in the air.

"Ivy," Nick said. "It's nothing more than a pair of midge nips. I promise."

This didn't seem to stop her from squealing and batting at her dress. Then he saw them, Lord Tinsdale and Miss Feeney standing beside the hired high-perch phaeton tied to the hitching post.

"Ivy, stop." He pressed her up against the tree trunk and held her there with his thighs and chest. "Ivy, *please*." His mouth hovered just above hers as he whispered calmly to her.

Just then, she quieted, and peered up at him, though her chest still rose and fell with excitement.

"Aye, Dominic?" Her tone was as silken as her skin. An invitation, more than a question.

And then he felt himself rising with excitement.

The sound of footfalls muted by the grass touched his ears just then.

Damn it all. Too late.

It was too late to warn her that Tinsdale and Miss Feeney had found them and would be coming around the tree at any minute to find them . . . in a most compromising position.

So, he did the only thing he could do. Use the situation to further Ivy's plan.

He would kiss her.

She must have seen the decision in his eyes, for her gaze softened, her golden green eyes suddenly became darker, more seductive, as she stared up at him.

A copper curl was tangled in the ribbon tie of her bonnet. It was all of the excuse he needed to touch her. He loosened the satin bow at her throat and drew the lock from it, dragging his fingertips along the sensitive skin of her throat. She closed her eyes and drew in a short breath before looking up at him again.

His fingers moved upward, meaning to stroke the side of her face. She turned her cheek into his palm, brushing her lips against it without, he was sure, truly meaning to.

Her eyes widened, and her lips parted in astonishment at her own reaction. But he wasn't going to let her turn away.

Whether it was *the plan* or simply the need to unleash his own yearning for her, he lowered his mouth to hers until he felt the sweetness of her breath upon it. Then he pressed his lips to hers, urging her mouth open until his tongue could slip inside.

Ivy moaned softly. He knew she had no notion that Tinsdale and Miss Feeney had arrived, and yet still she lifted her arms around him, moving her warm lips so passionately over his that the cut of his breeches was growing tighter, making matters far more complicated.

"Lady Ivy!" Tinsdale's voice boomed, startling Ivy to such an extent that her gasp sucked the breath right out of Nick's mouth.

Curling his fingers around the edge of the bonnet, Nick took it from Ivy's hands and held it at his middle as turned to face the viscount and Miss Feeney.

"Ah, there you are!" Nick said enthusiastically. "Thought we might have to start without you."

Miss Feeney colored and giggled into her hand.

But Tinsdale's gaze was fixed on Ivy's flushing face, which was deepening with color by the second.

"And what, pray would you be starting without us? Or dare I even ask?" His tone was scathing, which intrigued Nick. For why would a man who had jilted a woman care if she kissed another?

Ivy managed to steel herself then. "Why, our picnic, of course."

Nick stepped forward and clapped a hand over Tinsdale's narrow shoulder. "We just decided we'd start with dessert first."

And, just as Nick guessed, Tinsdale stiffened like an oak tree.

"What sort of dessert?" Miss Feeney chasséd over to hamper and began working on the leather strap holding it closed.

"Tarts." A mischievous smile tickled Ivy's lips.

"Tarts?" Miss Feeney glanced up at Nick, fluttering her thick lashes. "I would adore one."

In a burst of uncharacteristic generosity, Ivy hurried over to the hamper and quickly opened it. "Allow me to serve, won't you, Miss Feeney?" She retrained her gaze onto Lord Tinsdale as she handed up a small plate with what appeared to be an apple tart upon it to Miss Feeney. "I simply cannot wait to hear what you think of them . . . you being somewhat of an authority on tarts."

Miss Feeney scowled down at Ivy as she popped a large bite into her mouth.

Ivy smiled. Aye, it was going to be a lovely day
. . . after all.

After their alfresco meal, Nick sat down upon the
blanket, settling a comforting hand upon Miss
Feeney's back. He was fairly sure Ivy hadn't poi-
soned her, not intentionally anyway, but the tart
she'd gleefully served had caused Miss Feeney to
retch and sent her running to the Serpentine, where
she promptly heaved up the dessert.

Miss Feeney raised her eyes and glared. Nick followed her focus and saw Ivy leaning against the
phaeton, giggling like a maid. Nick glared too as
he noticed Tinsdale's arm propped casually on the
vehicle, his hand disappearing behind Ivy's back.

Nick came to his feet. Yes, his goal this day was
to flatter and charm Miss Feeney, but was it not
also to display his affection for Ivy? Had she not
bid him to make love to her—those were her words.
"Are you feeling any better, Miss Feeney? Or shall
I ask Lord Tinsdale to escort you to your home?"

She looked up at him, her face appearing a mossy
green in the waning afternoon light. She started to
say something, but a gurgling welled up from her
belly, and she clapped a hand over her mouth.

He lowered a hand to her. "No need to speak. I
understand. I shall fetch your escort promptly." He

bent and collected the basket, then strode across the green toward their carriages. His pace quickened as Tinsdale pretended to pluck something from Ivy's sleeve, allowing his hand to linger on her arm overlong.

Tinsdale didn't notice Nick's approach until he was but a few strides away. He dropped his hand to his side immediately. "Ah, Counterton. Is she feeling better?"

"Indeed she is not. Miss Feeney wishes to quit the park and be taken home to convalesce." Nick moved between Ivy and Tinsdale and lifted the hamper into the phaeton. He turned and settled a hand at Ivy's waist and handed her up into the phaeton. "I will return directly, dear one," he said to Ivy.

Nick pressed a hand into the middle of Tinsdale's back and started him down the gentle slope back to Miss Feeney.

"Good heavens, you look a fright!" Tinsdale exclaimed as he helped her find her feet and stand.

Nick lifted her hand and patted it. "I do you hope you are well very soon, Miss Feeney, for I hope to see you at the Winthrop musicale."

She smiled weakly, but her eyes revealed her pleasure at his comment. Not daring to open her mouth to speak, she gave a slight nod.

Nick bade them both good afternoon and returned to the phaeton carrying Lachlan's coverlet. He untied the team and climbed up into the perch, taking the reins, this time, himself.

"If I haven't yet mentioned it, you need to be wary of Mrs. Wimpole's special receipts," Ivy said. He looked at her, expecting a mischievous smile to be hanging on her lips. But there was none. "The tarts weren't spoiled, only an unfortunate blend of ingredients. I'd hoped to dispose of the tarts before anyone could wish to taste one. Sadly, Miss Feeney and Lord Tinsdale were upon us before I could do so."

Nick held the reins tightly, allowing the phaeton to roll slowly down Rotten Row. They were only just in sight of the gates when another carriage barreled past them, startling the team.

"Damn it all!" Nick looked up as he struggled to control the horses only to see that Tinsdale was cracking a thin whip, urging the team drawing his own carriage past them.

"*Tinsdale.*" Nick snapped the reins, and though given his lack of experience with such a fast carriage, he urged the team into a gallop.

"Good heavens!" Ivy reached out for the reins, but he would not allow her to take them. The phaeton picked up speed, and within a minute it had overtaken Tinsdale's carriage.

Tinsdale's gleeful expression fell from his face as they passed. His eyes were squinted with anger, and he raised his whip in the air again.

"Oh, no," Ivy gasped as they slowed to drive through the gates to Park Lane. With a pleased smile on his lips, Nick turned to see how close Tinsdale's carriage was behind them when he saw they had stopped.

Miss Feeney was doubled over on the bench. Tinsdale was standing on the earthen row, ripping off his dripping coat.

Nick's stomach turned at the sight. "Thank you for the warning about Mrs. Wimpole's special receipts."

"Not at all," Ivy replied, setting a hand over her mouth.

Nick snapped the reins and turned quickly onto Park Lane. "The evening is fine. What say you to a drive to allow me to master the phaeton?"

"Drive on, Lord Counterton," Ivy replied.

It wasn't yet dark as the carriage rolled into Mayfair, but in August the cloak of night fell late upon London . . . hardly seeming to come at all in Scotland, Ivy recalled. It seemed so long ago, and yet it was only a few short months past that she and her brothers and sisters were cast out of Scotland.

How deeply she missed her home. She sighed. She'd miss London too—if her plan failed. And she knew it might yet, for there was now only a clutch of days left before her father arrived and sealed her fate. It was inevitable if Tinsdale did not offer his ring very, very soon.

Today, while amusing at times, had sadly not been as successful an outing as she had hoped.

Ivy turned her head and looked at Dominic sitting beside her, his brow drawn in deep concentration as he struggled with the reins that barely held the phaeton's spirited team under his control.

Aye, he had performed his task perfectly. Miss Feeney was smitten with him. But Tinsdale, rather than fawning over Ivy as she expected he would once he saw that Miss Feeney's favor had shifted, had not offered up his affections. Nay, he almost seemed angry with her for allowing herself to be courted by another—when it was he who had tossed her aside.

As she swayed in time with the horses' strides, she became more introspective about the day. She could argue that Tinsdale had no cause to be angry with her. Tinsdale, himself, had forced this plan of hers into existence. For had he simply asked her to marry him—as she was sure he had been about to do before he abruptly transferred his affections to Miss Feeney—she would never have had to take such extreme measures to win him back.

She would never have had to engage Dominic to assist her!

The carriage turned a sharp corner. Ivy's hand shot out for support, catching Dominic's thigh. Her eyes flashed up at his as he glanced down at her for an instant before returning his eyes to the road. "Sorry."

"I'm not." She could see he was grinning.

But, truth to tell, she was glad that she had engaged Dominic. Ivy gazed at him thoughtfully. She enjoyed his company, the way he made her laugh, even the way he compelled her to consider things about herself and beliefs. The way he made her feel when he kissed her.

A flush bloomed on her chest as she relived in her mind the way he pressed her against the tree beside the Serpentine—and touched her, kissed her.

Aye, that kiss had made every part of her tingle. More importantly, though, she knew that his blood had pumped hot in his veins when their mouths touched—because he wanted her. She couldn't believe it at first, for she had been so sure that he was the sort of man who preferred the company of other men. But there was no ignoring the hardness of him pressing against her belly as he held her and moved his mouth over hers. Had it been a small matter, she might have been able to count his reaction to her as something else. A covered knife, or a watch. Any number of things. But when he kissed her today, there could be no mistake. What she felt was evidence of his desire, and that was no small thing at all.

She smiled inwardly. Despite his close relationship with his man Felix, which was confusing to her to say the least, there was no denying Dominic's physical attraction to her. None at all. His body confessed everything, and more. He liked women. More importantly, he liked *her*.

It occurred to Ivy then, that it wasn't the houses and parties and museums she'd miss most if she had to leave London. It would be Dominic. Aye, she'd miss him quite a lot. Most of all.

When the phaeton turned onto Berkeley Square, Ivy saw a young man sitting on the steps that descended from the walk to the road. As the evening was warm, his sleeves were rolled to his elbows and his coat lay in a crumpled heap on the step beside him.

At least he waited, she told herself. As late as they were returning to the house, he might have departed and levied another two guineas for another day's use of the phaeton.

He came to his feet, shoving back his sweat-damp hair from his eyes when the phaeton rolled to a stop before the Counterton house. In an instant, he was standing below the carriage gesturing for her to stand. When she did, he raised his arms, and to her surprise, without so much as a word, plucked her from the perch and settled her down upon the steps.

Dominic handed down the tail of the ribbons to him and leaped down from the phaeton.

The young man stepped up into the vehicle. "Will you be needing it again, my lord? I was meant to inquire as to your plans when I left it this morning." The horses' bridles jingled as they pranced in place. The driver tightened the reins in his hands.

"The phaeton? I . . ," Dominic glanced at Ivy, and she shook her head vehemently. "No, my good man, I think not," he replied. Dominic dug into his pocket and seized a coin, which he flipped to the driver.

"My thanks, my lord. Good evening to you both." With a snap of the loosened reins, he set the horses in motion, and the phaeton wheels began to roll quickly from the square.

"Damn me," Dominic muttered as the phaeton

turned the corner and disappeared from view. "I should have driven to Grosvenor Square to deliver you. I apologize, Ivy."

Ivy shook her head. "We were late returning the phaeton as it was. A hackney will do." Hiring a phaeton for the day was an extravagance, and an unnecessary one at that. Miss Feeney had been too green about the gills to have been impressed by Lord Counterton's high-perch phaeton.

Dominic glanced down the row of town houses as if to be certain no one had observed them. "Please, do come and wait inside. I will send a footman to hail a hackney."

Ivy paused. An unmarried miss could not enter a bachelor's house. It was time she followed the rules of propriety more rigidly. Tinsdale would expect nothing less of his betrothed, so she might as well begin immediately. She had already tempted Fate too many times.

"Better than calling attention to ourselves standing on the corner waiting for a hackney to appear." Dominic raised his eyebrows. "Come now, you know I have the right of it."

Ivy relented and took his arm and allowed him to hurry her toward the front door. "I suppose you do, this time."

Moments later, Ivy found herself seated in the

parlor with a crystal of sherry in her grip. While Dominic excused himself to speak with Mr. Cheatlin about locating a hackney, she leaned back in her chair and peered out the front windows sipping the sherry.

A deep, clear voice broke the silence of the room. "How was your afternoon in Hyde Park?"

She flinched at the unexpected intrusion, spilling more than a gulp of sherry into her mouth as she bolted upright in her chair. It was Dominic's man, Felix. She swallowed hard. "I beg your pardon?"

"The picnic. Did you enjoy it?" Felix hurried across the parlor and sat down in the chair across from her. "The day was rather warm, but I vow I have rarely seen a sky so blue in the month of August." He smiled expectantly and leaned toward Ivy, waiting for her reply.

"It was . . . lovely, I suppose." She paused then, her mind drifting to Miss Feeney and the tart incident.

Felix detected the delay and set his hand on her forearm comfortingly. "You can tell me. Dominic always does . . . eventually."

Ivy had just withdrawn her arm from his grasp when the knocker slammed down against the rest on the front door, startling her. "I cannot be found here," she stammered. "I cannot!"

Felix rushed from his chair and flattened his cheek against the window in order to see who was standing at the front door. He gasped and whirled around to face Ivy. "It is Lord and Lady Winthrop!"

Ivy jumped to her feet. "Hide me—somewhere," she pleaded. "They cannot find me here! *Please*, you must help me."

Chapter 10

It is better to want what you have than to have what you want.

Proverb

ll right, I'm comin'. Bloody impatient swells."
Cheatlin stalked up the hallway, not noticing
Ivy and Felix standing petrified in the parlor
as he shrugged on his butler's coat and passed. "Like
I have nothin' better to do with me time than trot to
the door every time somebody pounds on it."

The door squealed open. "Ah, Lord and Lady
Winthrop, please, do come in," Mr. Cheatlin very
nearly chirped. "Lord Counterton has just returned
home, and I am sure he would be delighted that
you have come to call . . . so unexpectedly."

Ivy implored Felix with her eyes. *Help me,* she mouthed.

A barrage of footfalls pounded in the entryway. "Please, would you take your ease in the parlor while I inform his lordship you are arrived?"

Panic visibly tore through Felix at that moment. *Help me.* Oh, God.

A scant second before Mr. Cheatlin led the Winthrops into the parlor, Felix grasped Ivy's arm and pulled her along with him behind the curtain. He laid his index finger vertically over his lips and motioned for her to stay quiet and still. Then he emerged from their hiding place.

"Lord and Lady Winthrop," he began.

Lady Winthrop gasped at his sudden appearance behind them.

"Might I offer you both a sherry?" Felix asked.

Ivy winced from behind the curtain. He wasn't acting the least bit like a footman, but like the Winthrops' esteemed host.

The Winthrops both murmured something in reply.

"Good, good. Though, Lord Winthrop, we . . . Lord Counterton," he corrected, "possesses an extremely smooth brandy which I highly recommend. Would you prefer it to sherry?"

Ivy covered her eyes. *Dominic, please, please help him.*

Then, as if summoned by her silent prayer, Dominic's voice interrupted Felix's chatter. "Lord and Lady Winthrop, how delightful that you have come to call."

"L-lord Counterton," Lady Winthrop stammered.

Ivy grasped the edge of the curtain and peered around it with one eye. The Winthrops were standing with their backs to the window where she hid. Dominic, as well as Felix, who was in the process of handing them their libations, were positioned in front of the guests.

It was then that Dominic spied Ivy. "Oh!" He quickly redirected his focus to Lady Winthrop. "I am so pleased that you have come, but it is so close in here. I fear the windows have been shut to the air all afternoon. Let us move to the garden." He offered his arm to Lady Winthrop, then flashed an urgent gaze at Felix. "I would dearly appreciate your opinion on the flowers and foliage. I have been told that my uncle collected exotic specimens from India, but I have no knowledge of such things—though I have heard that you are quite the expert horticulturalist, Lord Winthrop."

Lord Winthrop laughed off the assertion, though

quite unconvincingly. "I would not label myself an expert, Counterton, but I would gladly offer my opinion. Lead the way to your garden, man, and let us see what you've got."

"Come this way then. I do appreciate this," Dominic told them. "I know so few of the Quality in London, I vow I did not know who else to consult on such matters . . . and so many others."

"Well, my dear Lord Counterton," Ivy heard Lady Winthrop say, "that will change completely tomorrow evening at my musicale in your honor."

"Really, Lady Winthrop," Dominic replied. "You are too kind. I do not know how to show my sincere gratitude enough . . ."

Ivy listened for the voices and footsteps to fade as Dominic and the Winthrops walked down the hallway toward the back of the house. After she heard the French windows to the garden open and close again, she burst out from behind the curtains, her hands jammed atop her hips. "Does she suppose that we Sinclairs have done nothing to introduce Counterton to proper Society?"

Felix gulped. "Well, actually—"

"Stop." Ivy poked her finger at him. "That is only because welcoming him into Society is not my purpose. If it were my efforts would far surpass Lady Winthrop's dreary musicale tomorrow evening."

The door at the back of the house opened and closed again. Felix grasped Ivy's arm and hurried her to the front door and opened it. "You must leave, my lady, else I fear you will be discovered."

"Wait." Dominic was hurrying toward them from the far end of the passage. "Felix, as we passed the dining room, I noticed one of the . . . ehem . . . maids entwined with one of the carpenters on the dining table. I distracted the Winthrops, but would you please see to it that the pair are finished before the Winthrops leave?"

Though it was Felix he was speaking to, Dominic did not remove his eyes from Ivy.

"I should think Cheatlin would be better suited for such a task," Felix retorted.

"Felix. Please." Dominic strode forward and moved Felix aside to reach Ivy.

"They are upon the dining-room table, you say?" Felix turned and stomped like an angry child down the passageway.

Dominic stood only a breath away from her, gazing into her eyes.

"I must go," Ivy whispered, but she could barely hear her own voice over the pounding of her heart. Her fingers scrabbled for the latch of the door behind her.

Dominic reached behind her and pulled her fingers from the brass latch. He angled his head and leaned down until his lips brushed hers.

Ivy's eyelids fluttered, and she drew in a staggered breath.

"Will Her Ladyship still be needin' the hackney?" Mr. Cheatlin interrupted.

Dominic did not pull away. He meant to have his kiss. And she desired nothing more.

But she needed to leave the house at once. Needed to leave before she crossed the threshold of what must never be.

"I do, Cheatlin," she managed to say. She bent her knees and slid down the door until she could duck by Dominic and open the door into the night air. Into a less-heated frame of mind.

The next night
The Winthrop residence
Berkeley Square

While Counterton House, in its current state of repair, was quite suitable for a counterfeit marquess, the Winthrops' house, one of the largest and the grandest on Berkeley Square, was fit for a prince.

To claim that the grand old home was impressive would be an understatement. Only one other house on the square, Lansdowne House, was larger. It was a huge residence that stretched across the southwest corner of Berkeley Square and had once served as residence for the Prime Minister, William Pitt.

Ivy and her sisters were standing just outside the French windows from the aubergine drawing room, which Siusan found far too dark and oppressive to wait inside for the musicale to begin.

The Sinclair brothers, at Grant's suggestion, had begged off the Winthrops' welcome musicale for the Marquess of Counterton—which did not please Ivy in the least. Instead, they were to begin the night at White's, then head off to wherever that might lead them to manufacture their own wicked entertainment.

While Siusan and Priscilla gazed out over the lush garden, Ivy was leaning against the marble balcony rail. Her arms were folded over her chest as she stared back into the house.

Dominic was surrounded by a circle of matrons, and judging from their periodic laughter and playful raps with their collapsed fans, he was being his usual diverting and utterly charming self.

Miss Feeney was sitting in the first row of chairs set up for the concert. From her fine-featured profile, Ivy could see Miss Feeney was looking rather out of sorts. She was sure the fish gelatin tart was not still to blame. In her situation, any woman would be—especially when the man of her dreams (or so Ivy hoped) was standing only two strides away. And the man of the moment, Tinsdale, was standing like a sentry behind her, his hand set possessively on her shoulder.

Ivy felt a little sorry for her. But only a very little. This was the course Miss Feeney had chosen for herself. One that Ivy hoped to reverse. Soon.

"He needs to be speaking with Miss Feeney, not all of the ladies of the *ton*," Ivy huffed. "That's the true reason we are here. I do not care a groat if he is accepted in Society."

"Dear, it is not as if he has a choice in the matter," Priscilla argued. "The moment he was announced, he was encircled by hopeful mamas."

Ivy exhaled her frustration. "But he needs to focus his charms on Miss Feeney—else I shall never win Lord Tinsdale back from her."

"Why, pray, are you so set upon reclaiming the thoroughly uninteresting Viscount Tinsdale, whose sole mission seemed to be to squeeze the exuberant nature from you and bring you into formation?" Siusan probed.

Ivy turned around and leaned her hips against the railing and peered up at the crescent moon.

"Why, Ivy? Why, when your Lord Counterton adores everything about you. It is so plain in his eyes. How can you not see it—feel it!"

"And . . . good heavens," Priscilla added, "just look at the man." She looked over her shoulder and exaggerated a dreamy sigh. "Were I you, Ivy, I would be scheming to find a way to see him into my bed, not into someone else's."

"Priscilla!" Ivy thumped her sister with her fan.

"What? You know it's true." Priscilla lifted a single eyebrow at Siusan. "Or it should be, eh?"

"There are two very good reasons why Dominic and I can never be together but I am not going to explain them to the two of you." Ivy spun around and started toward the French windows of the drawing room. "Suffice it to say, Tinsdale is my match, and I would like it very much if you both supported my efforts—as you promised—to take him back from Miss Feeney."

A few minutes later, the musicians assembled, and, for an hour, the Winthrop aubergine drawing room was filled with song . . . and thirty-nine guests who were trying their best to keep their eyelids propped open.

Only Lord and Lady Winthrop, and one other,

seemed to be immune to the lulling effect of music in the crowded, stuffy room.

That one other was Lord Tinsdale, but then, he wasn't truly paying attention to the musicians. Not at all, in fact. His full notice was upon Ivy, and Lord Counterton, who was whispering in her ear and making her shoulders bounce in silent laughter.

He didn't much care for her behavior, but he knew that she was not truly the one at fault. It was Lord Counterton.

Tinsdale had heard all about him. His penchant for seducing women, then tossing them aside. And now, Ivy had fallen under Counterton's spell. And he knew he was wholly to blame.

Being a motherless Scot, she had looked to him for guidance regarding proper behavior in Society. It was something she'd said her father valued above all else. And something he was quite willing to teach her. It just hadn't been as easy as he'd thought it would it be. His teaching methods were sound. But Ivy was like a young filly, still wild and untamed. She had yet to be broken, but Tinsdale was actually looking forward to that undertaking with great excitement.

Until he met Miss Feeney. She was everything Lady Ivy was not. She did not challenge him on the issues of the day. She did not call undue attention to herself, except by virtue of her great beauty, which of course, she could not help. She was gentle and sweet, and sought after by every unmarried man in Society. And somehow, he'd won her. And all of London had taken notice of his spectacular conquest.

Only now, he was growing rather bored with his lovely doll.

And the appeal of breaking Lady Ivy was growing. He hadn't realized, until he saw her with the scoundrel Counterton, how desirable she was. How intelligent, and, though not a classical beauty like Miss Feeney, she was moderately attractive. But most importantly, she was the daughter of a duke—the most wealthy peer in all of Scotland.

There was only one flaw in her that he could see—but it was also one he would relish correcting.

But to do that, he'd have to do something about the Marquess of Counterton. Seeing him press her against a tree and kiss her like that, well, it was too much. Had anyone else witnessed their intimacy, Lady Ivy would have been ruined in the eyes of Polite Society.

And then, it would be too late to exert his will over her. To transform her into a proper lady.

No, he knew he had to separate her from the Marquess of Counterton. And soon.

Miss Fiona Feeney adored music, but not the sort the Winthrops had chosen for the entertainment this night. Her tastes in notes were a little more . . . passionate. Give her the sounds of a fiddle and drum, and she would be dancing in the clouds in heaven.

That's how she remembered Inis Thiar, where she grew up, a rocky emerald green island off the west coat of Ireland. Life was hard, and you had to be passionate about it if you were to survive long enough to put a penny in your pocket.

Fiona was a great beauty though, and she knew she wasn't meant to live out her days on the wee cropping of land framed by the sea. And her mother knew it too, which was why when she had the chance to pack Fiona off to London to become the charge of her wealthy yet ailing great-aunt, Mrs. Cavanaugh, she did just that.

But London was so foreign to Fiona, with all its rules of propriety, that within six months she was writing to her mother every day begging to return to the simplicity of Inis Thiar.

And once a month her mother would write back, telling her to wait, for as the charge and sole heir of Mrs. Cavanaugh, she would one day become the great lady she was destined to become. Until one gray misty day, another letter arrived from Inis Thiar, telling Fiona that her mother had died of a fever. Fiona was alone, except for her great-aunt, who grew weaker every day.

Fiona knew what she must do. She had to find a wealthy husband, a titled husband before her great-aunt passed and her connection with Society withered with it.

And so it came to pass that Mrs. Murphy, a friend of her great-aunt's and an ancient fixture of the *ton*, had been tapped to promote Fiona within Society when Mrs. Cavanaugh could no longer do so. And she did so with great success.

The black-haired beauty quickly nudged out vibrant Lady Ivy Sinclair as the toast of the *ton*, and that attention brought her the enviable gift of being free to choose a favorite from more than a dozen of London's most eligible bachelors.

And the one she selected from this glittering pool was the best by far. She knew this because one of the Sinclair heiresses, Lady Ivy, had already chosen him for herself—Viscount Tinsdale.

Of course, Fiona reveled in her success. Tinsdale seemed entirely devoted to her. So smitten was he with her that within two weeks of knowing her,

Tinsdale had already acquired a special license, and she knew he'd ask for her hand soon.

But now that Lady Ivy reemerged into Society with a knee-weakeningly handsome marquess on her arm, Fiona began to doubt her choice. She wondered if Lord Tinsdale really was the best selection after all. What was worse was that her great-aunt's condition was worsening every day. She didn't have time to investigate Counterton's suitability, but neither could she simply walk away from him and be content with Tinsdale.

Fiona pretended to drop her fan so that she could steal a glance at Counterton, who was sitting behind her at the musicale. His gaze met hers briefly, and he bent down and retrieved her fan for her.

She gave him a shy smile of thanks, then faced forward again.

Oh, she couldn't concentrate on the music being played. It was as dreary and predictable as Tinsdale. While Lord Counterton . . . well, he made her heart pound with all of the fierce passion of a *bodhrán* drum.

The night air was soft and the sky clear enough that the crescent moon above lit the square as efficiently as a gaslight. And so Ivy decided that rather than join her sisters in the carriage to return directly to Grosvenor Square, she would take the air and walk with Dominic.

It was just a short distance around Berkeley Square to Lord Counterton's town house, and there, as long as she was not observed entering his residence, they could privately discuss their progress with the plan that evening.

Siusan and Priscilla, whose primary goal that Season was to be accepted fully in proper Society, agreed to Ivy's proposal—only if she would permit them to follow behind. They would act as chaperones of sorts, at least until they were all obscured by trees and shrubbery on the square's green.

Ivy begrudgingly accepted this condition, but the moment they were blocked from the view of any guest who might be leaving the Winthrops' palatial home, she raised her hand and summoned the carriage driver who'd been stalking them around the square.

"We will send the carriage back for you," Siusan told her, "and I urge you to make use of it before the sun rises in a few hours. Wouldn't want anyone to get the wrong notion."

Priscilla leaned her head before the window. "Or *would* we?" She tossed a wink at Ivy and Dominic, then leaned back into the darkness of the carriage.

They could hear her wicked sisters laughing even as the carriage turned from the square.

"Lady Siusan is right, Ivy. You are risking quite a lot by being alone with me right now. We arrived with one another and were seen leaving together."

"We left in the company of my sisters." Ivy plucked a tiny leaf from a boxwood hedge and rolled it between her thumb and index finger. "Remember, I am a Sinclair. No one expects one of the Seven Deadly Sins to follow the rules . . . precisely. Though, I am trying. Really, I am."

"Nevertheless, Ivy"—Dominic laced his fingers behind his back as he walked—"Society does have certain expectations. Scoff at those, and there are doors that will never open to you—*or Tinsdale*—again."

Ivy stilled her step, then turned and looked at Dominic. She hadn't realized it, but she hadn't thought to learn if Tinsdale had yet left Winthrops' House or not.

That was very silly of her, wasn't it?

She'd entirely forgotten about Tinsdale the moment he was no longer in sight. She had been more interested in convincing her sisters to return home so that she could talk with Dominic about the plan.

And yet, she'd forgotten the whole point of the

ruse and the primary reason for even coming to the musicale this night—to win back Tinsdale from Miss Feeney.

"How extraordinary."

"What was that?" Dominic asked, stopping at the steps of Counterton House.

In the moonlight, his features were even more chiseled, perfect and, Lord above, the way he was looking at her was making her remember the hardness of him as he had pressed her against the tree beside the Serpentine.

Unexplainably, she found herself wanting to feel his lips on hers again, his tongue on her mouth. And more.

And that too was extraordinary. He was . . . an actor, for God's sake. He no more wanted her than . . . than she wanted Tinsdale.

Without realizing it, she licked her full lips, drawing Nick's attention to her mouth. He wanted to taste her again, wanted to feel her body softening beneath his.

He wanted to caress her, touch her silken naked skin, and press the hardness of himself into her softest, most intimate of places.

Her breath was coming fast. Her eyes were impossibly wide.

And in those eyes, damn it all, he could see it.

She wanted him, too.

Barely contained desire crackled between them, closing the distance between their bodies.

He ached for her. Needed to be with her, to make love to her now.

To let his touch prove to her what she could not allow herself to believe. That he loved her. Already, he loved her.

No longer able to endure this game, Nick took a step toward her, reaching out his hand to her.

Without hesitation, she slid her slippers forward a stride and grasped his hand with a sureness that surprised him.

Pulling her to him, he settled his hands on her hips. Her face was a breath away from his.

But there was a question to be asked, and so he posed it with his eyes, and she nodded, silently.

His chest swelled with emotion as he bent and brushed his lips against hers, then took her hand again and gently led her to the door.

There would be no retreat now.

Chapter 11

Envy consists in seeing things never in themselves,
but only in their relations.
Bertrand Russell

The passage was dark as they stepped inside the
house, and Dominic latched the door behind
them. No servant stirred, and the only sound
Ivy could hear was the creak of floorboards beneath their shifting feet.

Her mind whirled, and impossible thoughts
crowded her mind. Dominic grasped her shoulders
and, without a word, walked her back against the
wall and pressed his body firmly against hers.

His hardness wedged urgently against her pelvis,
and Ivy wrapped her arms around his neck and
wriggled against him. She rose on her toes and

raised a knee slightly, centering him in a softer place between her legs.

With a groan, Dominic slid a palm down her waist to her hips and caught her knee, then leaned more fully into her as he trailed hot kisses along her throat.

Ivy moaned and squeezed his shoulders with her fingers, trying to steady herself, but her heart slammed against her ribs, and her body trembled with anticipation like a new leaf in the wind.

A door closed below stairs, and there was murmuring. Ivy tensed and pulled herself against his chest, resting her chin on his shoulder, listening. "Shh."

Someone, one of the staff, had come home. "Upstairs," Dominic whispered to her, his tone transforming the word into a question.

She turned her eyes to his, knowing how she should reply . . . to tell him she should wait outside for the carriage to return. But those weren't the words that came from her lips. What did was spoken so softly that it was hardly a sound at all. "Aye."

But he'd heard her. To Ivy's surprise, Dominic drew back, then bent and scooped her roughly into his arms and carried her up the stairs.

The passageway sconces were not alight this night, but it was clear that he knew exactly where he was taking her. He whisked her down the passage, nudged open the door, and burst into his bedchamber, where he set her on her feet at the edge of his tester bed.

Without Dominic to cling to, she barely managed to keep her balance. She was shivering, as though cold, but she was anything but chilled. Heat pumped through her, surging strong along with her desire.

"There is no need to be afraid." Dominic reached her and cupped his hand around her lower back, pulling her against him again as he kissed her deeply.

She broke the seal of their lips for a gasp of air. "I'm not afraid." That much was true. She was just . . . inexperienced.

This would have surprised him.

He would have heard the rumors. Everyone had. And he would believe that the Sinclair brothers and sisters were every bit as passionate as they were wild.

She had done nothing to counter the notion. In fact, from the very first moment Dominic met her outside The Theater Royal Drury Lane, and she pulled him to her and kissed him, she could have only bolstered the impression that she was a complete hoyden.

But that wasn't quite the truth of the matter. In fact, he, and the members of the *ton,* would be surprised to learn that despite the gossip that flooded London all Season long, Ivy was, in fact, still a maid.

He kissed her again, letting his hot lips drag over her throat. "I want to kiss all of you," he whispered oh so seductively. "Would you mind terribly if I did?"

"Nay." Ivy felt a clench between her legs and a moist warmth growing there.

Dominic drew a finger down her throat and slid it down to where her neckline met the swell of her breasts. He tugged at the satin ribbon between her breasts, the thin cord that cinched her bodice closed.

She gasped as the gown opened, and his hand skittered across her chemise. The heat of his fingers pressed through the wisp of silk, searing her skin like a brand.

Oh God. She wanted this. Wanted him.

He eased his hand around her, loosened her stays, and released her breasts from their confinement, then eased her back onto the bed. With her knees together, her position on the bed made her back arch. Seeing this, Dominic nudged her knees apart and moved between them.

He leaned over her and molded one bare breast in his hand and kneaded it gently, as he took her other nipple into his mouth. It pebbled at the wet, searing touch, and she writhed, bowing up against him, but this time for a very different reason.

And then, he reached a hand behind him, and she felt it on her ankle, then riding up beneath her gown. His fingers moved up her silk stocking to her thigh and between the part in her pantalets.

He was going to touch her. Right *there*.

And she wanted him to. So badly.

She didn't care what her father might think. What others might. That isn't why she had never been touched like this before. It wasn't the reason that her virginity was still hers to offer.

It was because, until now, this moment, it hadn't been right. But she hadn't been in love. But she was now.

She could barely wait. Her heart quickened in anticipation as he removed his trousers.

Centering the rough pads of two fingers just between her cleft, he slowly ran them upward between her passion-slickened folds. Suddenly, she felt the pressure of his thumb, and he used it to circle her most sensitive part.

He lifted his head and pressed his mouth to hers as he tantalized her below. Prodding her feminine lips apart, he nudged her knees wider and knelt between them.

She could feel the hot tip of him touching her, could feel him dipping just into her moistness before pulling back. Heat surged within her below. She wanted to feel him inside her completely.

Dominic leaned low over her and slipped his tongue into her mouth, just as he pressed his full tip between her nether lips, pausing for just a moment before thrusting deep into her—breaking through the resistance it met.

There was a sharp sting, and she jerked, gasping at the surprise of the pain.

Dominic ripped his mouth from hers. "Bloody hell!" He shoved up from her and came fully to his feet. He stared down at Ivy, his expression one she could only read as utter horror. "You're a—virgin."

She hadn't expected this to happen. Hadn't wanted him to stop. She only wanted to be with him. As close as a man and a woman could be.

Ivy leaned forward and shoved her gown down, covering herself. The heat was already rushing into her cheeks. "Aye." She propped herself up on her elbows. "I *was* a virgin."

Suddenly, she felt ridiculous and naïve—and as if she was going to cry. But she couldn't allow that to happen.

Not now. She was a Sinclair after all . . . and Sinclairs were not weak.

"What of it?" She lifted her chin defiantly and peered up at him. "It is not as though it changes anything."

"Yes, Ivy, it does!" Dominic was nearly sputtering. "Do you not understand? Nothing can *ever* be the same between us again. *Ever.*"

In the light of the crescent moon cutting through the front windows, Nick could see the shimmer of tears in Ivy's eyes.

He moved toward her, wanting to hold Ivy in his arms, but suddenly the sound of footfalls on the stairs echoed up the passageway. The bobbing light of a chamber lamp cast a glow into the dark hall.

Damn it all. He'd left the bedchamber door open.

Ivy heard the sound too and scrambled from the bed just as Felix stepped into the doorway. Without taking even a moment to smooth her gown or tuck her stray locks back from her face, she silently marched past Nick, then Felix too, and descended the stairs.

Nick started after her, but Felix braced an arm across the doorway. "I would not advise going after her just now," he said, more forcefully than Nick would have expected. "I may not be privy to what happened here, but I saw her face. Anything you said right now would be met with a backhander across the face. Believe me."

Nick batted his cousin's arm aside, but at that moment the front door slammed. He could just hear the clop of hooves on the square outside.

It had changed everything.

Had he been just a diversion, no matter how he felt about her, Nick would have been able to abide by Ivy's wishes to follow her father's dictates and step aside so that she could marry Tinsdale.

But no longer. He could never allow it now.

What happened this night was not folly. Despite the air of nonchalance she now donned, Ivy had given him her body, but more importantly her heart.

He knew this now.

She had *chosen* him.

It was too late.

Damn it.

Ivy stood upon the steps, frantically scanning the passing conveyances on Berkeley Square for the Sinclair carriage. It hadn't returned for her yet. Why would it have? Her sisters had left her and Dominic on the square perhaps only a quarter of an hour ago. A short few minutes that changed her life forever.

But it was just as well the carriage hadn't yet arrived. Grosvenor Square was not so very far and, just now, a walk in the night air would do her good. Ivy swiped her palms over her cheeks, wiping away the tears running down them. She caught up her skirt, raising her hem from the steps, and hurried down to the pavers, mindful that Dominic might be in pursuit.

She didn't slow her pace until she turned off the square onto Davies Street, and even then, she kept walking until she had passed four houses and was sure that she was no longer within view of the Counterton residence. Grasping a wrought-iron rail that ran in front of a stately brick house, she finally paused to catch her breath. But with the air that filled her lungs came the tears she thought she'd left behind in Berkeley Square. Her knees crumpled beneath her, and she slid down the fence to the pavers.

What a fool she'd been, giving in so utterly to her passions, her emotions. Ivy leaned back against the fence and rested her head in her hand.

Why had she done it? Tinsdale was the one she wished to marry—not Dominic.

She didn't even know who Dominic was, not

really. She didn't even know his true name. Everything about him was an act. It wasn't real . . . even the way he made her feel. That's what actors were paid to do after all—make their audience feel what the playwright wished. Only this time, she had crafted the script. His role was to charm and make his audience fall in love with him.

And she had.

She had allowed herself to fall in love with naught but an illusion—and one of her own creation. How imprudent she was. How gullible. Such a fool.

A breathy laugh pressed through her lips as cold realization overtook her. She'd been drawn in by her own ruse.

Reaching up, Ivy caught a rung midway up the fence and slowly pulled herself to her feet. And though her heart pained her like never before, she straightened her back and willed herself to walk back to Grosvenor Square.

Noon
The Sinclair residence
Grosvenor Square

Her stomach growled and ached as Ivy descended the stairs from her chamber, but she didn't feel much like eating breakfast. She knew, though, her sisters, and perhaps her brothers too, would be waiting for her in the dining room. Not because of their impeccable manners, though they had been well trained by their governesses and tutors as children. Or because they were deeply invested in the success or failure of her plan to steal back Lord Tinsdale from Miss Feeney.

Nay, Ivy knew it was because of the worried little man who was standing beside the newel post, waiting for her, at the bottom of the staircase had also awaited her return from Berkeley Square last night. "My lady, when the carriage returned without you, I went searching for you myself, and—"

Ivy descended the last three steps and laid her hand on his shoulder. "And I thank you for that, Poplin, but as you can see I am here, safe and quite well."

The butler peered at her through squinting eyes as if assessing the truthfulness of her last word. He paused for several moments, then gestured for her to follow him to the dining room. "Mrs. Wimpole has set a fine meal this day."

Ivy lifted her brow. "Really, I am not hungry. I thought I might convince my sisters to join me at the Garden of Eden for tea and cake later."

He exhaled. "You needn't fret. She didn't cook anything . . . special. Just dished some cold beef, fruit, toasted bread, and cheese." He bent slightly at the waist and extended his hand again. "Please. Your family is waiting, Lady Ivy." When she didn't follow him promptly, he added, "I-I might have mentioned that you did not return in the carriage last eve. They know you are at home now, of course—one of your sisters checked your bedchamber this morn—but they seem rather concerned about you."

Ivy set her fingers to her temples and rubbed as she reluctantly followed him down the passage toward the sound of clinking silver mingled with low murmurs.

Blast. All of her brothers and sisters, save Sterling, were there at the table . . . waiting.

"Good noon to you all." She smiled as brightly as she could.

"Weel, that expression says it all, doesn't it?" Siusan, who'd come to her feet the instant Ivy entered with Poplin, waved a dismissive hand, and reseated herself.

A saucy smile crossed Priscilla's lips. "I'll say."

Ivy scowled. "And what, pray, are you two implying?"

"I wasn't implying anything," Siusan replied, "but then, there is no need. Poplin told us that you did not return in the carriage last eve, but here you stand, smelling of April and May, grinning like a gleeful fool."

"Whatever it is you are guessing at, you are likely very wrong." Ivy looked down her nose at her sister. "Rather than waiting for the carriage, I walked back to Grosvenor Square, then I went directly to my bedchamber." She looked at Poplin. "I apologize if I worried you."

Killian chuckled and tapped his hand on the chair beside him. "Do sit here next to me, Ivy. I fear our sisters are overly partial to your actor fellow and are quite envious of a plan which allows you to spend so much time with him. Just ignore them."

Priscilla and Siusan gasped at their brother's jibe, but, before either could utter a word, Lachlan raised a hand as he swallowed a wedge of beef and washed it down with some weak-looking tea.

Siusan slid the newspaper across the table to Ivy, then pinched the corner, and flipped it open to the second page. She poked at a short column. "I think you might wish to read this—the *on dit* column. I believe the report mentions you."

Ivy peered up at Siusan, then saw that everyone else at the table was waiting breathlessly for her to do just that. "Nothing . . . scandalous, I hope." Certainly the long-nosed columnists could not have learned of what she and Dominic had shared last evening. Good God, she hoped not. But somehow, the blasted columnist seemed to notice everything of late. She began to scan the column when Priscilla complained, desiring her to read aloud.

"Very well. Though I do hope you are not making this request of me to increase my embarrassment." Ivy let her gaze flit around the table to be sure before beginning. " 'The fine weather yesterday brought Londoners out of doors by the score, with many Society notables making Hyde Park their destination of choice. There many enjoyed a picnic luncheon along the Serpentine and walks beside the water, while others such as Lord C. and Lady I. S. chose the high excitement of phaeton racing. The victors celebrated with sherry, while those left behind on Rotten Row, Lord T. and Miss F., finished the afternoon with a wash bucket and flannels, cleaning the excitement of the day from the carriage.' "

Priscilla laughed. "Do tell us, who gave back their noon meal to Mother Nature? Please tell me it was Lord Tinsdale."

Ivy scowled. "What a thing to say. It was Miss Feeney . . . thanks to Mrs. Wimpole's fish-gelatin tart."

Grant chuckled. "Aye, caught a whiff of one of those." He shuddered for effect.

"Speaking of Tinsdale and Miss Feeney. How goes the ruse, Ivy?" Lachlan asked. "Any progress?"

"I should say so," Grant interjected. He nodded to Poplin, who scurried out into the passage, then returned a moment later with a silver salver.

"Lady Ivy," the butler said, moving the tray before her, "for you."

Her sisters exchanged confused glances, but Grant could barely contain a smile.

Ivy lifted the letter and broke open the seal. "It's . . . from Lord Tinsdale." She looked up at Grant.

"Tinsdale's footman delivered this last night," he informed her. "Damn it, Ivy, stop staring at me and read it."

Ivy shook the letter from its folds. She could hardly believe what it said. She clapped a hand over her mouth. "He wishes an interview at four of the clock." She jerked her eyes from the missive and looked back to Grant. "What shall I do?"

"How is it that you do not know, Ivy?" Grant peered at her for a long while before speaking. "Is not this what you wanted—for Tinsdale to return his attention to you?"

"I—I . . ." Ivy looked down at the missive again. "Well, of course it is. It was the whole purpose of the ruse—the reason for all of my efforts." She turned her gaze upward again but was completely taken aback by what she now saw.

No one was smiling, or seemed pleased for her at all, at this new development. Instead, they were all looking back at her with expressions so dour one would believe someone had died.

· She came to her feet at once. "Why are you all looking at me like that? Tinsdale's coming to call is a very positive sign. He would not have requested the interview if he was still infatuated with Miss Feeney. He must intend to return his affections to me—if I will accept them." The tone of her voice started to resemble a whimper. "Why aren't you happy for me? You know that this is exactly what I needed to happen—what I wanted."

Ivy especially couldn't bear the way Grant was looking at her. It was as if he somehow saw into her heart and her head and knew what had happened last night. A rush of confused emotions flooded Ivy's senses.

"Aye," Grant said softly, "it *was* what you wanted. But, Ivy, is it still?"

Ivy swallowed and peered down at the letter. Tears began to catch in her lashes. "Aye, it is," she whispered, trying to convince her brothers and sisters. Trying to convince herself. She raised her gaze. "It is exactly what Da would want. What I have worked so hard to achieve."

But she knew Grant would not let her leave it at that, though her sisters might. And so, she spun around and left the dining room without another word.

Chapter 12

Malice may be sometimes out of breath, envy never.
Lord Halifax

From her bedchamber, where she'd taken refuge from her family, Ivy heard the door knocker strike two different times before the tall case clock tinged three in the afternoon. She came to her feet and stood in the center of her room both times, but Poplin never came for her, and no cards were delivered.

Ivy had expected Dominic to call for her, if not to make sense of what had passed between them last night, then at least to ensure that she had arrived home safely.

But he hadn't, and now, when the clock sounded

the hour and the doorknocker slammed into its rest, she knew Tinsdale had arrived.

He was never tardy. In truth, his punctuality was as predictable and reliable as the sun taking its perch each morn, which, she decided, was probably a very good quality in a husband.

As were his calm demeanor and common sense. She'd never had to worry about Tinsdale backing her into a wall and kissing her with a passion that would make her mad with wanton desires. With him guiding her and setting a fine example, she would become the respectful woman her father demanded—a Sinclair worthy of the family name.

Ivy had been staring blankly at the door, reminding herself of the list of qualities that recommended Lord Tinsdale, when she suddenly noticed Siusan standing before her, waving her hand.

"Gorblimey, Ivy," Su was saying. "Are you well? I've been calling to you from outside your door."

Blinking, Ivy focused on her sister. "Aye, I was thinking."

Siusan nodded knowingly. "About how to break it to Tinsdale that you have set your heart on Counterton."

"What?" Ivy shook off the notion like a dog that had just come in from the rain. "Good Lord, no! I mean to encourage his interest in me, if that is why he has come."

"Och, why would you do that?" Siusan huffed a sigh as she sat down on the edge of Ivy's pallet. "Dominic's feelings for you are true. Everyone can see that, and I suspect yours run just as clear and strong as his."

"You do not know what you are talking about, Su. Dominic is just playing the role I paid him to, and he happens to excel at his position, that's all." Ivy thrust her hands forward. "I don't even know his real name, or anything about him."

Siusan set an elbow on her knees and propped her chin in her palm. "Have you asked him?"

"Well, no, I haven't. In fact, I asked him not to tell me so I wouldn't accidentally bungle the ruse by addressing him by his true name, or mentioning where he grew up." Ivy, feeling flustered again, folded her arms tightly across her chest. "The point is, it is impossible to have fond feelings for someone you do not even know."

Siusan abruptly sat up straight. "And why do you think you don't know him at all? He is a very kind, intelligent, charming, and diverting man. No matter how skilled an actor, if he were not truly all of these things, we certainly would have seen a very different Lord Counterton. No actor could remain immersed in his character for so long without breaking and exposing his true self—which is why I believe, sister, you do know him very well."

"It doesn't matter anyway. Father would never consider an actor a suitable match for his wayward daughter." Siusan was studying her now, getting her nerves on edge. Ivy started for the open door. "Believe me when I tell you that if Tinsdale has come to reestablish our relationship, I shall accept him without delay and close the curtain on Lord Counterton."

"I shouldn't do that *yet* if I were you, Ivy," Siusan called after her.

Ivy whirled around. "Why not?"

"Because Priscilla spied Miss Feeney and Lord Tinsdale walking together along Pall Mall only an hour ago." Siusan rose from the pallet.

"T-today?" Ivy tried to clarify.

"Aye, *today,*" Siusan replied, slowly and quite deliberately.

Ivy stiffened. Very well. Perhaps it had just been wishful thinking, especially after her disastrous encounter last night with Dominic, that Tinsdale was now in the parlor waiting to tell her he had set Miss Feeney aside for her. But he was here to see her right now, and that was at least a start.

"You may be right that I shouldn't release

Dominic from our agreement just yet," Ivy said. "Besides, I have paid for the house and staff on Berkeley Square until the end of the month." With that, she turned again and descended the stairs to the parlor, where the man she intended to be her future husband awaited.

Ivy paused outside the parlor, leaning against the wall as she prepared herself to greet Tinsdale. Her heart thumped inside her chest, and her nerves twisted and wriggled like a nest of warring spiders.

Lud, she'd never felt so conflicted about meeting Lord Tinsdale before. Why then did she now? She was being such a great goose. She had just drawn in a deep, fortifying breath in preparation for turning into the room when Tinsdale stepped around the corner and in an instant was standing before her.

"I thought I heard you come down the stairs," he said, "and I wondered if you thought I was waiting in the garden."

Ivy shook her head stupidly. "My hair had shaken loose on my way to the parlor, and I was simply tucking it back into place." A smile was in order, and she fashioned one for him.

Skirting around Tinsdale, she started for the parlor, one of the only rooms in the house they'd had funds enough to furnish properly. And it was lovely, and usually she was happy to entertain in the parlor, but today she saw it as naught but a cage. "But the afternoon is beautiful and the weather mild. I rather like your suggestion to visit in the garden." She and Tinsdale whirled to reenter the passage, where they almost collided with Poplin.

The little man nearly dumped the large silver tray he held. The tea service atop it shifted, but aside from a biscuit that rolled off a serving plate into an open pot of jam, nothing spilled to the floor. "Your Ladyship, will you be taking tea in the—"

"Garden," Ivy inserted.

Poplin followed Ivy and Lord Tinsdale to the French windows leading out to the portico and the garden beyond. Ivy reached for the door latch, but Tinsdale cleared his throat, and so she paused.

Tinsdale looked at Poplin, though the elderly man who walked up behind them was weighted with a heavy tray.

This was ridiculous. The Sinclairs had but a two-member house staff. She could easily open the door for Poplin. Ivy made for the latch again, but Tinsdale caught her wrist and pulled her arm down against her side.

She bit her lip, knowing that Tinsdale was not truly being rude, just reminding her of her proper place in the house, even in one so poorly staffed.

Poplin's shaggy white eyebrows lifted for an instant, but then he settled the tray on a table in the passage and walked back to open the door for Ivy and Lord Tinsdale.

As they walked to the garden table and sat down, Ivy watched over her shoulder to be sure that the door hung open for Poplin. When she was certain that it had, and that the butler had sidled through with the weighty tea tray, she returned her attention to Tinsdale.

"I must admit, Lord Tinsdale, I was greatly surprised to receive your missive," Ivy said, as Poplin laid the tea service.

"Pleasantly so, I do hope." Tinsdale's smile was cloyingly sweet.

"Absolutely, it was merely unexpected." Ivy lifted the porcelain teapot and topped a cup with hyson tea. She breathed in the scent of dark amber broth. The family never drank it. Hyson was ruinously expensive and because of the Sinclairs' reduced means, was reserved only for esteemed guests— and today that meant Lord Tinsdale.

"I do hope my request for an interview was not entirely unforeseen after our conversation at the Argyle Rooms. We never finished our discussion, not during the picnic or even the Winthrop musicale." He took the tea she offered but allowed his fingers to brush over hers and remain in that position without drawing the dish of tea to him directly.

After a few moments, Ivy lowered the dish of tea to the table and pulled back her fingers. "Actually, my lord, I thought we had concluded that particular conversation, and I would have thought that my continued association with Lord Counterton would have confirmed that for you."

"Perhaps so, if I truly believed he was in love with you." Tinsdale leaned forward over the table and snatched up Ivy's hand into his. More firmly this time. "But I do not. He cannot love, not anymore. He is a scoundrel. His string of conquests is legendary throughout Lincolnshire."

Ivy struggled to pull her hand away, but he held it firm. "And how do you know this?"

"I . . . made some inquiries." Tinsdale's pale cheeks flushed with a mottled red color.

"Word in Averly is that when he was young, he once loved the daughter of an earl and she loved him as well. But Dominic Sheridan was the son of a mere gentleman. Her father would not approve of the match and hastily married her off to a widowed baron. She died in childbirth one year later." Tinsdale pinned Ivy with his gaze, waiting for her reaction.

But there was none. Why would there be? This man, this scoundrel Tinsdale spoke of, was not her Lord Counterton—the actor.

"Do you not understand me, Ivy? He doesn't love you because he cannot love anymore. He casts off women as regularly as his neckcloths."

"Lord Counterton is not the man you speak of. Believe me, I know."

Tinsdale's brow furrowed. "Ivy, you are only his choice of the moment. Have you not seen him hover about Miss Feeney lately? You are about to be replaced."

"In the same way you replaced me with Miss Feeney?" Ivy knew those words were too sharp. She knew she should use this moment to feign sadness and make it easy for Tinsdale to return to her and offer up his slightly bruised heart.

But she couldn't.

She was still angry with him, and hurt, by the way he had cast her aside without a word of explanation. Reining in her emotions was impossible at this moment and, before she knew it, she had lashed out at him. "Do you not fear, Lord Tinsdale, perhaps *you* are the one being replaced this time?"

Tinsdale stared at her, utterly thunderstruck.

Ivy pushed up from the table and stared down at

him. Then, without a further word of explanation, she left him in the garden.

Alone.

At two in the afternoon, when Nick had knocked at the Sinclair front door the first time, he was promptly told by Mr. Poplin that Lady Ivy was not taking visitors that hour. And so, he waited an hour longer before knocking again, hoping three of the clock was a more suitable hour to accept a very sincere and genuine apology. But the response remained the same.

Nick decided to wait an hour more, hoping that Lady Ivy, who oft enjoyed taking tea with her sisters at that hour, might emerge from the house. If he approached, she'd have no choice but to listen, at the very least, to what he had to say.

But when he peered down at his pocket watch and saw the hour hand sitting atop four, the front door opened, and instead of Ivy stepping outside, a blond gentleman, who could be none other than Lord Tinsdale, was invited inside.

Anger surged through Nick, and he stalked across the green and straight up to the door of No. 1 Grosvenor Square and instead of knocking politely, he charged straight into the house.

"Oh dear me. No, no, no!" Mrs. Wimpole came

hurrying up the passageway toward him. "You can't be here, my lord. You can't!" She grabbed his arm and drew him into the parlor. "She's got that other fellow here. The yellow-haired one."

"Where are they?" Nick made no effort to hold his voice low. "I must see Lady Ivy at once."

"Well, you can't, my lord," she whispered. The heavyset cook set her chubby hand against his chest to hold him in place while she leaned back and peered down the passage. She turned her head back to him. "Here comes Poplin. He'll know what to do. Just give me a tick." She thumped his chest once more. "Stay here, and please don't say a word."

She cast a look of warning to him and raced into the hall.

Nick heard whispers of varying tones, growing more and more urgent, but a moment later, Mr. Poplin and Mrs. Wimpole appeared at the open parlor door. "Where-is-she?"

Poplin raised his knobby-knuckled hand in the air. "Stay in here, and I will let her know you are in the parlor presently." He looked worried, and very little blood pinked his gaunt visage.

Nick nodded. "Three minutes, my good man. Three minutes, then I am coming to look for her."

* * *

Having just closed the French windows behind her, Ivy clapped a hand over her mouth. Gorblimey, she couldn't believe the things she'd said. But she'd meant them, every last one of them.

She lowered her hand and turned slightly to glance back out of the French window. Lord Tinsdale was still sitting where she had left him, staring at her empty chair.

Blast! She might have ruined everything. She wished she could rush back out to the garden and snatch back her spiteful words from the air—every last one of them.

Ivy set her hand on the door latch, intending to make amends, when she heard footsteps. She turned her head around to peer into the passage. Poplin was hurrying toward her.

It was all the incentive she needed to reverse her decision to go to Tinsdale. She released the latch.

"Please see Lord Tinsdale out, will you please, Poplin? I-I . . . please. As quickly as possible." She continued walking up the passage, making for the refuge of her bedchamber, when she noticed the oddest expression on Poplin's ancient face. "My God, what is it?" She halted just before him.

"I apologize, my lady. But you have a visitor waiting for you in the parlor." Poplin looked ready to burst into tears. "I did not invite him inside; in fact, I told him twice over that you were not accepting visitors. He just barged in. There was nothing Mrs. Wimpole nor I could do. He means to see you, now."

Ivy's eyes went wide. "Who? Who just barged in?" But she knew already. Dominic, or whatever his name truly was.

"Lord Counterton," Poplin sputtered. "He's in the parlor."

Good heavens. Ivy shot a worried glance behind her. "Please escort Lord Tinsdale out directly. Do not tarry or pause for any reason outside the parlor."

When Poplin nodded, Ivy sidled past the butler, then lifted her skirts and ran down the passage to the parlor.

Chapter 13

There is much less envy of the rich by the poor than there is of the happy by the unhappy.

Dennis Prager

hat are you doing here, Dominic?" Ivy hissed as she pressed the parlor door closed behind her.

Dominic strode toward her, but Ivy stopped him in midstride by raising a stalwart hand.

"You are a very intelligent woman, Ivy. You know exactly why I have come."

"Shh! Dominic, you can't stay," she whispered hoarsely.

"Where is Tinsdale?" His eyes were like steel.

"In the garden." She turned and leaned her ear to

the door and listened, then turned back to Dominic. "Please, you have to go—now."

"I won't until we discuss between us what happened last night." He opened his arms and stepped toward her.

"No. Dominic, not now."

"It must be now. Tinsdale is already here, wishing to claim you. But I won't let him. I can't."

"Why not? This has always been our agreement. This is why I hired you. You know this." She was doing it again. Using her words to wound when what she meant to sound strong, sure, convincing—like a Sinclair. Her heart clenched like a fist, drawing a whimper into her throat.

"Because you love me. I know you do."

"What an absurd thing to say." Ivy twisted the key in the lock and set it upon the table nearest the door. "Ours is a business relationship, nothing more."

Dominic prowled toward her, and she retreated one pace and then another until her back pressed against the door. Another moment, last night, was immediately called to mind.

"You are lying, Ivy. You know it as well as I." He stood too close, only a breath away. Just as he always did before he kissed her.

Ivy hadn't heard any sound in the passageway. Hadn't heard the click of the front door opening. "Please, lower your voice."

"Why? So he can't hear us. Ivy, I don't care. Do you know why? Because I will not be party to his claiming you. I won't do it. I can't. Not after last night."

Ivy set both hands against his chest, holding him back from her. "We have an agreement. I *paid* you."

Dominic flinched, her words stinging as surely as she had slapped his cheek.

"Ivy, I love you." Gently, he stroked her hair back from her face. "And I know you feel something for me as well, else you would not have offered yourself to me."

He leaned against her then, his lips hovering just above her own.

There was a pounding of boots in the hallway just outside the door. Ivy froze, but Dominic did not. Instead, he tilted her head slightly with his hand and moved his lips over hers.

The front door slammed shut, awakening Ivy to her more logical senses. "You suppose too much, sirrah." It was so hard looking into his eyes, knowing he spoke the truth. But it was a truth neither of them could ever live. Her father would never allow it.

"I want you, Ivy. I have since the first moment

our lips touched outside the theater." He kissed her again. "I have never met a woman like you. I have never loved anyone the way that I love you. I want you, Ivy. I want you in my life forever."

Ivy couldn't seem to breathe. He was too close, making promises she could never allow him to keep. Her eyes grew watery and hot. She had to push him back emotionally, even if she could not bring herself to do it physically.

"Is it me you truly want? Or the life I have, the life I have given you?"

Dominic stepped back from her, his eyes confused.

The tears were coming into her eyes, and she hated it. "Because I have nothing." She waved her hand about the room. "This is all false. The chandeliers, the silk draperies, the fine furnishings. It's all we have. All my brothers and sisters can afford since our father banished us from our home in Scotland. All we have until, like our brother Sterling, we reform and show ourselves to be respectable and worthy."

"Ivy, none of that matters to me."

Ivy gave a forced laugh. "Really? Then come with me. Let me show you the reality of my life if I do not marry Tinsdale." She snatched the key from the table, turned it in the lock, then grabbed Dominic's hand and led him upstairs, away from the splendor of the public rooms of the house.

* * *

The druggets on the stairway were worn and threadbare, and with each step they took, the house began to look more forlorn.

Ivy tugged at Nick's hand and pulled him up the staircase faster still, until they reached the next floor.

"This is where my sisters and I reside. It's rather luxurious, at least compared to the attic garrets where my brothers, the sons of a duke, sleep."

"Ivy, you don't need to do this. It doesn't matter to me. You are all that matters in my life. Nothing else."

Ivy marched him down the passage, then flung open a door and led him inside. The room was barren, devoid of furnishings save a little table near the window with a small, hazy mirror upon it. Against the far wall was a pallet, barely a bed at all, blanketed by a worn old coverlet.

Releasing his hand, Ivy stepped into the center of the room. "This is my reality, Dominic. This is who I really am."

Nick set his hand on the door and shut it. Ivy blinked at him in confusion. "Ivy, I don't care about the trappings of Society." He closed the gap between them in two short strides. "You are every-thing. You are all I need."

Her eyes were bright, still wet with tears as she scrutinized him.

"Don't say anything, Ivy." He took her into his arms, and from the expression on her face, he wasn't sure if she would push away. She didn't. Ivy folded against him, and he felt her surrender.

Nick ran his fingers through her copper locks. Splaying his fingers, he loosened her silken hair, removing any hairpins he found, dropping them to the floor, until her hair hung free about her waist.

He smoothed his hands around her, turned her face up to him, and kissed her. Her lips were sweet as sugared tea, and she parted them for him and welcomed his tongue inside.

She murmured something as their kiss deepened, and she slid her arms around his neck, drawing him closer still.

He felt the tip of her pink tongue gliding over the roof of his mouth, then urging his tongue into her mouth and, to his surprise, sucking on it.

His groin tightened, and he tried neither to imagine her naked in his arms nor think about the tiny bed only a stride away from them.

The door hinges squealed behind him. Startled, Ivy broke their kiss and looked around his shoulder. "Su, have you ever heard of knocking before entering a bedchamber." She didn't break away. It was almost as though she clung to him to keep her footing.

"I-I apologize, Ivy," Siusan stammered. "I heard Lord Tinsdale and . . . I wasn't aware that you had a another caller." He could tell from the tone of Siusan's voice that she was not so much surprised at finding him there as amused. "Good afternoon, Dominic."

Nick started to turn, but Ivy's hold on him prevented it. "Siusan, I trust you are having a lovely day."

"Och, aye. Very diverting."

He heard the whisper of slippers behind them, then the creak of the pallet. Turning his head slightly, he saw Siusan leaning back and gleefully kicking her feet over the low edge of the pallet like a little girl. The grin on her face was huge.

"Is there something you wanted, Su?" Ivy leaned her forehead against Nick's chest, and, from the upward curve of her reddening cheeks, he could tell she was smiling too.

"Oh, come think of it, there was. I came to remind you that we are leaving for the fête at five of the clock."

Ivy exhaled. "I had quite forgotten."

"There are so many festive activities at this time of year that everyone, in Society, will be there. I do hope you will join us, Dominic. The whole family is attending." It was clear that Siusan could barely contain her laughter, for it leaked through and heightened the tone of every word she spoke. "I know Ivy will be very disheartened if you refuse— as will I, of course."

Ivy's grip on his shoulder tightened, but he did not know how to read what it meant, whether he should join them or refrain. And so, he went with his own heart. "I should greatly enjoy joining your family at the fête."

Ivy looked over at Siusan. "Is that all, sister?"

Coming to her feet, Siusan walked straight over and, from a distance no wider than the circumference of a teacup, she smiled at them both. "No, that is all. I . . . well, then I will see you both directly in the parlor then."

Nick couldn't tell for certain, but from the thump and wisp on the floor, he guessed that Siusan had just skipped from the bedchamber.

Ivy looked up at him and laughed. "Sometimes I want to wring my sister's neck like a Christmas goose's."

"I hardly heard a word she said, which—given that she had found her sister in her bedchamber in the arms of her hired hand—were probably all quite derisive." Nick touched his forehead to Ivy's, and their noses brushed.

"Nothing contemptuous at all," Ivy told him. "Though you did accept an invitation to attend a fête, and I fear Siusan will never let you wriggle out of it."

"When she came in, all I could think about was making love to you."

"Well, it was fortunate she came in when she did . . . because I was having the same wicked thought."

To his dismay, Nick hardened again, and his breeches were feeling rather tight.

"Are you ready to meet everyone in the parlor?" Ivy broke their embrace and stepped back. Her gaze dropped below his waist. "Oh my." Her words rode a giggle. "Maybe not just yet."

Thimbletweed
Regent's Fête

Flaming branches and twigs crackled and smoked, burning brightly in more than two dozen cresset baskets framing an open field just outside of Thimbletweed.

The quaint village, which really was no more than a crossroads bordered by two dozen thatched-roof cottages, was known for only two things: the annual fête and the popular Thimbletweed buns, which were carted to teahouses, restaurants, and bakeries in London each morning.

The moment the crowed Sinclair carriage arrived at the fête, Grant immediately made for the stand selling hot and buttery Thimbletweed buns, while the others strolled through the center of the fête.

Colorful flags and tents dotted the flame-illuminated field, while dancers, musicians, and low actors in bright harlequin performed on a litter of stages.

"La, only a guinea to actually ride an elephant in the ring!" Priscilla was nearly jumping up and down with excitement as she pointed at a tired, dusty beast.

"A guinea? Are you serious?" Lachlan stared at his sister. "We don't have coin to waste on elephant rides."

"Go and have a look, Priscilla," Killian said to his twin. "I am headed for the refreshment stall for a pint of porter. Anyone want to join me?" Lachlan was at his side in a moment.

"Since I am quite sure Ivy and Lord Counterton have their own plans for the evening"—Siusan turned their way and tossed them a wink—"I will stay with Priscilla beside the elephant. But bring me a tip of something wet with you, will you, Killian? The dusty drive from London has left me quite parched."

Killian agreed, and the group split into three sets.

"What do you suppose Siusan meant by our having plans of our own?" Dominic asked Ivy, as the other four disappeared into the crowd in opposite directions.

"I did not speak a single word to her in the carriage. I think she knows to give us some time alone to allow us to . . . finish our discussion." She glanced sidelong at him.

Dominic grinned wickedly, but Ivy would have none of it and thumped him playfully with her reticule. "I mean it, Dominic, we have much to discuss."

"Do you?" came a male voice from just behind them.

Ivy turned, knowing whence it came. "Tinsdale," she said, smiling when she saw another gentleman at his side.

"Lady Ivy, such a surprise to encounter you here," Tinsdale replied.

"Really? We had discussed the event several times. I believe you even suggested we attend the fête together; but then, that was more than a month past, and so much has occurred since then." Ivy shrugged.

"I do beg your pardon, Lady Ivy, I had quite

forgotten, I'm afraid." Tinsdale bent and, without leave to do so, lifted her hand and kissed it. "The Marquess of Counterton." Tinsdale turned to the man at his side. "May I make known to you both Lord Rhys-Dean?"

Rhys-Dean barely glanced at Ivy but tipped his hat somewhat politely in her general direction. Now he was peering queerly at Dominic. "Sheridan?"

Dominic stared blankly back at him. "Yes, Dominic Sheridan. Counterton now. I recently inherited the Counterton title from my late uncle, the fourth marquess."

"Damn me," Rhys-Dean uttered, with no concern that a lady was present. "You've changed. I would not have recognized you."

Dominic's eyes grew wide. "Rhys-Dean . . . why you are—" He paused then, raising a finger as though the answer were on the tip of his tongue.

But Ivy knew it was not. This man obviously knew the real Counterton. *Oh dear God.* Dominic was going to be exposed—and in the presence of Tinsdale!

"Do you not remember me? We were at Shrewsbury together." He set his hand on Dominic's shoulder. "Only, you do not look at all the way you did. You were so thin and pale, and I am sure I would have remembered your substantial height—"

Dominic slapped his hand on Rhys-Dean's back, knocking the man's hand from his shoulder. "Rhys-Dean, of course I remember you. We were caught for"—he tossed a glance over his shoulder at Ivy—"well, *you* remember." He winked.

La, Dominic was a clever actor.

Rhys-Dean laughed heartily. "Indeed I do." He turned to Ivy. "Do not worry, Lady Ivy. Our offense was not so egregious." He elbowed Dominic. "We were allowed to finish out at Shrewsbury after all, were we not?"

Tinsdale gazed at Dominic, as if appraising him. "You knew each other at Shrewsbury, then?"

Rhys-Dean nodded. "But damn if you haven't changed, Sheridan."

"As have you," Dominic interjected, clearly before the man could expound on just how he'd changed. "Lucky for us both, eh?"

Everyone laughed, but it seemed that only one of the circle of four was amused.

"Have you seen your mother's brother yet?" Rhys-Dean asked.

"M-my . . . uncle?" Dominic managed.

"Yes, yes. Pittance. Ran into him down at Carlyle House just this morn. We're both in town for just the week. My wife can't stand the ridiculous rain in Somerset of late and begged me to take her to London," Rhys-Dean rambled. "I was damned lucky I ran into Tinsdale on Pall Mall earlier, else I would be spending this night with my sister-in-law. Not that she is not a charming woman, you understand." He looked at Ivy, sheepishly.

"It was lovely to meet you, Lord Rhys-Dean." Ivy grasped the moment for escape. "Lord Tinsdale. Do give Miss Feeney my best. I assume she did not wish to intrude on your evening with Lord Rhys-Dean."

"You've got that right," the other man said, "just the menfolk tonight."

"Well, then we should not impose on your time any longer. Good night, Lord Tinsdale, Lord Rhys-Dean." She smiled and even dipped into a curtsy.

Dominic made a halfhearted promise to remain in contact with Rhys-Dean, then he and Ivy lunged into the crowd and left the two men behind.

They trudged through the dried grasses until they nearly crossed the commons dedicated to the Thimbletweed fête before stopping for breath.

"My God, Dominic, we're going to be exposed!" Ivy clutched frantically at his shoulders.

"Rhys-Dean seemed to believe me well enough, so don't fret, Ivy." Dominic started to wrap her in his arms, but then, thinking of the crowd half-filled with members of the *ton,* guided her behind a row of red-and-green tents. He climbed up the three short steps to the door of a wooden caravan and knocked. "No answer." He opened the door and peered inside, then finding it empty, reached down and grabbed Ivy's hand and pulled her up with him

"Why did you bring me in here?"

"So we can talk without running into Tinsdale, or Lord knows who else." Dominic squeezed her hand and gestured to the floor in the same gallant manner he might urge her to sit on a silk ottoman.

The caravan was filled with straw and smelled strongly of livestock, but the bedding seemed fresh, so Ivy warily sat down.

"Truly, Ivy, we have nothing to fear from Rhys-Dean. I know it."

"Perhaps not from him, but did you see the way Tinsdale was watching the two of you? He knows something is not as it seems, and I do not doubt he will go to great lengths to discover just what that inconsistency is. You did not see him in the garden earlier."

Dominic set his arms around Ivy's shoulder and drew her against him. "What could he possibly do?"

Ivy sat straight up, knocking Dominic's arms

from her. "Expose us both. If my father hears the details of my plan to win back Tinsdale, the lengths to which I have gone, he will disown me forever!" She sat up on her knees. "And Dominic, he could make it worse for you. Impersonating a peer is illegal. All Tinsdale would need to do is to speak to some of his cronies at the courts, and you could be thrown into Newgate! Dominic, we have to stop now. You have to leave London. Disappear. It's the only way I know you will be safe!"

"I can't." Dominic reached out and pulled Ivy against him. "I can't leave you—ever. I love you. I have no fear of Tinsdale and his connections at all."

"But I do! Please, Dominic, pack your bag, go—and leave me to the future that is expected of a proper Sinclair."

"No. Ivy, trust me. Trust your heart. Forget everything else because it doesn't matter. Trust me."

She stared up him, wanting to believe him, needing to trust him. Her fingers caressed his cheek as she opened her mouth to reply when Dominic suddenly tumbled her back onto the bed of straw and leaned over her mouth and kissed her.

Ivy moaned with pleasure. It was so easy for him to make her forget the rest of the world . . . the complicated lives she'd foolishly constructed for them. But she didn't regret anything she'd done.

For had she been more responsible, less audacious and daring, she would have never met Dominic.

But then, a set of rusty hinges screamed behind them, and the caravan's plank door opened wide.

They sat up, their eyes blinking and burning as their vision adjusted to the bright torchlight in front of the door.

"Who's in there? Ah, a couple of lovers, eh?" The old man standing on the top stair of the caravan was nearly toothless. His clothes were colorful but nearly threadbare, and he smelled strongly of drink. "Well, I'm not rentin' a love nest. This is Ginger's bed, so get your bleedin' selves out!"

Ivy stared, stunned, as a huge Tamworth pig trod up the stairs behind the old man and peered into the caravan. Ginger, the pig, squealed loudly, startling Ivy to her feet in an instant.

As Ivy and Dominic moved forward, the pig charged straight in. They leaped to the side to give her room as she angled herself, then flopped down heavily on her side.

Ivy and Dominic squeezed past the old man and descended the steps. They both stared at each other mutely in astonishment, until Dominic pointed at the painted side of the caravan.

Ginger, the learned pig

Ivy cupped her hand over her mouth, but neither she nor Dominic could stifle their laughter as they walked around to the front of the row of brightly colored tents.

"Ivy, look this way!" Priscilla called out to them. Ivy glanced about until she noticed Siusan beside the elephant ring, pointing into its center.

"Gorblimey!" Ivy slipped her hand into the crook of Dominic's arm and hurried them both to the ring. Priscilla was perched atop the huge elephant, seated on a satin mat as though she were riding a palfrey. She waved down to them, giggling, then looked suddenly worried and grabbed at the harness with both hands to maintain her balance. "Lud, I cannot believe she spent an entire guinea to ride an elephant around a ring."

Siusan reached over and exaggeratedly plucked two pieces of straw from Ivy's hair. "Some of us spend what little we have on elephant rides. Others"—she brushed a tangle of straw from Dominic's shoulder and looked back at Ivy—"on lovers."

Ivy flushed. "Though some would say certain guineas were better spent." She glanced up at Dominic through her lashes, and a tiny smile budded on her lips.

Chapter 14

The envious man thinks that if his neighbor breaks a leg, he will be able to walk better himself.
Helmut Schoeck

The next morning
The Sinclair residence
Grosvenor Square

Thunder woke Ivy early the next day, well before the Sinclairs' usual time to rise—just before their noon-hour breakfast. Yawning, she started to open her eyes, but had to squeeze them shut again against the bright daylight . . . which seemed rather odd given the volume of the thunder. She opened one eyelid. Sun was shining through her window and a robin chirped on the branch just outside. She opened the other eye, then sat up.

The sound of thunder rolled through the house, upstairs perhaps, and she could hear her brothers shouting frantically to one another.

There was a rumble of footsteps on the staircase, then someone pounded on her door. And then across the passage on Siusan's and Priscilla's too. She leaped from her pallet, ran to the door, and flung it open.

Poplin stood in the center of the passage, as if he were waiting for all three doors to open. "Your father. He sent a footman with a card—he is in London and will be here—at noon!" His hands shook nervously, shaking tiny dust clouds from the featherduster in his grip.

"Da is coming?" Priscilla, her face blanching, tore back inside her room.

"Lord Grant sent me to rouse everyone. It is already half past eleven." Poplin spun around and hurried back down the passage muttering something about Mrs. Wimpole and the baker.

Siusan stared mutely at Ivy, then they both raced into their bedchambers to prepare themselves for their father's arrival.

The Duke of Sinclair had mentioned that he had an agent who provided him with weekly reports about the goings-on at the Sinclairs' Grosvenor Square residence. Neither Ivy nor her brothers or sisters knew who this agent was, or how information was collected. It was for this reason that the Sinclair family shared very little with anyone outside the house, and yet, even so, the detail of events echoed in their father's letters was often startlingly precise.

For a time, they pointed accusing fingers at one another. That is, until it was pointed out by Sterling, before he accidentally ingratiated himself with his father, that the reports painted them all with an equally harsh brush of truth.

Ivy and her two sisters sat rigidly on the blue settee while their brothers stood shoulder to shoulder before the window, waiting for their father to speak. He sat in a small chair beside a cold hearth, which clearly aggravated him even though the day was quite mild.

The Duke of Sinclair looked at each of his children with an air of disappointment . . . until his eyes fell upon Ivy. And then, to everyone's astonishment, he smiled warmly at her.

Ivy's shoulders relaxed. Clearly, he did not know about her ruse, else he'd be marching her to the street just now.

He raised his hand and summoned one of his three liveried footmen to his side. The footman withdrew a letter from a leather pouch and handed it to the duke.

Grant, who, like Ivy, was probably worried that their father was about to read aloud from another dreaded report, gave her a quizzical glance. She replied with an almost imperceptible shrug.

The duke cleared his throat, then shook open the letter and set his spectacles atop his nose. "I received a missive, penned nearly a month ago, from Viscount Tinsdale." He looked over the bridge of his spectacles at Ivy as if waiting for her to tell everyone what the letter said. But she had absolutely no idea. If Tinsdale sent the letter a month ago, it might have been either before Miss Feeney stole his fancy—or after. She felt her back stiffening again.

"He requested an interview with me at my earliest convenience, which was not until now, to discuss his suitability as a husband for my daughter, Ivy." He peered at her again.

Ivy could do naught but swallow and peer back. This was a complete surprise. Tinsdale had not said a word about petitioning her father for her hand.

"I must say, he is of fine stock, a solid, respectable, landed family. I wish I could say his financial standing was as solid, but your generous portion will be more than adequate to sustain his properties both in Town and out."

"M-my portion?" Ivy stood. "I have no portion—anymore."

"But you will again, assuming this Tinsdale fellow is as suitable as my agent believes. I sent a card to Lord Tinsdale this morn, and he had agreed to meet with me here at one of the clock." He tipped his spectacles and studied Ivy's appearance. "Do change into something more appropriate for the daughter of a duke, Ivy." He looked at her sisters. "I would greatly appreciate it if the two of you assisted her. You might learn something from Ivy."

"Learn something?" Priscilla came to her feet and Ivy shook with fear that her sister was going to tell their father all about Ivy's outrageous ruse.

"I summoned all of you here, instead of dear Ivy alone, so it would be clear to you how simple it is to become a respectable member of this family. And with respectability comes reward." He tipped his head to the second footman, who carried a parcel to Ivy. "A new gown of blue satin. Go now, and dress."

Ivy stepped forward and kissed her father's cheek, then hurried out of the parlor. *No, no. This cannot be happening! My fondest dream is coming true, only now it is my greatest nightmare.*

Grant was a godsend of a brother. He persuaded the duke to join him and his brothers in the garden for a whisky-heavy noon meal while Ivy and her sisters prepared for Tinsdale's arrival.

Siusan and Priscilla barely spoke to her as they pinned her hair and helped her dress, but their eyes expressed the concern that their words did not. When they had finished, her sisters kissed her cheeks, then with bowed heads, they left her bedchamber.

There was no way to avoid the next hour, and so she decided to face her future directly. She would wait at the door for Tinsdale to arrive, then she would tell him, before he could speak to her father, that she did not love him and would never marry him.

After that she would take the consequences.

She packed what she could fit into a small portmanteau, set that beside her bedchamber door, and descended the stairs to wait for Tinsdale. The tall case clock warned her that in two minutes Tinsdale would arrive. He was never late.

From the parlor, she peered out the window, watching the square, then glanced again at the tall case clock in the passage. At one minute before one of the clock, Tinsdale's carriage drew up before No. 1 Grosvenor Square, and he walked up to the door.

Poplin, who was peering up at the clock, turned to go to the door, but Ivy raced past him and opened it, catching the brass door knocker before Tinsdale could lower it to its rest. Ivy turned to Poplin. "Please,

Poplin. I only need a minute alone with Lord Tinsdale." The short butler nodded and excused himself. Ivy dispensed with formality, grasped Tinsdale's hand, and pulled him hurriedly into the parlor.

Tinsdale was already scowling at her.

"I know why you are here. My father told us all. But I will admit to you now that I will not marry you. I cannot." She glanced into the passage, making sure her father's footman had not alerted him that Tinsdale had arrived. "I am in love with Lord Counterton."

A snarl spread over Tinsdale's lips. "Who? Lord Counterton . . . or that actor you hired to impersonate him?"

"What?" A jolt shot through Ivy, and she staggered backward until the back of her legs struck the settee. She sat down. "H-how—"

Tinsdale strode confidently over to her and sat down beside her. Too close. His thigh brushed against hers. "I knew something was not as it seemed from the moment you first introduced us. And then, at the fête, when Lord Rhys-Dean did not recognize his old school chum, Dominic Sheridan, then I was sure something was afoot. And so I watched and waited. And when he left the Berkeley Square residence of Lord Counterton, I went to the door and spoke to the butler, Cheatlin."

"*Cheatlin,*" Ivy muttered beneath her breath.

"Oh, it cost me a month of tenant rents, but in return he gave me a fortune. Yours."

"What do you mean?" Ivy whispered. "I have nothing."

"No, but your father does, and when I marry you, I expect quite a lovely dowry to be attached to my lovely bride." Tinsdale snatched up her hand and stroked it roughly with his thumb.

"What about Miss Feeney? You left me so readily for her," Ivy spat.

"And I came back to you. Your Lord Counterton, your actor, made me doubt my decision to leave you. Seeing the two of you together, so happy, made me envious of what he had. What I could have had." Tinsdale followed Ivy's gaze to the clock in the passage and moved restlessly. He was going to be late for his interview with the duke. He looked back at Ivy and spoke more quickly. "And so I thought more carefully, and compared your assets more prudently. In the end, you were both beautiful, but you, dear Ivy, have a name and a fortune, while she does not."

"I will not accept you." Ivy tried to stand, but he held her hand and tugged her next to him again.

"Oh, I think you will, if you love him as you say." Tinsdale leaned his mouth to her ear and whispered to her. "What he did is illegal, and I can make sure he pays for his crime in Newgate . . . for a very long time. It's a hard life in prison, and I doubt he'll look quite so handsome when, if ever, he is released."

Ivy's eyes heated with coming tears. "No. Please, just let him leave London. I can make sure he does. I-I will do whatever you ask . . . please, just don't turn him over to the magistrates."

Tinsdale finally released her hand but pressed his hand to her shoulder, keeping her seated, as he stood. "Well, now, that all depends on what your father offers in the way of a dowry."

"But I have no say, no control, over that, you must know that, Tinsdale," she called out to him, not bothering to lower her tone now.

He didn't turn back to her until he reached the passage. "Then wish me luck, darling. Your Lord Counterton will need it."

Poplin appeared at the parlor doorway and gestured for Tinsdale to follow him to the garden.

A cold sweat broke over Ivy's skin. She sat very still, too stunned to move. Until she realized that she had to warn Dominic. Had to convince him to leave London.

Right now.

She rose and hurried into the passage. Snatching her bonnet from the row of hooks, she dashed out the front door, not caring if she had to run all the way to Berkeley Square.

Chapter 15

Envy shoots at others and wounds itself.
English proverb

The Counterton residence
Berkeley Square

It wasn't Cheatlin who opened the door of the Counterton town house, as Ivy had hoped, but Mr. Felix Dupré, in full butler costume. "Lady Ivy." He smiled nervously.

She started forward, expecting to be welcomed into the house at once, but instead he stepped outside and closed the door behind him.

"I need to see Dominic. Please, let me inside." She tried to step around him, but he moved his body in front of the door, blocking her.

"You should know that he has an important guest—his *uncle*." Felix widened his eyes and Ivy took his meaning. The man whom Lord Rhys-Dean had mentioned crossing at the hotel was there.

Blast. Was there anything worse that could happen this day?

Ivy scanned the square behind her for Tinsdale's carriage. She didn't have much time before Tinsdale concluded discussions with her father—and made his decision about marrying her. Would he allow Dominic to leave London or have him arrested out of spite? "Has he been exposed? Does the uncle know he is not Counterton?"

Felix shrugged his shoulders. "They are in the garden, and I haven't been able to hear a word said."

"By chance, is Cheatlin in the house?" She eyed the door latch as she spoke.

"I believe so. He's in the kitchen with one of the . . . *maids*." Without probably realizing it, he glanced at the outside stairs leading to the kitchen below.

"Thank you, Mr. Dupré. I shall return in but a moment to call on Dominic."

His brow furrowed in confusion as Ivy whirled around and descended the steps to the kitchen.

She flung the door open and spotted Cheatlin

immediately. He was groping a very willing maid against the pantry door. He jerked his head up from her heavily painted lips as the heavy kitchen door hit the wall.

"Bloody hell!" he howled, yanking himself around to face her. "What are you doing 'ere?"

Ivy had forgotten how hulking and menacing Cheatlin was. She fixed her hands to her hips to look as confident as she might. "I will ask you the same thing. Had I betrayed *both* of my employers, the true Lord Counterton and me, I would have left Town right away."

Cheatlin set one booted foot on the seat of a chair before the kitchen table. He rested his elbow atop it and leaned forward menacingly. "Lord Whatever-his-name-is paid me nearly twice what you did for the house and staff. And all he wanted was a little information about the current occupant, which I happily supplied. He was very pleased when I told him about your little ruse."

No doubt. Her heart pounded like a bird's, and she started to feel light in the head.

Cheatlin must have seen the ebb of her confidence. He chuckled, releasing putrid fumes of gin into the air. "His Lordship told me if anything came out about my role in the *crime,* I could say I was duped like the rest of Society into believing that this actor fellow was the true Lord Counterton. So you see, Lady Ivy, I ain't got nothin' to worry about."

"Except that you illegally sublet Lord Counterton's house to me—a noblewoman—not a mere actor." Ivy narrowed her green eyes.

"Only you ain't going to give me up, Lady Ivy. If you do, you're sinking yourself in the muck as well." Assured in his position, Cheatlin folded his hands over his barrel chest. "What have you got to say now?" Realizing she didn't want to be any part of this exchange, the maid backed out of the room and slipped away, leaving Ivy and Cheatlin alone.

"I would say that I honestly don't know what I might do, Mr. Cheatlin. Not yet. Because Lord Whatever-his-name-is hasn't decided what *he* will do with the information you gave him. He may hang me along with my Lord Counterton, and, if that happens, I promise you it will be a scandal that heads every newspaper in London. You can be assured that I will not forget to mention your name as the unscrupulous carpenter who rented out his employer's house and aided in the illegal impersonation of a peer."

Cheatlin stared at her, his mouth flapping like fresh-caught salmon on the riverbank.

"That's right. You'll be in Newgate Prison before you can say 'I should not have said anything to

Lord Whatever-his-name-is.'" Ivy lifted a smug smile to her lips. "Were I you, I would be on the North Road out of London within the hour."

She was shaking as she turned her back to him and walked out the kitchen, then up the steps to the street.

There, she took a deep breath and walked up the front door, where Mr. Felix Dupré was still waiting for her.

Nick walked on the shell path beside Mr. Garland Pittance through the beautiful but neglected Counterton rose garden. Though the sky had grayed to deep ash, the day was still pleasant enough that *Uncle Pittance,* as he had asked to be called, would not think it unusual in the least that his nephew, Dominic, would suggest taking sherry in the garden.

"I can't help but be amazed at how you've matured," Pittance commented.

"I am a man, full grown now. How many years has it been since we've seen each other," Nick probed.

"Since your mother died. And I apologize for that. It pained me too much to see you. You have her eyes, you know."

Nick averted his gaze and pretended to busy himself kicking a twig from the pathway.

"But not now," the uncle added. "Oh, they are the same dark blue, but the expression is altogether different now."

Nick looked up from the crushed-shell path and turned to face Pittance. "Life is hard for a boy without parents."

The older man nodded dolefully. "I suppose it would be." He smiled then, as a new thought seemed to enter his mind. "You were still quite a young a lad, all gangly arms and legs, and teeth!" He chuckled then. "You hadn't grown into your features yet. But look at you now, son." He clapped him on the back. "Mrs. Pittance and I were not in London for an hour when we encountered Lord and Lady Rhys-Dean. Her Ladyship wasted no time in telling us how the handsome new Lord Counterton is the talk of the ladies. I bet you have your pick, don't you?"

"I have my pick, yes, sir." *Ivy.* Nick's gaze strayed to the French window, and he turned. There she was, standing there, with Felix watching him. Nick tipped his head toward Pittance, then looked back at Ivy, silently asking her if she wished to join them.

When she shook her head, he saw how pale her countenance was, and even from a distance he could see the haunted expression in her green eyes.

"Uncle Pittance"—he turned his gaze from the house—"I have another engagement just now, and must away. Please forgive me."

"Only if you agree to join Mrs. Pittance and me for dinner this night at the Clarendon Hotel. I fear she would not forgive me if I didn't introduce my famous nephew to her." He laughed at his own play on words. "What do you say, man, eight of the clock?"

"I believe that can be arranged, sir." Nick faced the house again and turned Pittance along with him. Ivy and Felix disappeared into the shadows of the house.

Pittance stopped abruptly and dug something small from his pocket and palmed it. "When my wife decided we needed to escape the rains and go to London, I decided to bring this along to give to my nephew." He grasped Nick's hand and dropped an emerald ring into it.

Even in the muted light, the emerald gleamed in Nick's hand and recalled to mind Ivy's eyes, just before she cried. He closed his hand and pushed it toward Pittance. "I cannot accept this."

"Why not? It's yours—it was your mother's, and your grandmother's before that." Pittance pushed Nick's hand back against his chest and held it there. "I cannot let you refuse this gift, Dominic. Giving you this ring is the fulfillment of a promise I made your mother, shortly before she passed. She didn't want it sold, or taken from you, and so she asked me to hold it for you until the time was right. And it is. Look at you now, son. Look at you now." He was smiling warmly and proudly at Nick.

A way he'd never seen anyone look at him so fondly and warmly . . . except Ivy.

A few minutes later, Mr. Garland Pittance was in a carriage returning to the Clarendon Hotel, and Nick was headed for the parlor, where Felix had informed him that Ivy was waiting.

The moment he entered the room, Ivy was on her feet, running toward him. She threw herself against his chest and clung desperately to him.

He grasped her shoulders and eased her back enough that he could look into her eyes. She was shaking. "My God, what is it, Ivy?"

"So much has happened, Dominic. I don't know where to begin." Her voice was thick, as though she'd been crying while she waited for him. "After our encounter with Lord Rhys-Dean, Tinsdale became suspicious of you. He paid Cheatlin to tell him whatever he knew about you—and Cheatlin told him everything. Tinsdale knows about the ruse. You have to run, Dominic. You have to leave

London now." She fumbled in her reticule, then, in frustration, pushed the whole bag at him. "It's all I have left, but it should be enough to see you far from here."

"I am not going anywhere. I won't leave you, Ivy."

She shook her head frantically. "No, no! You must go. My father has come down from Scotland, and Tinsdale is asking for my hand right now. If I don't agree, he is going to expose us both. I will be banished from my family, and his cronies at the courts will see you to Newgate." She blinked back a tear and stepped back from him. "Don't you see? We have no choice."

"You can't marry Tinsdale, Ivy." Nick silently slid his hand into his pocket until he felt the emerald ring between his fingers. "You don't have to."

"I do." Ivy swiped away her tears and walked past Nick and opened the parlor door. "I am sorry, Dominic, but I do."

As the front door closed, Nick released the ring he held and removed his hand from his pocket. He walked over to the cold hearth, and rested his hands on the marble mantel. Damn it all! He couldn't be the cause of Ivy's being cast out of the family she loved so dearly. He couldn't cause her such pain.

But neither could he allow her to marry Tinsdale.

The creak of the floorboards caught his notice. "Felix," he asked without turning.

Felix quietly walked into the parlor and set his hand upon Nick's shoulder. "So, the game is over."

Nick turned his head to the side and peered at his cousin. He stared for several moments in silence as an idea spun and formed in his mind.

"Nick?" Concern tightened the skin around Felix's blue eyes.

Nick pushed back from the mantel, letting his cousin's hand fall from his shoulder, then started from the parlor. "No, Felix," he called out as he turned into the passage. "This game has just begun."

Chapter 16

People hate those who make them feel their own inferiority.

Lord Chesterfield

The Sinclair residence
Grosvenor Square

When Ivy burst through the front door, she found her brothers and sisters gathered in the parlor. Her cheeks were damp with perspiration from running, heedless of who might have observed her, from Berkeley Square all the way back to Grosvenor Square. She peered down the shadowy passage toward the French windows leading to the garden, then turned her questioning eyes toward Siusan.

"They're still talking," her sister told her.

"Negotiating," Grant said. He lifted an eyebrow at Lachlan, who guided Ivy into the parlor and settled her into an armchair.

Killian handed a small crystal of whisky to Ivy over the arm of the chair. "Scottish fortitude."

With a trembling hand, Ivy grasped the glass and took a sip.

Priscilla came to her and sat on the tufted footstool beside Ivy. "Isn't this what you have wanted all along, Ivy?"

"Aye." Ivy brought the glass to her lips and took in just enough of the amber liquid to wet her tongue.

Priscilla stroked Ivy's free hand. "If Da accepts Tinsdale's offer, then he will welcome you back into the family. You will have your life back."

Ivy nodded. "I know."

"Then why aren't you smiling?" Priscilla stared up at her with her shadowed eyes.

"Because . . . I will never be happy." Ivy's eyes began to well with tears.

Siusan looked pointedly at Ivy. "Then don't do it. You do not have to agree."

Ivy turned her chin downward, and a tear rolled down her cheek and dripped from her jaw into her glass. She watched the circular ripple radiate from the middle until it had swept the entire surface.

Ivy raised her eyes and peered back at Siusan. "I have to. There is no other way."

A door opened at the far end of the passage. Everyone heard it and knew what it meant. The negotiations for Ivy's future had concluded.

Ivy and her brothers and sisters all came to their feet and waited for their father and Tinsdale to appear. One look would tell all.

And it did. Two of the liveried footmen preceded the Duke of Sinclair and Viscount Tinsdale into the parlor and took posts on either side of the door. The duke entered next, his face devoid of all emotion. But Tinsdale was beaming. He'd been successful in his dowry request.

The duke sat down and looked at Ivy. Her face was still wet, and her eyes were still stinging with tears. "Sit down, Ivy." He continued to look at her but dismissed her brothers and sisters with flick of his hand.

Grant paused at the door. "You don't have to do anything, Ivy." His eyes held hers far longer than Ivy would have considered wise, given that their father did not suffer his wayward children lightly.

"I know," she mouthed. Then closed her eyes for a long moment, letting her brother know that she would be all right. Only then did he quit the parlor.

Her father turned his gaze to Tinsdale. "Ye'll

make the arrangements fer the announcement this day?"

Tinsdale bowed to the duke. "I will send notice to the *Morning Post* right away, Your Grace."

"Then ye may go, Lord Tinsdale." He flicked his fingers again.

"Ah, if I may, Your Grace." Tinsdale gave a quick glance at Ivy and the duke nodded. "Lady Ivy, I should like it very much if you would join me for a drive in Hyde Park on the morrow. Noon—"

The duke shook his head, and, though Tinsdale was no longer facing the old man, he somehow saw the movement.

"Two of the clock? Would that be convenient?" Tinsdale was looking at Ivy, but his head was by then turned so that he could better discern the duke's expression.

"Aye," Ivy muttered. She lowered her gaze, then peered at the tea table, where she'd set her whisky when her father had entered. "Two of the clock."

Within a minute more, Tinsdale had made his farewells, and then hurriedly departed. Ivy was left with her father.

"I am verra pleased with yer choice, lass. Viscount Tinsdale is everything my agent reported him to be and more. I shall be pleased to welcome him into the family, and with him, ye as well."

Ivy nodded, but did not say anything in response. If she opened her mouth, she feared that she would scream.

"Lord Tinsdale requested that the engagement be announced tomorrow night at Almack's as well. I have agreed. The wedding will take place within the week. A special license has already been procured from Doctors' Commons."

Ivy gasped. "S-so soon?" This was all too much to comprehend.

"Is there any reason to delay? I came to London to see ye wed, lass, and so I shall."

Ivy wanted to tell her father that she would never have enough time to be ready to marry Lord Tinsdale. That there was only one man she wanted to marry . . . the man she loved, Dominic.

But that was a bliss that could never be.

Her life would be with Tinsdale—full of parties and balls, and trinkets galore. She'd have her inheritance, more money than she'd ever be able to spend in her lifetime.

And she would lament every minute of her good fortune.

Though the shelves were barren, save a single, cracked-spine edition of Shakespeare's sonnets, the library was a welcoming room. The afternoon sun streamed through the windows, making it a serene place to collect one's thoughts without the likelihood of interruption.

Ivy sat before a small desk near the great window, dipping her pen into a pot of India ink. The tips of her fingers were stained with ink, and several sheets of foolscap, each with a number of lines struck out, lay discarded in a pile at the corner of the old desk.

She was trying to write to a letter to Dominic, but the words weren't coming. Not the right ones anyway, phrases that would soothe and make him understand that, while she loved him, accepting Tinsdale's troth was something that she must do for the good of everyone.

In the end, she stopped trying to coat her words with honey, deciding that he would seek to change her mind, and that she could not allow.

And so, she sprinkled pounce over the short, inked letter and tapped it on the table. She read it once more, then withdrew the shining lucky sixpence her sister had tucked in her slipper when Tinsdale arrived to ask for Ivy's hand, and slipped it inside the folded letter. She melted scarlet wax over the single candle on the desk and added her stamp, an I entwined with English ivy.

Blowing out the candle, Ivy rose from the desk to

find Mr. Poplin and beg him to deliver her letter to the Counterton residence. She paused at the door, closed her eyes, and gave the letter a parting kiss—something she would not be able to give to Dominic herself.

Ten minutes past two of the clock
The next day

Tinsdale had arrived exactly at two, as Ivy had expected, and now, minutes later, they were nearly to Hyde Park. She hadn't said a single word to him, but she doubted he noticed. He had too much to say to her.

"My mother agreed that the benefits of an association with the Duke of Sinclair, his influence and, of course, his coin, far outweigh any detractions attached to your brothers or sisters." He glanced across at Ivy as he snapped the ribbons and urged his team faster. "What do you think of my phaeton?"

Ivy shrugged.

"I bought it the day after our picnic in Hyde Park, when I saw the one Lord Counterton was driving. Had to have one. Even when I learned that Counterton was an impostor, I decided to keep the phaeton. Miss Feeney told me she finds a man who drives a high-perch phaeton to be quite masculine in demeanor and appearance."

Ivy looked away from Tinsdale and rolled her eyes.

He took the ribbons in one hand, wanting her, she guessed, to admire his driving skills, but she didn't. He didn't know what he was doing. He was allowing too much slack in the reins. The horses could bolt at any moment. And she wouldn't care. She didn't care about anything anymore—except making sure Dominic left London that day, before her engagement to Tinsdale was publicly announced.

"Certainly you will be permitted to visit your brothers and sisters from time to time, but never alone. Mother and I have discussed this at length. I will accompany you, for guidance, to make it easier for you to avoid their bad influence."

Ivy eyed the reins. She wanted nothing more than to snatch the ribbons from him and turn the phaeton back to Grosvenor Square.

"My mother will instruct you in the manners of Society. You will be expected to be kind, courteous, and grateful to her for condescending to train you."

Ivy couldn't take his patronizing prattle any longer. She grabbed the ribbons from his hand

and halted the horses, then shoved the reins back at Tinsdale. Dangling her feet over the edge, she made to leap down, but Tinsdale grabbed her arm cruelly and pulled her back.

"Agree to everything I said, dear Ivy, and your actor will be safe." He skewered her with an ice-cold stare.

With a nod, she acquiesced and lifted her feet back into the phaeton.

A smug grin slid over Tinsdale's mouth. "Very good, Ivy. You made a wise choice."

No, I only realized that I have no choice at all. Ivy looked straight ahead and waited for Tinsdale to snap the reins.

Chapter 17

Sympathy one receives for nothing; envy must be earned.

Robert Lembke

Almack's Assembly Rooms

I vy swept up the short train of her peacock blue silk ball gown, then took her father's arm and walked up the staircase and into the assembly rooms. Tinsdale and his mother followed closely, with the Sinclair brothers and sisters trailing behind.

Naturally, the engagement would be announced at Almack's, the most rigid and proper of the assembly rooms in London . . . or England, for that matter. Ivy decided that the location fit Tinsdale like a finely tailored coat.

Judging from the endless train of carriages lining the street outside, everyone of the *ton* would be in attendance. Even those who had not planned on using their subscriptions that evening must have abruptly changed their minds. How could they not? For the *Times* had somehow discovered and promptly reported that the Duke of Sinclair and his notorious offspring would grace Almack's with their presence that very night for a momentous announcement.

The ballroom was abuzz with chatter when the Sinclair party entered. Ladies of all ages, and gentlemen, too, crowded around to get a look at the Duke of Sinclair.

Tinsdale and his mother were standing in their midst, but no one seemed to notice. The guests, instead, peered around, and Ivy heard murmurs from the gathering that sounded like a chorus of "Lord Counterton."

An excited jolt wriggled through her, when at first she thought Dominic had ascended the stairs behind them. It took but a moment more to realize what was truly happening. The members of the *ton* had witnessed her public romance with the man they thought to be Lord Counterton—and now they assumed that the announcement to be made that night would be the engagement of Lady Ivy and the Marquess of Counterton.

Oh dear heaven, if only it could be.

Her father was smiling proudly at Ivy, and she tried with all that she was to force an answering smile. But it was impossible. She would be doing well not to cry . . . or become ill upon the floor.

The night moved as slowly as sap from a tree in winter, and, though it was a ball and the attendees were there to dance, Tinsdale waited nearly two hours before he led Ivy onto the floor.

The orchestra, led by a Scotsman, seemed to favor lively tunes. As Ivy reluctantly took her place on the floor for a Scottish reel, the first few notes of "Revenge" lifted into the air.

Though the reel was a spirited dance, Ivy felt like she was moving languidly in her sleep. She barely heard the music or felt Tinsdale's hand holding hers. Instead, her eyes scanned the crowd ringing the dance floor, searching for Dominic.

She hadn't mentioned the ball in her letter to him, merely begged him to leave London, but the article in the *Times* almost assuredly guaranteed his attendance this night. And foretold that the ball would end with her cheeks awash with tears.

She could just make out the silhouette of Grant, who was easily a head taller than any other man, save another Sinclair, in the room. He was positioned at the head of the staircase, at her request, to prevent Dominic from entering the assembly rooms if he could, or to enlist the aid of his muscled brothers if Dominic would not listen.

But this was all taking far too long. As much as she was loath to do it, as the song ended, she turned to Tinsdale and forced a sugary smile. "I have noticed that people are beginning to leave. Should we not announce our engagement soon?"

A worried look crossed Tinsdale's eyes. "Yes, yes, I want everyone to hear the announcement. I shall collect my mother. Would you please locate the duke and join us before the orchestra?"

"Certainly." Ivy would do anything to see this night over before Lord Counterton arrived, for he certainly would. It was only a matter of moments now.

Ivy found the Duke of Sinclair standing on the perimeter of the dance floor conversing with several gentlemen. A string of older women stood behind the men, chatting and laughing as they took turns stealing peeks at the Scottish duke.

"Da," she interrupted. "The announcement. Would you join us please?" Ivy couldn't bring herself to link her name with Tinsdale's for even a moment. How strange this was, because only two weeks before, such a moment would have been her crowning glory. Her greatest success.

Her father excused himself from the circle of conversation. Ivy had just turned to lead him to the orchestra, when, at the other end of the dance floor, Dominic appeared.

Grant was standing beside him and beckoned Ivy forward.

What was her brother about? Grant was meant to stop Dominic from entering the room. To prevent his presence from piquing Tinsdale's ire and having Dominic hauled off to Newgate!

The duke was standing just behind her; Tinsdale next to his mother before the orchestra. All of this, she knew, but Dominic was all she could see. Everything else blurred around him, around her.

The first lilting bar of a slow waltz rose up and bloomed, spreading out through the assembly rooms. Dominic strode forward, his hand reaching out as if to claim the dance.

Likely expecting the "announcement" the *Times* had reported, the other dancers scattered and drew back along the edges of the dance to watch, leaving Ivy and Dominic alone in the center.

And suddenly, Ivy realized she was moving, running to Dominic. Their hands touched and held as they fell together. He stared down into her eyes, saying nothing, and yet everything.

He grasped her hand and raised it high, and she felt

his other hand encircle her back, holding her close against him. The beautiful music seemed to swell, and Dominic moved her across the dance floor.

This was not the slow waltz Ivy knew. This was an expression of passion. This was Dominic.

As they reached the center of the floor, Dominic abruptly tipped her backward, supporting her with his strong forearm. A surprised gasp rose up from the ladies in the room, who had clearly never seen such a display at Almack's. From her inverted view of the crowd, Ivy saw dozens of fans flip open to cool their owners' pink cheeks.

Just then, her eyes met her father's heated gaze.

Dominic whipped her back up again and into his arms. "It's your life, Ivy. You have a choice. You do not have to marry Tinsdale."

Ivy glanced back over her shoulder at her father and bit her lower lip. She tried to sound sure, but her throat had gone dry. "I have to."

His hand pressed against her lower back, making her arch against him as he turned her around and around. The crowd applauded, and couples hurried to join them on the dance floor before the waltz ended.

The spinning was making her dizzy, and she leaned in to him just as he lowered his head, their temples resting against one another's.

"You don't have to, Ivy." Dominic's heart pounded through the thin silk of her gown, making her own heartbeat quicken. He said something else too, but she couldn't make it out with the music filling her ears.

"What?" She drew back her head and looked up at him.

"I have a plan that will turn everything around for us. Trust me, Ivy. Put your faith in me. Everything is not as it appears."

She peered into his eyes and saw the emotion there.

"Meet me outside, as soon as you can manage it."

She nodded, just as the music ended. Dominic released her then, and in that moment, he disappeared into the churning crowd.

Grant had her arm in an instant and was pulling her from the dance floor at a fast trot.

"What is going on?" Ivy was frantic. Her father would no doubt be furious with her outrageous display and certainly have angry questions to pose.

As Grant pressed her forward, Ivy whipped her head around toward the orchestra dais. Tinsdale had her in his sight and was racing toward her through the throng.

"You'll know soon enough," Grant said. He urged her through the doorway and hurriedly down the staircase. "Dominic only needs a few minutes to explain, but I fear you will need a goodly amount of understanding if this is to work."

A liveried footman opened the door to the street, and Grant rushed Ivy through the lines of nearly identical carriages to one parked nearby.

When they neared, the door to the cab opened, and she saw Dominic waiting there. Grant gave Dominic a nod.

"Trust him. Trust your heart, Ivy," her brother told her, then spun around and dashed back in the direction of Almack's.

Dominic reached down and grasped Ivy's waist. She squealed in surprise as he lifted her and pulled her inside. He jerked the door closed behind her.

"Dominic, what is this all about? Do you know what you have done?" Ivy searched his eyes, but she saw no worry there. "Tinsdale will certainly—"

"Tinsdale isn't worthy of you." He rapped on the front wall of the town carriage and the driver urged his team slowly through the gauntlet of vehicles outside Almack's.

He reached inside his waistcoat pocket. "But I hope you will find it in your heart to find me worthy of your love."

Ivy's eye's widened. Between his fingers was large

emerald ring, its cut stone glowing vivid green in the lantern light of the cabin.

She peered up Dominic. "This can never be. We can never be—"

He took her hand, peeled off her glove, and slipped the ring onto her left hand. "We can be. All you have to do is say . . . *yes*."

Chapter 18

*Envy is blind and she has no other quality than that
of detracting from virtue.*

Titus Livy

"-aye," Ivy said.

Nick smiled. "Close enough." He eased his arms around her and pulled her back into the thickest shadows of the carriage as they inched past Almack's.

Tinsdale was standing at the door, his face red and pinched as he shouted at Grant, who was shrugging nonchalantly in response.

Ivy huddled against him. "This is madness, Dominic, you are aware of that. Tinsdale will expose and bury us both. We'll need to leave tonight."

"Tinsdale may try, but he will not be successful. Trust me, Ivy. I have made sure of that."

"And my father . . ." A sudden look of sadness fell over her visage, and she turned her face from him. But then, she caught sight of the emerald ring on her finger and lifted her hand slightly from his chest to peer at it.

Nick hooked a finger under her chin and turned it up toward him. Her eyes were dark with worry, and even though a child could have walked faster than the carriage was moving through the squash of vehicles, she made no move to leave his side. She had made her decision.

She loved him.

She trusted him. Enough to walk away from the life she knew, and, for all she was aware of, from the family she loved as well.

And now he had to trust her too—with the truth.

Fine feathers of smoke rose like blue specters from the cheroots and pipes of dozens of carriage drivers, passing the time, bantering and laughing, as they waited outside Almack's for their passengers.

Their carriage horses were slow, hardly moving at even a walking pace. Dominic knocked on the forward carriage wall again.

"Damn it, can't he move this thing any faster?"

The driver on the perch of their carriage responded by calling down to the other drivers and footmen, urging them to move their vehicles to allow him through. There were shouts in return, and twice Ivy thought she heard the unmistakable clink of coin being tossed to the pavers.

Every muscle in her body was tense, and she imagined that at any moment Tinsdale, or worse, her father, would fling open the carriage door and pull her onto the pavers and back inside the assembly room. She nestled closer to Dominic.

His fingers smoothed her hair, soothing her, but his breathing grew more and more shallow. His expression was pensive.

"Dominic?" Ivy leaned back from him, and when he still seemed lost in thought, she shook his shoulder.

"Nick." He met her gaze. "I prefer Nick."

Ivy broke their embrace entirely. Dominic. Nick. What did it matter which he preferred? It wasn't his name!

Unless . . . *it was.*

"I know, when we first met, then when you agreed to help me, I told you I didn't want to know your true name. It would make the ruse easier if I didn't stumble and use your real name in conversation." She swallowed hard. "When I began to care for you, began to love you, I wanted with all my heart to know who you really were."

"Not enough to ask."

"No. I didn't ask because I couldn't let myself know. Not knowing who you were let me pretend that what was happening between us wasn't real—because it couldn't be." Her voice quavered uncontrollably. "But I love you. I want to be with you, as your wife, for the rest of my days. I don't care if we have to live hand-to-mouth, or live out of a portmanteau moving from town to town. I know what matters most in this world. It is love and happiness. Nothing else. And I have that with you. I know that." A steadiness settled over her then, as if saying the words aloud had somehow imbued her with a new strength, a confidence she had not possessed even a moment before.

A tiny smile tugged the corners of her lips upward. "The only thing I don't know . . . is your name."

He didn't answer right away, which surprised her. Several more moments passed, and still he said nothing.

Why wouldn't he want to tell her, especially after all she just confessed? Her heart began to thrum harder in her chest. "Please, you have to tell me now. I can't endure waiting anymore." She tilted her head downward a bit and prodded him. "Your name is Nick . . ."

He nodded slowly, then clasped her hands firmly in his. The expression on his face became one of apprehension. One of guilt.

"Yes, my name is Nick," he admitted.

Squinting her eyes, Ivy mentally braced herself for what he would say next.

"As in . . . Dominic Sheridan."

Ivy's mouth dropped open. She blinked, not quite able to comprehend exactly what he was saying.

So he said it for her. "I am Dominic Sheridan," he told her, "the true fifth Marquess of Counterton."

"The *real* Lord Counterton?" Ivy didn't know what she had expected him to say, but it was not that. Confusion and anger flooded her senses. "Why didn't you tell me?" Her eyes began to sting, and she knew she'd be overtaken with tears in a moment. "I-I would have married Tinsdale to protect you!" She struggled to pull her hands from him.

"Ivy, please. Hear me out."

She slipped from his grip, leaving behind the emerald ring in his palm. "I can't. Not now." Flinging the door open, she hiked up her ball gown and jumped from the slow-moving carriage. Her momentum slammed her against a carriage parked along the road, and she slid down its side to the rain-dampened pavers. A footman, who had been standing beside it, rushed to her and helped her to her feet.

Dominic appeared in the open cab doorway. "Ivy!" She saw him gauging the distance to the ground. He meant to jump.

"Don't follow me, Dominic. Please." The tears rolled down her cheeks. "I am begging you. Do not follow me."

He paused then, his eyes filled with anguish.

That was all the additional time she needed. Whirling about, she ducked between two parked carriages and ran back down the street toward Almack's.

Chapter 19

Love envies not.

St. Paul

Grosvenor Square

Ivy peered out into the wet streets of London as the carriage trundled through Mayfair. She felt numb and utterly confused, and all she wanted was to crawl into her tiny bed and sleep, and pray that in the morning she would find that what happened this night had all been a dream.

At Grant's instruction, the hackney driver halted the carriage at the northernmost corner of Grosvenor Square. Her brother handed her down, and they began to walk the short distance to their home.

The clop of the hackney's lone horse bounced off the houses around the square, but other than the soft song of a nightingale somewhere nearby, there were no distinctive noises. And so, as if to preserve the quiet of the square, they walked in silence until they were but three houses away from the Sinclair residence.

It was then that Grant grasped her arm and prevented her from going any farther. "What are you going to do?"

She raised her palms skyward and shrugged. "I don't know, Grant, I wish I did." Her throat was raw from crying, and she could scarcely force the words into the air. "But I will not marry Tinsdale."

Grant wrinkled his nose. "Well, after tonight, Ivy, I truly don't reckon you'll have to worry about that eventuality . . . at all."

"What of Tinsdale? I saw him talking with you when the carriage passed Almack's. Did he make any threats?" She was sure he must have, for telling her father, and the courts, about her ruse was the only control he had over her. But now she had humiliated him before the *ton*. Her passion for Dominic was undeniable. Grant was right, Tinsdale could never marry her now. But he could, and likely would, try to follow through with his threats.

Not that his threats carried so much weight anymore. He'd sully her name. And her father would surely fling her to the street. But she had earned that eventuality.

"Tinsdale did the talking, but no, he didn't promise to reveal your game. He was, however, quite adamant that I tell him where you had gone—he had no doubt you were with . . . *the actor*." There was an unusual glint in her brother's eyes when he mentioned Dominic.

Ivy stared deeper into Grant's eyes. "You know what Dominic said to me, don't you?"

"If you mean that he is Dominic Sheridan, the Marquess of Counterton, then aye, I do."

At his response, Ivy faced forward and started walking again. For some reason, his knowing Dominic's true identity before she did stung.

Grant lunged and caught up her arm again. "But he admitted nothing more, I promise you. I swear to you, Ives, that I didn't know he was the true Lord Counterton until tonight."

Ivy shot him a doubtful look.

"Well, I might have had my suspicions that he was more than a stage actor, but that is all. He told me tonight."

"Tonight?"

"Gads, he had to give me a damned good reason

to let him into the assembly room you had me guard like a sentry."

At the mention of Almack's, high emotion surged through Ivy again. "I am sorry, Grant. It is only that I don't understand—why didn't he tell me sooner? Why? I was willing to risk everything to protect him from Tinsdale."

"I wish I could tell you." Grant hugged her tight, drew her back, and, bending a bit at his knees, leveled his head with hers. "Listen to Counterton. Let him tell you. He will if you give him the chance. He's a good man, Ivy. He'd never hurt you. I think you know that."

Ivy rubbed her forearm across her damp cheeks. "In truth, I do not know what to think anymore. None of this would have happened if I hadn't been so envious of Miss Feeney. I never loved Tinsdale. I only wanted him back because she had stolen his attentions from me." She gave her brother a weak smile. "Oh, I have made a royal jumble of things, haven't I?"

Tilting his head to the side so she'd have to look at him, he raised his eyebrows and smiled in that upside-down way of his. "As only you could, my dear outrageous sister."

Though her eyes still welled, he forced a wee laugh from her.

"See here, Ivy. You love him. I know you do. And he loves you too," Grant told her. "The rest will sort itself out. I'm always right about these things. Come now, you know I am."

Ivy nodded and turned to face the front door again. "Da is inside, isn't he?"

"I cannot say, but I would expect so." He reached down and squeezed her hand. "Be truthful and candid with him. He may not agree with your actions and decisions, but he will respect your honesty."

"I will." Ivy sucked down a deep breath as Grant opened the door.

She slowly removed her wrap and set it on a hook near the door. Every one of her muscles protested each step into the parlor, where she knew her father would be impatiently waiting.

Fear tightened her chest, making it harder to breathe than wearing an overtight corset. She reminded herself then that it had been her choice to come directly home after she found Grant at Almack's. She could have delayed this inevitable confrontation with her father for a time.

She could have prevented this moment altogether and turned away from Dominic when he appeared on the dance floor. She could have gone to Tinsdale, and let him make the announcement that would have sealed her fate. She could have married the man who sought only to use her family's connections to enhance his own standing with Society, in order to protect the man she loved.

Then, too, she could have remained in the carriage and listened to Dominic's explanation. It was the alarm of hearing that he was the true Lord Counterton that had driven her to leap from a moving vehicle. It was shameful, the lengths she had gone to secure Tinsdale's offer—lying, hurting Miss Feeney, stealing a gentleman's identity with no more than a fleeting thought of how doing so might affect others, including the true Lord Counterton.

It wasn't that she didn't love him. She did.

And it certainly wasn't that she doubted his love for her.

The truth was that it was time at last that she took responsibility for her behavior. It was time to become an adult.

It was time to atone for everything she'd done when driven by envy.

Ivy lifted her head, and, though she shook with fear and dread, she forced herself to put one foot before the other until she was standing before her father.

Alone in the parlor, her father was peering through a quizzing glass at a newspaper. At first, she didn't think he'd heard her come into the room, but then he spoke.

"So, ye've returned." He did not look up at her.

"I have." She glanced sidelong at the settee, but she didn't dare sit though her legs felt weak and in danger of giving out beneath her.

"Weel, what have ye to say for yerself, lass?" He raised his eyes then, letting the quizzing glass fall and dangle upon its chain. He stared at her for what seemed like a lifetime.

It was not as if Ivy hadn't expected this question. In fact, she'd auditioned several curt answers during the short hackney ride from Almack's to Grosvenor Square. It was the coldness of his demeanor that surprised her and stole the words from her head. Had he shouted in anger, a heated response would have been justified. But now it wasn't.

There was no explanation that could remove the slap of humiliation her father surely felt when she left one gentleman waiting alone upon a dais to announce his betrothal to her while she displayed her love for another upon the dance floor.

There was no explanation he'd accept or understand.

Grant was right. All that was required was honesty.

"There are no excuses for my public behavior this

night, Da. I apologize for the distress my actions no doubt caused you." Ivy clasped her hands behind her back and wrung them. "But I am in love with Dominic Sheridan, the Marquess of Counterton. Tonight, he asked me to marry him, which I plan to do if he will still have me."

The duke abruptly lurched forward in his chair, causing Ivy to take a step backward. "What of Tinsdale?"

"I never loved him. I set my cap at him because I knew you would accept him. If I married such a respectable member of Society, you would welcome me, your wayward daughter, back into the family. My fortune would be restored, and life would return to the way it was meant to be for a Sinclair." Ivy lowered her head so her father wouldn't see the shame in her eyes. "I convinced others to do terrible things, take part in potentially illegal acts, all to win Lord Tinsdale away from a woman who wished to marry him." She raised her eyes and met her father's gaze.

He looked startled. "Y-ye're *ashamed*."

"Aye. For possibly the first time in my life, I am ashamed of what I have done—and of the reasons I considered valid to justify my actions."

The old man remained calm, his face devoid of emotion.

"I know after tonight you will wish me gone from this house. I will abide by your wishes. I will be greatly saddened if you never wish to see me again, but I cannot endure living my life without Dominic. I learned that tonight." She walked over and kissed his cheek, as though saying good-bye, then turned for the passage.

"Where are ye going, Ivy?" He jabbed his cane into the carpet and stood.

She turned around. "To my bedchamber to pack a small bag. And then I am going to find Dominic and attempt to make amends for everything I have done. I love him, Da. For the first time in my life, I am in love." She swiveled and began walking toward the stairs.

"Leave the bag," he ordered.

Ivy didn't turn around to face him. It hurt too much. Her father was casting her out without so much as a brush for her hair. She walked for the front door instead, leaving her wrap upon the hook.

She paused at the front door, then looked back over her shoulder, hoping Grant might still be about so she could hug him and bid him good-bye. To her surprise, her father was standing behind her.

He lifted her mantle from the hook. "There's a chill in the air. Take this." There was a curious expression in his eyes as he settled the wrap around her shoulders, and she didn't know what to make of it.

"Thank you, Da."

"After ye've spoken with yer lad, bring him back with ye."

"H-here? To Grosvenor Square?" she stammered.

"Aye. If he wishes to marry ye, I want to talk with him first." He smiled then, something he so rarely did, and Ivy thought she'd topple over.

She hugged her father to her and gave him a tight squeeze. "I will, Da."

Releasing him, she depressed the latch and darted outside, closing the door behind her.

Poplin was waiting on the pavers with the Sinclair town carriage. He let down the steps and opened the door for her. "Lord Grant thought you might need a ride, Lady Ivy."

Ivy grinned. "Indeed I do."

The Counterton residence
Berkeley Square

As the Sinclair carriage approached Lord Counterton's town house, Ivy could see that there was a lone candle burning in one of the windows of the crimson parlor. No other light shone through the windows above, and so she assumed that if

Dominic—Nick was at home, that is where he would be. The carriage began to slow, and so she rapped on the forward wall. She leaned out the window and asked the coachman to take the carriage around the corner before stopping.

The dampness of the night set loose a chill through Ivy. She bundled her mantle tighter around her shoulders and crept up the front steps to the door. She leaned on the wrought-iron rail as she peered into the window. Nick was sitting with his back to her. A bottle was on the table, a folded swatch of paper—her missive she assumed—and an empty glass accompanied it.

He set his elbow on the table then, turning something between his fingers. She leaned closer, and in the haloed candlelight she saw what it was—the emerald ring. Her heart clenched.

She didn't risk lifting the brass knocker. Felix, or worse yet, Cheatlin, might answer and refuse to allow her inside. And so, Ivy tentatively pressed the door handle, and luck was with her. It opened.

Her gait was swift, and if her footfall made a creak on the floorboards, Nick didn't hear it. His head was bowed, and his eyes closed, but she saw the muscles of his throat work, and she knew he wasn't asleep.

Her eyes were wide against the near darkness as she moved stealthily through the parlor until she stood silently at his side. Raising her hand, she touched his hair, meaning to caress his head soothingly with her hands, the way he had comforted her in the carriage earlier that night.

His fingers were around her wrist in an instant, and he was staring at her as though she were his mortal enemy.

"Domin—*Nick*," she gasped, "it's Ivy."

He shot to his feet without releasing her wrist. "Ivy." Her name floated on his breath. "God, Ivy, is it really you?"

As she looked up at him, she saw that his eyes were brilliant and glistening in the candlelight. The distraught tightness of his mouth softened as he peered down upon her face. His lips parted and moved as if he were saying something she could not hear.

"Nick." She slid her hands up over his chest until she wrapped them around his neck and pulled him against her. "I am so sorry . . . for everything I've done. I was confused and surprised, and, aye, more than a little ashamed when I learned who you truly are, that's all." She ran her fingers through his hair, and she pressed her lips to his.

When she broke the pressure of the kiss, he drew back his head and stared at her for several moments before he drew her to the settee with him.

"I should have made clear to you who I was sooner."

"Why didn't you tell me?"

"I tried in the carriage at Drury Lane, but you stopped me then, and when I learned your mission was to hire someone to impersonate me—live in my town house—I decided to go along with your ruse for bit. I wanted to learn the truth of your reasoning for such a plan. I could scarce believe the plan was to win over Tinsdale."

"It was." She lowered her gaze for a moment. "Once you knew, why didn't you stop me?"

"Because I quickly came to enjoy being with such a beautiful and diverting woman." He wedged a finger beneath her chin and made her look at him. "You were like no one I had ever met, nor likely will."

"I can understand that much, but why didn't you tell me who you really were . . . when you realized that you loved me?" Ivy bit into her lower lip, trying to rein in her emotions as she awaited his reply.

He took her hands into his and looked down at them as he spoke. "I was in love once before, but her father required her to marry a man of higher rank. My brother was Counterton's heir, not I. I managed our land. I farmed. I wasn't enough for her father. She died a year later giving birth, but I never stopped wondering that if, had she loved me even a little more, she would have resisted her father's wishes and married me."

Ivy blinked up at him. "I don't really understand."

"Do you not?" Nick exhaled as he gathered up his words. "When we met, you wanted me to help you win back a man your father would approve of you marrying—not a man you loved. Your father's approval meant everything to you."

"It did. I admit it. His approval meant everything—until I fell in love with you." She pulled one hand from his and caressed his cheek. "From that moment forward, the only thing I truly cared about was you, my love."

Nick closed his eyes and let her stroke his face. "I feel foolish that I realized the depth of your feelings too late—and by that time, I had almost lost you because you loved me, because you would have sacrificed your own happiness, your own future, to protect me." He opened his eyes. "I am sorry, Ivy."

"I am too. I have done some appalling things and I only hope that you can forgive me, and that we can be together," Ivy said softly. "I love you, Nick. I do."

"I love you too." Nick breathed a great sigh of

relief, and she felt the rigidness of his back muscles relax. "Lord above, you can't believe how happy I am right now. When you took the ring off—"

"I never did! It slipped off when I pulled my hand away." Ivy nestled herself against the curve of his chest. "I want nothing more than to be your wife, to be with you . . . forever."

Nick bolted from the settee and snatched the emerald ring from the table. He knelt before her and took her hand gently into his. "Marry me, Ivy. Say you will marry me *tomorrow*." He poised the ring over the tip of her finger.

"I will marry you," she said, not able to stop the gentle, delighted laughter that rode her words, "and were it possible, as soon as tomorrow."

He slid the ring over her knuckle and pressed it to the base of her finger. "Tomorrow it is then." Just then a small clock on the mantel pinged the midnight hour. Nick turned and looked at it, silent until twelve bells finished sounding. Then he kissed her. "It's our wedding day, Ivy."

"What?" She blinked at him. He was jesting with her about marrying tomorrow, was he not?

He tipped his head at the table with the candle upon it. "That's a special license from Doctors' Commons. I had it with me tonight, in the carriage."

Ivy's breath seized in her lungs. "S-so that means—"

"We can marry whenever we like."

Ivy grimaced. "Well, not exactly."

Nick gave her a quizzical look.

"I promised my father I would bring you to speak to him first."

"Your f-father?"

Ivy nodded slowly. "A courtesy, Nick. Nothing more. I love you, and no one can stop me from marrying the man I love."

He stood and opened his mouth, but she leaped from the settee and pressed her lips hard against his, stifling any words.

She ignored a brief murmur of protest, easing her hands around his waist and pulling him against her. Her mantle fell to the carpet as his chest, hard and warm through his thin lawn shirt, pressed against her breasts. "It is our wedding day, after all," she whispered.

A low chuckle welled up from inside him. "That it is," he said, as he lifted her and carried her up the stairs to his bedchamber.

Chapter 20

Who at one time has not envied the happiness of a bride on her wedding day or the groom on his wedding night.

Unknown

Feverish with desire, Ivy frantically tugged at the lacing of Nick's lawn shirt and just managed to lift it over his head as he unfastened the last tiny pearl button at her back and pushed her gown into a blue silk puddle on the floor.

Never had she so urgently wanted anything in her life as she wanted Nick at that moment—and it seemed he needed her just as much. He reached behind her and unfastened her corset as Ivy fumbled with the buttons of his front fall. Balance was sacrificed at that moment and they toppled together in a tangle onto the huge tester bed.

Nick rolled beside her, his fingers opening her chemise, inching it downward until she was spilling out of it. He cupped her, and she felt his breath, sweet with brandy, hot on her throat. His thumb flicked over her nipple, then he gently squeezed it, rolling it between his thumb and index finger. She squirmed against him.

Ivy caught his wrist and tried to stop him, tried to pull him on top of her, but he wouldn't allow it. He pinned her hands above her head and lowered his mouth to her other nipple, drawing it between his lips. There was a draw, and something lit through her, racing down through her body, between her legs. "Dominic—"

"Nick."

She bucked against him, but he didn't stop, and his hand moved over every bit of exposed skin, easing over every contour, making her writhe, before finally dipping under the hem of her chemise and centering on the wet cleft between her legs.

Her free hand caught the waist of his trousers and she felt the last remaining button beneath her fingertips. She fumbled with it until at last she was able to edge it through the buttonhole. The front fall opened, and she felt his hard erection spring free against her hand.

Ivy didn't know what to do. She'd heard whispers and stories when in Edinburgh, but hearing was very different from doing, especially when she couldn't see beyond Nick's head and shoulders.

She curled her fingers around his thickness, feeling its heat in her palm. The heat of his hardness seared her hand. She tried to lean up and look at him there, but Nick pressed down harder upon her.

Since she could not see that part of him, she decided to feel every part of his hard manhood and see with her fingertips.

She ran her fingers along the satiny skin of his length until she reached a round-edged ridge. She caged the ridge with her fingertips and slowly moved her hand upward, until she reached a divot in the plum-shaped head.

She ran her thumb around the tip of him, using the same circular motion as he was doing between her legs, before gripping him and running her hand down to his base and skittering over the soft hair covering the tight balls of flesh she found below.

Nick groaned, and that encouraged her to tighten her grasp around his erection and slide her hand up and down him again, faster and faster each time.

He raised his head from her breast, and in the muted moonlight, she saw him squeeze his eyes shut, his breathing becoming pants. She felt the whole of his body tightening, the same way hers was. "Christ, Ivy." His voice was ragged and low.

She released him and fisted her hand in his hair, dragging him back to her lips, needing to feel his hot tongue thrusting inside her mouth.

As their lips met, his fingers dipped into her, as his thumb circled the tiny bud at the joining of her folds, making her more and more sensitive to his caresses everywhere else as well.

Her heart was pounding in her ears and between her legs. Her body jerked, and her breath caught in her throat. She arched her back and raised her hips against him, pinning his hand between them.

"Now. Please, Nick, now," she gasped.

"Not yet."

She tugged at his shoulder, urging him over her. He obliged, but then slid down lower and opened her legs. Her breathing came faster as she waited for him to enter her. But he didn't. He lifted one of her legs over his shoulder, then she felt the smoldering wetness of his tongue on the pink pearl at her core.

God, she hadn't expected this. She felt shamed, but thrilled as he fed upon her most private of places, sucking her, gently flicking her bud while his fingers moved inside her and curled just a bit, caressing a place that made her dizzy with pleasure. She reached down to pull him up again, but she couldn't reach his shoulder and found her fingers running through his hair, pressing his head harder between her legs as she arched against his fingers' thrusts.

Her head was spinning, and her body tensed, but she didn't want it to end this way. She needed to feel him inside her, filling her with his length.

Almost as though he heard her thoughts, he slipped his fingers from inside her and kissed the silken skin of her inner thighs. He lowered her leg and nudged her legs wider, as he knelt between them. Her whole body pulsed with excitement, and gooseflesh swept over her skin.

He leaned over her then, at last, supporting his weight on one hand beside her shoulder, and with the other stroked the head of penis between her wet nether lips. She was writhing against him, needing more, and she dug her heels into the bed and forced herself down, driving his hardness inside of her.

He moaned as the scalding tip of his erection entered her, and he couldn't endure the wait any more than she could.

He thrust into her, burying himself until his body met her damp curls. Pausing, he looked down at her face with passion-glazed eyes and then bent to kiss her mouth. "Christ, Ivy, you are so beautiful . . . so passionate. I love you."

She peered up at him, her eyes welling. "I love you, too."

Slowly, he began to thrust inside her, nearly drawing out completely before pumping into her again. Ivy grasped his broad shoulder and brought her legs higher, feeling him slam deeper inside her. She moved her legs around his trim waist, trying to lock her ankles to allow him to pound into her harder, deeper still.

A sheen of sweat gleamed upon his back, and he groaned as he thrust into her. Heat spiraled at her core, and just when she thought she'd reached the pinnacle of sensation, he pushed one thigh from his side and leaned up, circling his thumb over the bud between her legs. Molten heat suddenly flooded her body, and she arched her hips up against him, driving him hard inside, as she felt her muscles contract around him, grasping him tight.

Nick moaned with pleasure and arched hard into her.

Reaching up, Ivy set her hands on his shoulders and drew him down to her. He kissed her gently and relaxed his body over hers. "I love you, Ivy."

Ivy wove her fingers through his hair and kissed his lips. "I love you, my soon-to-be-husband." She grinned wickedly up at him. "And just think, once we're married we can do this every night—and morning."

Nick laid his head next to hers and laughed. "About that," he began, "do you think it would be acceptable to wait until morning to ask your father for your hand?"

Noon
The Sinclair residence

Before Ivy entered the dining room, she paused in the passage to check her appearance in the large mirror in the entryway. She knew her copper locks were neatly brushed and her rosebud day dress, one of Priscilla's actually, was perfectly respectable and fashionable as well. It was her complexion she fretted over. Her cheeks specifically. For since last night, they'd seemed to be perpetually flushed.

And so they were now. She scowled at her reflection in the silvered glass until she remembered that brides were supposed to be blushing. At that moment, Ivy convinced herself that her pink cheeks were befitting of a young woman about to married to a dashing gentleman, and so she put it out of her mind, and there it remained for the entirety of the quarter minute it took for her to walk from the passage into the dining room, where her brothers and sister awaited.

"Isobel didn't blush until after our wedding night."

Oh dear God. Sterling, her eldest brother, and his new wife Isobel were sitting at the head of the table.

"You know that's not true, Sterling," Isobel said, "Do not mind your brother, Ivy. I admit I blushed every time I thought of him, even before the wedding."

"Thank you, Isobel," Ivy said, circling around the table to embrace her sister-in-law and brother. "I spent too much time in the cool air last eve, and my cheeks are . . . chapped, 'tis all." She set her hands on her hips. "How is it that you two came to be here on such an auspicious day?"

"Da told us nearly a month ago that you'd be getting married this week and that we should be in attendance," Sterling told her. "And he was right, wasn't he?"

"He was, only he didn't get the name of the groom right." Grant winked at Ivy.

"He is a handsome fellow, tall and strong too," Isobel added. "Fits perfectly with the Sinclairs. I am not surprised you accepted him."

What was that? Ivy tilted her head and peered

at Isobel, who was smearing marmalade on her toasted bread. "You've seen him?"

"Oh, yes. He met with your father in the garden early this morning." Isobel looked around and realized that everyone, except her husband, was staring at her. "You were asleep. I, on the other hand, have still not adapted to Sinclair hours, and I shared tea in the garden with the duke and your Lord Counterton shortly after they concluded the interview."

Ivy grasped Isobel's shoulders. "How did they seem? Are you sure Da accepted him, agreed to our marriage?"

"Good heavens, Ivy," Siusan chided. "Allow Isobel to finish her noon meal, she has to nourish two, you know."

"Two?" Priscilla came to her feet. "Do you mean there will be a baby soon?"

Sterling could not help but grin then. "Aye. We wanted to wait until after the wedding to tell everyone—only somehow Su seems to have learned of our news."

Siusan laughed. "No one told me. I simply noticed . . . a slight change in Isobel's slim build. I honestly didn't know for sure, Sterling, until you admitted it."

Ivy was delighted with the news of a baby, but

at this moment she had her own concerns. "Isobel, about Da and Lord Counterton—"

"If ye would like to know about our interview, Ivy, please join me in the parlor." Her father, wearing his dress kilt, stood leaning on his cane in the doorway of the dining room.

"The wedding will be tonight, as you know, in the Counterton rose garden," the Duke of Sinclair told Ivy. "It shall be a private ceremony. Only our family, Counterton's cousin, Mr. Dupré, and his uncle and his wife will be in attendance."

Mr. Dupré is Lord Counterton's cousin? Ivy was flabbergasted. *No wonder there is a resemblance.*

"Poplin and Mrs. Wimpole, of course, since it seems that the Counterton staff . . . is not as well able to handle such a grand occasion."

To say the least, Ivy thought, *but they'd probably do no worse than the Sinclair staff.*

"Da, please, tell me"—she swallowed hard—"do you support my marriage to Lord Counterton?"

He paused for a long moment. "Aye, but likely not for the reasons ye might expect—that his father and I had been acquainted in our youth or that he has a large estate and a title."

"No?" Ivy had forgotten that Nick had once told a story that their fathers were acquainted, but at the time Ivy had believed the notion to be only a fabrication of a gifted actor's lively imagination.

"Nay. I accepted him because he is a good man. He loves ye, and . . . because yer love for him brought about a change in ye I honestly dinna think possible—ye learned the value of putting others and their needs before those of yerself. Ye came to love someone, not for the things he had that would make ye the envy of others, but for the man, the good man, that he is."

"Da, are you saying that . . . I am worthy of the Sinclair name at last?" Ivy held her breath.

"Aye, my dear Ivy. My approval had nothing to do with whom ye married, but who ye became."

Ivy sprang from her chair and wrapped her arms around her father. "Thank you, Da."

The duke smiled at her and summoned one of his footmen forward, who presented him with a leather purse. "Now, ye haven't much time before the wedding. Best collect yer sisters and head off and see if ye canna find something suitable to wear."

The Counterton residence
Berkeley Square

Nick had just arrived home from his interview with the Duke of Sinclair when he entered the parlor to find Felix sitting atop the trunk of clothes that had gone missing for nearly a month. "I don't believe it! After all of this time—my clothing!"

"The trunk might have arrived . . . oh, two or three days after Lady Ivy moved you in here. I can't quite remember," Felix said, shrugging.

Nick narrowed his eyes at his cousin. "Are you telling me that you forgot to mention this to me or that this omission was in fact purposeful?"

"Well, we agreed you needed clothing more appropriate for life in Town—"

"You were alone in that notion, Felix. I only agreed to purchase a suit of clothes because I had nothing else!" Nick stalked forward and pushed Felix off the trunk.

Felix rolled up off the floor. "Well, aren't you glad you have everything now since I haven't time to find something appropriate for your wedding?"

Nick pointed his finger at Felix and had just opened his mouth when the knocker pounded urgently upon the front door. Nick and Felix exchanged glances, and his cousin walked from the parlor and opened the door.

There was a pounding of footsteps and into the parlor strode three magistrates, Mr. Cheatlin, and Lord Tinsdale.

Tinsdale turned to Cheatlin. "Go on, Cheatlin, tell them all about it."

Cheatlin's face contorted with apparent confusion. "I don't know what you mean, my lord."

The magistrates were studying Nick quite keenly.

"How may I help you, good sirs?" Nick asked, though he knew exactly why they had come.

"Tell him about the ruse concocted by Lady Ivy Sinclair and . . . this man—an actor," Tinsdale charged, thrusting his finger at Nick. "He isn't Lord Counterton. He is impersonating the marquess and living in his house!"

"Lord Tinsdale, you have met me many times before," Nick replied, talking very slowly as if to someone addled. "I am Dominic Sheridan, the fifth Marquess of Counterton. Have you forgotten?"

"No!" Tinsdale scowled and turned his gaze toward the magistrates again. "I am telling you, he pulled the wool over everyone's eyes. The real Lord Counterton is up north in Averly, but I will ensure he hears of this!"

It was clear from their puzzled frowns that the magistrates had begun to doubt Tinsdale's story. "Um . . . my lord, just where did you learn that this man is not truly Lord Counterton?"

"I've had my doubts for sometime. Lord Rhys-

Dean, who went to Shrewsbury with the true Dominic Sheridan, did not recognize him when I introduced them. I knew something was afoul at that moment." Tinsdale pinned Cheatlin with an angry gaze. "And then I inquired here, at this very house, and this chap, Mr. Cheatlin, told me all about Lady Ivy and this man's plan to imperson-ate Lord Counterton. Cheatlin even sub-rented the house to Lady Ivy in order to give credence to the claim that this *actor* was truly Lord Counterton."

The largest of the magistrates rolled his eyes, but addressed Cheatlin. "Did you tell Lord Tinsdale about this scheme?"

Cheatlin shrugged again. "I've never even met Lord Tinsdale. I only came to the house just now because I need to finish some carpentry work before the wedding this eve."

Tinsdale's eyes went round. "No, that's not true. I asked him to meet me here to tell you about the impersonation!"

"Lord Tinsdale, why would I pretend to be the Marquess of Counterton?" Nick asked softly. "There must be a reason." He glanced at the mag-istrates and nodded and looked expectantly at the increasingly anxious Tinsdale.

Tinsdale's face reddened. "To assist Lady Ivy in

winning back my affections. Is that not abundantly clear?"

"The same Lady Ivy I am marrying this very night?" Nick chuckled resignedly. "Oh, dear."

"Marrying Lady Ivy? Preposterous! The duke would never hear of it!" Tinsdale raised his chin. "He already accepted my offer for her."

"Did he now?" Nick addressed the magistrates. "Sirs, would you please assist me by removing this man from my home. I have a wedding to prepare for."

"Absolutely, Your Lordship," one of the magistrates replied, while the others took Tinsdale's arms and marched him out the door. "Dreadfully sorry for the inconvenience, my lord."

Felix closed the door behind them.

"Thank God that's over." Nick collapsed into the armchair and ran his hands through his dark hair.

"Timing could have been a bit better, Cheatlin," Felix complained, as he directed the carpenter down the passage. "What if he had waited until this evening and interrupted the wedding?"

"I came when he contacted me. Wouldn't work otherwise, now would it?"

Nick exhaled. He'd had more than enough games

to last a lifetime. All he had to do now was look forward to his wedding.

One week later

The Times

Recollections of the Wedding of the Marquess of Counterton and the Lady Ivy, daughter of the Duke of Sinclair by Mr. Felix Dupré, First Cousin of the Groom.

The moon was bright in the clear night sky, and the garden's lush roses scented the air with fragrance at the hour the wedding of Lady Ivy Sinclair and Dominic Sheridan, Fifth Marquess of Counterton, commenced.

A column of cresset baskets illuminated a glowing pathway for the Duke of Sinclair to lead his daughter to her betrothed and the rector of St. George's, Robert Hodgson (who had already wed three other couples at the church that day alone), was charged with binding them in holy matrimony.

The Ladies Ivy, Siusan, and Priscilla wore simple white gowns from Edinburgh adorned with vibrant green satin ribbons, with pearl and crystal pins in their hair.

The groom's attire, a dark blue coat, white neckcloth, and white kerseymere waistcoat and breeches befitted a gentleman of his elevated position. At his side, his groomsman, Mr. Felix Dupré of Davies Street, was impeccably garbed in a bottle green kerseymere coat, a gold neckcloth with a coordinating gold-shot silk waistcoat, black breeches and slippers. Mr. Dupré has recently accepted the role of Gabriel in the upcoming production of Tales Over Scandalbroth *opening in two weeks at Astley's Theatre.*

The Duke of Sinclair and his sons the Marquess of Blackburn, and Lord Grant, Lord Lachlan, and Lord Killian, in keeping with Scottish tradition, wore the Sinclair clan dress tartan, topped with black woolen coats and accented with sealskin sporrans.

After a visit to Lincolnshire to visit the ancestral mansion, the Marquess and Countess of Counterton will—

"Well, you know the rest—except for *this*: 'We notice the London Society also bereft of the enchanting Miss F.F., who just this week (after a hurried trip to Gretna Green) has returned to Ireland with her new husband, the Duke of O . . .'" Felix said, smiling proudly as he folded the paper and stashed it under his arm.

Ivy's jaw dropped open. "This is all . . . true?"

Felix nodded excitedly. "Absolutely true! Miss Feeney has claimed her happily-ever-after as well. Or so we hope." He grinned. "You know, everyone who is anyone, that is, has commented on my Recollection column. I reckon it's only a matter of days before the editor of the *Times* requests another Society column from me. And at last, for the first time since I began writing my columns nearly a year past, I shall finally be able to share my *on dit* with all of London—without the need to conceal my doings."

Ivy furrowed her brow suddenly. "So you—you have been the source of the regular mentions of the two of us in the *on dit* columns!"

Felix snickered at that. "Well, certainly I was. Had I not used my connection with Nicky here to glean whispers for my columns, others would have begun digging into your lives. Believe me, I squashed a number of reports regarding your escapades. My columns ranked, however, because I admitted from the beginning that Lord Counterton was my cousin."

Ivy studied Felix, watching his face for any sign of deception. But there was none. "Then, Felix, I thank you for your observations, and your protection."

"Allow me to add my thanks. Though I do not agree with your spying and eavesdropping on me, I know you did it out of love," Nick said as he hurried Felix from the carriage. "Good night, cousin. We'll see you next month when we return to London."

"Gads, that's right. When are you leaving for Lincolnshire?" Felix called out from the pavers.

"First thing on the morrow," Ivy called back. "Must away though, we have one more stop to make this evening." She waved to Felix. "Good night, Felix."

Nick closed the door and the carriage rumbled down the road. "We have one more stop to make?"

Ivy nodded. "I thought, since it's been so long, we'd stop at The Theater Royal Drury Lane."

Nick gazed at her through suspicious eyes. "But . . . Felix claimed that the Drury Lane is dark."

Ivy smiled wickedly at him as she drew the shades down over the windows. "So is the carriage, my love."

And now
a sneak peek at
The Duke's Night of Sin
the next captivating title
in The Seven Deadly Sins series
from Kathryn Caskie
Available from Avon Books in 2010

Autumn 1816
Blackwood Hall, outside London

The ancient hall was bustling with excited guests waiting for the introduction of the new Duke of Exeter. It was to be the handsome bachelor's first appearance in London Society since ascending to the title—which, of course brought everyone with a daughter even close to marriageable age to the glittering event.

But the gala, orchestrated by his grandmother to celebrate the occasion, had begun over four long hours ago, and there had been no sighting of the duke—at all.

The novelty of the evening was wearing ever thinner for Lady Siusan Sinclair.

She hadn't wanted to travel eight miles out of the city for another dreary Society gathering. Especially not tonight of all sad nights. In fact, she and her wayward siblings, known within proper Society as the Seven Deadly Sins, had only accepted the invitation for one simple reason—they were willing to try anything to earn back their father's approval. And that was only because the money provided by the Duke of Sinclair was only enough to meet their most basic of needs, and that was dwindling. No further funds were to come until they each changed their wild ways and earned the respect the Sinclair name deserved. Time was fast running out.

And, well, there was an unmarried duke to be had. What quicker way to restore respectability than to marry a duke?

Or so her sister Priscilla offered to her as she called out her claim on the new Duke of Exeter.

Siusan wiped an errant tear from her eye. Tonight marked two years. And despite her brother Grant's good intentions, no amount of whisky while enroute could lessen the sadness in her heart.

The moist heat emanating from the sweating hordes of ladies in pale silk gowns and gentlemen in dark coats thickened the air. It was hard enough for Siusan to breathe in her overtight corset, but the stays were a necessary evil if she was to fit into her sister Priscilla's cerulean gown.

The crush of perspiring bodies was unbearable.

What benefit would a beautiful silk gown be if it became sodden with perspiration? Nay, she had to remove herself from the crowds, even for just a few moments.

She made her way through the ballroom into a grand entry hall. The vaulted ceilings were high, but three small windows were no match for the heat of hundreds. Like the other Sinclairs, Siusan was extraordinarily tall and, by standing on her toes, she was able to see over the shifting sea of guests to a darkened passage just ahead to her left. She made for it, but the crush of humanity was too great. She could not move through the crowd.

Gritting her teeth, she came up with a plan. She called out to her sister, who in actuality was nowhere to be seen. "Priscilla! Priscilla, dear." A quartet of people before her parted to let her through. "I am coming. I see you." She pushed forward. "Please do excuse me. My sister is just *there*. Thank you. Thank you so much." She smiled and edged her hip sideways through the next gathering. She raised her hand into the air. "I am trying, dear. Just another moment." After three minutes of using this ploy to accelerate her forward momentum, she at last reached the passage she sought.

The temperature of the dimly lit passage was somewhat cooler, but her head was spinning from the heat, and what she truly required was an open window.

She hurried to the first door. Glancing around to be certain she was not observed, she pressed down on the latch and peered inside. A finger of moonlight reached between the drawn curtains, allowing just enough light for Siusan to discern an intimate library. She slipped inside and pressed the door with her hip, closing it behind her. She could smell the oiled books on the shelves lining the walls, though she could not quite see them. But for the thin swathe of moonlight coming through a break in the curtains, the room was dark.

She started for the window but within her first three steps, her knee slammed into something hard—a table, desk? She bit into her lower lip to stifle a whimper. Her knee throbbed.

She felt for a place to sit down, her hand finally finding a cushioned sofa. Limping around its arm, she sat down and hoisted her skirt up and pulled the ribbon at her thigh then drew down her stocking to rub her barked knee. It wasn't bleeding, which was a good thing, since this was her last pair of silk stockings, and she hadn't the money to buy another if they were ruined.

Just then, she heard the door open. Her breath seized in her lungs.

Moonlight just barely touched the angular face of a large man. He was hardly two strides away.

Her heart pounded. How respectable would it appear for her to be found in a room not meant for guests? Thankfully, the library was cloaked in night. If she didn't move . . . barely breathed . . . the man mightn't even know she was in the library with him.

But then, his eyes shifted to her, and she saw a smile roll across his lips. She followed his gaze and saw that shaft of moonlight was draped across her bare thigh.

"There you are. I couldn't recall if you said the ante-parlor or the library," he whispered, striding fast toward her. "Suppose I guessed right, eh."

Siusan sat stunned, her mind all a jumble about what to do.

"I apologize for leaving you to wait. Went out for a long ride. I cannot endure the crowds." He came and stood before her, his feet on either side of hers. His hand shot out and one finger slid alongside her jaw, easing her head back against the headrest.

Siusan's heart thudded harder in her chest. Panicking, she opened her mouth to tell him that she was not who he thought her to be, when suddenly his mouth was moving over hers. She shivered as she felt his tongue ease into her mouth and begin stroking her tongue and the insides of her cheeks. The peaty notes of brandy lingered on her tongue, and as she focused on the taste of his mouth, she didn't at first feel his other hand move between her legs and begin to caress her thigh.

When she did, she clamped her legs together. He lifted his mouth a scant breath from hers and exhaled a short laugh. "Come now, it is not as if it is the first time. And I know you like this quite a lot."

Siusan's eyes went wide. How, pray, could he possibly know this? Her mind was spinning. No one else knew. *Only Simon did—but now he's—* Suddenly he was lifting her, and her back brushed the seat of the long sofa. He stood beside her as he unbuttoned his waistcoat, dropping it to the floor. Within an instant, he'd unwound his neckcloth and pulled his lawn shirt over his head.

She peered up at him, his face, the score of his chest muscles, and the rise beneath his breeches clearly defined in the shaft of moonlight. He was so very male. To her own embarrassment, moist heat began to collect between her thighs.

What was she doing? Aye, she was no longer a maid, but no one knew. And it had only been Simon, her betrothed, the man she would have married . . . until two years ago . . . until Waterloo.

He moved from the light, and she felt him part her knees. The cushion beneath her gave, and she felt him move between her legs.

She couldn't see him now, and she knew he couldn't see her as he leaned over her and began kissing her again. She closed her eyes and remembered Simon. How she missed him. How she missed the feel of him.

She could let herself have this. Just one night. No one would know. Even he thought her to be someone else. Just one night of sin. That was all.

She raised a hand and ran it through his thick hair, holding him to her as she responded to his passionate kiss while she stroked his muscled chest.

"Mmm," he moaned, stealing one last kiss. He leaned back slightly and ran his fingertips over her breasts, making her arch into his touch. He moved lower and eased his hands over her belly, then beneath the rumpled skirts about her hips. He pushed up her silk chemise and petticoat to rest with her skirt. His mouth was searing as he kissed the insides of her thighs as he nudged her legs wider.

Siusan closed her eyes. *Oh, God, this is madness,* but she wasn't going to stop him now. His touches and kisses had wound her body so, so tight.

Simon. She would think of Simon.

His mouth centered on the heat between her thighs. He sucked on her core, flicking her, swirling his tongue with all knowing surety.

Simon. Simon. She tried to hold an image of him in her mind. Only, Simon had never done this. Never made her feel this way.

She trembled as his fingers spread her folds then eased inside her, pumping into her, curling up slightly as he circled her womanhood with his masterful tongue. She moaned and twisted as heat spiraled tighter and tighter inside of her.

Her legs began to quiver uncontrollably. An urgency grew within her, one that she knew only a man could quell.

With both hands, she grasped his head and turned it up toward hers. When his head turned to face her, she leaned down and caught his arms, dragging him back up to her.

In the darkness, she heard him laugh softly, and he moved and rose to kneel between her legs. She extended her arm until her hand felt his breeches stretched tight over his erection. She inched the fingers of both hands now, searching and finally finding the buttons to his front fall. Against the strain of fabric, she fumbled to release the buttons.

His hands came down over hers, then moved them aside to release each button himself. At once the front fall came down, and she felt the heavy weight of his cock bounce down against her before rising again.

She grasped its long thickness and skimmed her fingertips up its shaft to its plump head the way Simon had once shown her. A bit of moisture pearled at the tip.

The sound of the crowd in the ballroom swelled, and she felt his body twist. He was looking toward the door.

Nay, we've not gone this far only to stop now. Siusan pumped her hand once more, then set his plum-shaped tip against the entrance to her wetness.

He groaned aloud and arched his body over hers, poised to take her.

Her anticipation was so great, she could scarcely catch her breath, but when the musk scent of him filled her senses, her yearning grew ever more intense.

She thrilled at the sensation of his hot, muscled body between her thighs. She needed to feel him inside her. Needed to feed a hunger like no other she'd felt.

He eased his hardness into her moist folds, brushing past that place he'd made so sensitive with his skilled tongue. She shivered and brought her legs up and nearly around him.

In a low voice, he swore beneath his breath and then all at once, he grasped her wrists and held them on either side of her head as he thrust into her sheath. She gasped. Unbidden, her muscles gripped him, and she arched up, driving him deeper inside.

He slammed harder into her, filling her, almost to the point that she could not bear it. But not quite. His fully aroused penis stroking her so forcefully created a mutiny of sensation, pushing her to the edge of sanity.

A whimper of carnal pleasure slipped from her mouth, drawing his attention. He kissed her again, hard at first, then slower and more gently, all the while pressing into her again and again, making her even wetter.

She gasped against his mouth, then again and again. He thrust into her harder and faster, until her muscles spasmed with an intensity she'd never known, overwhelming every inch of her with ecstasy.

With his last stroke, he swore again and tried to pull back, but her legs held him in place. Too long. His body suddenly arched and jerked into hers until the weight of his body collapsed atop hers. A sheen of perspiration broke over his back.

Panting, he rested upon her. "I'm sorry. I tried—but you've never done that before. Christ, I've always been able to stop." He pushed up finally and came to his feet, busying himself with dressing.

Siusan slid to the corner of the sofa, her fingers scrabbling for the ribbon to her stocking. In the black of the room, she couldn't find it anywhere. So, instead, she rolled the top of her stocking to hold it in place, then, with a yank, she returned her skirts to her ankles. She sat still then, keeping to the darkness, until she could make her escape.

He bent to retrieve what Siusan took to be his waistcoat. This was her moment. As quietly as she could, she rose from the sofa, slipped around behind it, and started for the door.

"Wait." His hand curled around her wrist. "I would be remiss if I allowed you to forget this." There was a clink of coins as he pressed a small leather bag into her palm.

She couldn't help herself. Siusan turned, her face catching the moonlight as she looked down at the bag, torn between her dire need of the money and feeling like she would have sold herself if she took it.

He released her wrist, and his hand dropped to his side. "You are not . . . Clarissa."

"Nay, I am not." *Christ, I should not have said anything!* She dropped the bag on the floor, and when he instinctively bent to retrieve it, she opened the door and ran down the passage, chancing a hunted glance over her shoulder.

He stepped from the library just at the moment she reached the perimeter of the crowd. Suddenly the masses surged forward, and she disappeared into the swell.

She heard the bang of the liveried footman's staff on the floor. "All hail, His Grace, the Duke of Exeter!"

RULES OF ENGAGEMENT

Rules . . . are made to be broken.

This fall, meet four ladies—who won't let a few wagging tongues stand in the way of happiness—and the handsome gents who are willing to help them break with convention.

Turn the page for a sneak preview at delicious new romances from Laura Lee Guhrke, Kathryn Caskie, and Anna Campbell, and a gorgeous repackaged classic from Rachel Gibson.

Coming September 2009

WITH SEDUCTION IN MIND

A Girl-Bachelor novel by
New York Times **Bestselling Author**
LAURA LEE GUHRKE

Infamous author Sebastian Grant, Earl of Avermore, has seen better days. His latest play opened
to crippling reviews, his next novel is years over-
due, and, to top it off, his editor assigned feisty,
fire-haired beauty Daisy Merrick as his writing
partner (never mind she's the critic who thrashed
his play)! And yet, as frustration turns to desire,
it seems the one place Sebastian can find relief is
in the beguiling Daisy's arms . . .

Sebastian rolled down his cuffs and fastened
them with his cuff links, then gave a tug to
the hem of his slate-blue waistcoat, raked his
fingers through his hair to put the unruly strands
in some sort of order, and smoothed his dark blue
necktie. He went down to the drawing room and
paused beside the open doorway.

Miss Merrick's appearance, he noted as he took
a peek around the doorjamb, was much the same
as before. The same sort of plain, starched white
shirtwaist, paired with a green skirt this time. Ribbons of darker green accented her collar and straw
boater. She was seated at one end of the long yellow

sofa, her hands resting on her thighs. Her fingers drummed against her knees and her toes tapped the floor in an agitated fashion, as if she was nervous. At her feet was a leather dispatch case.

He eyed the dispatch case, appalled. What if Harry wanted him to read her novel and give an endorsement? His publisher did have a perverse sense of humor. It would be just like Harry to pretend he was publishing the girl and blackmail Sebastian into reading eight hundred pages of bad prose before telling him it was all a joke. Or—and this was an even more nauseating possibility— she might actually be good, Harry did intend to publish her book, and they truly did want his endorsement.

Either way, he wasn't interested. Striving not to appear as grim as he felt, Sebastian pasted on a smile and entered the drawing room. "Miss Merrick, this is an unexpected pleasure."

She rose from the sofa as he crossed the room to greet her, and in response to his bow, she gave a curtsy. "Lord Avermore."

He glanced at the clock on the mantel, noting it was a quarter to five. Regardless of the fact that it was inappropriate for her to call upon a bachelor unchaperoned, the proper thing for any gentleman to do in these circumstances was to offer her tea. Sebastian's sense of civility, however, did not extend that far. "My butler tells me you have come at Lord Marlowe's request?"

"Yes. The viscount left London today for Torquay. He intends to spend the summer there with his family. Before he departed, however, he asked me to call upon you on his behalf regarding a matter of business."

So it was a request for an endorsement. "An author and his sternest critic meeting at the request of their mutual publisher to discuss business?" he murmured, keeping his smile in place even as he wondered how best to make the words "not a chance in hell" sound civil. "What an extraordinary notion."

"It is a bit unorthodox," she agreed.

He leaned closer to her, adopting a confidential, author-to-author sort of manner. "That's Marlowe all over. He's always been a bit eccentric. Perhaps he's gone off his onion at last."

"Lord Avermore, I know my review injured your feelings—"

"Your review and the seven others that came after it," he interrupted pleasantly. "They closed the play, you know."

"I heard that, yes." She bit her lip. "I'm sorry."

He shrugged as if the loss of at least ten thousand pounds was a thing of no consequence whatsoever. "It's quite all right, petal. I only contemplated hurling myself in front of a train once, before I came to my senses." He paused, but he couldn't resist adding, "Hauling you to Victoria Station, on the other hand, still holds a certain appeal, I must confess."

She gave a sigh, looking unhappy. As well she should. "I can appreciate that you are upset, but—"

"My dear girl, I am not in the least upset," he felt compelled to assure her. "I was being flippant. In all truth, I feel quite all right. You see, I have followed your advice."

"My advice?"

"Yes. I have chosen to be open-minded, to take your review in the proper spirit, and learn from your critique." He spread his hands, palms up in a gesture of goodwill. "After all," he added genially, "of what use to a writer is mere praise?"

She didn't seem to perceive the sarcasm. "Oh," she breathed and pressed one palm to her chest with a little laugh, "I am so relieved to hear you say that. When the viscount told me why he wanted me to come see you, I was concerned you would resent the situation, but your words give me hope that we will be able to work together in an amicable fashion."

Uneasiness flickered inside him. "Work together?" he echoed, his brows drawing together in bewilderment, though he forced himself to keep smiling.

"Yes. You see . . ." She paused, and her smile faded to a serious expression. She took a deep breath, as if readying herself to impart a difficult piece of news. "Lord Marlowe has employed me to assist you."

Sebastian's uneasiness deepened into dread as he stared into her upturned face, a face that shone with sincerity. He realized this was not one of Harry's jokes. He wanted to look away, but it was rather like watching a railway accident happen. One couldn't look away. "Assist me with what, in heaven's name?"

"With your work." She bent and grasped the handle of her dispatch case, and as she straightened, she met his astonishment with a rueful look. "I am here to help you write your next book."

Coming October 2009

THE MOST WICKED OF SINS

A Seven Deadly Sins novel by
USA Today **Bestselling Author**
KATHRYN CASKIE

Lady Ivy Sinclair is used to getting her way. So when an Irish beauty steals the attention of the earl Ivy had claimed, she hatches a devious plan: distract the chit with an irresistible actor hired to impersonate a marquess. But can Ivy resist Dominic Sheridan's sinful allure, or will she fall victim to her own scheming?

D amn it all, answer me!" A deep voice cut into her consciousness, rousing her from the cocoon of darkness blanketing her. She could feel herself being lifted, and then someone shouting something about finding a physician.

She managed to flutter her lids open just as she felt her back skim the seat cushion inside the carriage.

Blinking, she peered up at the dark silhouette of a large man leaning over her.

"Oh, thank God, you are awake. I thought I killed you when I coshed your head with the door." He leaned back then, just enough that a flicker of light touched his visage.

Ivy gasped at the sight of him.

He shoved his bronze hair away from eyes that

looked almost black in the dimness. A cleft marked the center of his chin, and his angular jaw was defined by a dark sprinkling of stubble. His full lips parted in a relieved smile.

There was a distinct fluttering in Ivy's middle.

It was *him*. The perfect man . . . for the position.

"It's *you*," she whispered softly.

"I apologize, miss, but I didn't hear what you said." He leaned toward her. "Is there something more I can do to assist you?"

Ivy nodded and feebly beckoned him forward. He moved fully back inside the cab and sat next to her as she lay across the bench.

She gestured for him to come closer still.

It was wicked, what she was about to do, but she had to be sure. She had to know he was the right man. And there was only one way to truly know.

He turned his head so that his ear was just above her mouth. "Yes?"

"I assure you that I am quite well, sir," she whispered into his ear, "but there is indeed something you can do for me."

She didn't wait for him to respond. Ivy shoved her fingers through his thick hair and turned his face to her. Peering deeply into his eyes, she pressed her mouth to his, startling him. She immediately felt his fingers curl firmly around her wrist, and yet he didn't pull away.

Instead his lips moved over hers, making her yield to his own kiss. His mouth was warm and tasted faintly of brandy, and his lips parted slightly as he masterfully claimed her with his kiss.

Her heart pounded and her sudden breathlessness blocked out the sounds of carriages, whinnying horses, and theater patrons calling to their drivers on the street.

His tongue slid slowly along her top lip, somehow making her feel impossible things lower down. Then he nipped at her throbbing bottom lip, before urging her mouth wider and exploring the soft flesh inside with his probing tongue.

Hesitantly, she moved her tongue forward until it slid along his. At the moment their tongues touched, a soft groan welled up from the back of his throat and a surge of excitement shot through her.

Already she felt the tug of surrender. Of wanting to give herself over to the passion he somehow tapped within her.

And then—as if he knew what he made her feel, made her want—he suddenly pulled back from her.

She peered up at him through drowsy eyes.

"I fear, my lady, that you mistake me for someone else," he said, not looking the least bit disappointed or astounded by what she had done.

"No," Ivy replied, "no mistake." She wriggled, pulling herself to sit upright. "You are exactly who I thought you were." She straightened her back and looked quite earnestly into his eyes. "You are the Marquess of Counterton . . . or rather you will be, if you accept my offer."

Coming November 2009

CAPTIVE OF SIN

**An eagerly anticipated new novel by
ANNA CAMPBELL**

Returning home to Cornwall after unspeakable
tragedy, Sir Gideon Trevithick stumbles upon a
defiant beauty in danger and vows to protect
her—whatever the cost. Little does he know the
waif is Lady Charis Weston, England's wealthi-
est heiress, and that to save her he must marry
her himself! But can Charis accept a marriage of
convenience, especially to a man who ignites her
heart with a single touch?

C haris' eyes fastened on Sir Gideon, who waited
outside. A cloud covered the moon, and the
striking face became a mixture of shadows
and light. Still beautiful but sinister.

She shivered. "Who are you?" she whispered,
subsiding onto her seat.

"Who are you?" His dark gaze didn't waver from
her as he resumed his place opposite, his back to the
horses, as a gentleman would.

Charis wrapped the coat around her against the
sharp early-morning chill and settled her injured
arm more comfortably. "I asked first."

It was a childish response, and she knew he

recognized it as such from the twitch of his firm mouth. Like the rest of his face, his mouth was perfect. Sharply cut upper lip indicating character and integrity. A fuller lower lip indicating . . .

Something stirred and smoldered in her belly as she stared at him in the electric silence. What a time to realize she'd never before been alone with a man who wasn't a relative. The moment seemed dangerous in a way that had nothing to do with her quest to escape Felix and Hubert.

"My name is Gideon Trevithick." He paused as if expecting a response but the name meant nothing to her. "Of Penrhyn in Cornwall."

"Is that a famous house?" Perhaps that explained his watchful reaction.

Another wry smile. "No. That's two questions. My turn."

She stiffened although she should have expected this. And long before now.

"I'm tired." It was true, although a good meal and Akash's skills meant she didn't feel nearly as low as she had.

"It's a long journey to Portsmouth. Surely you can stay awake a few moments to entertain your fellow traveler."

She sighed. Her deceit made her sick with self-loathing. But what could she do? If she told the truth, he'd hand her over to the nearest magistrate.

"I've told you my name and where I live. I've told you the disaster that befell me today. I seek my aunt in Portsmouth." Her uninjured hand fiddled at the sling and betrayed her nervousness. With a shuddering breath, she pressed her palm flat on her lap. "We're chance-met travelers. What else can you need to know?" She knew she sounded churlish, but she hated telling lies.

In the uncertain light, his face was a gorgeous mask. She had no idea if he believed her or not. He paused as if winnowing her answers, then spoke in a somber voice. "I need to know why you're so frightened."

"The footpads . . ."

He made a slashing gesture with his gloved hand, silencing her. "If you truly had been set upon by thieves, you wouldn't have hidden in the stable. Won't you trust me, Sarah?" His soft request vibrated deep in her bones, and for one yearning moment, she almost told him the truth. Before she remembered what was at stake.

"I . . . I have trusted you," she said huskily. She swallowed nervously. His use of her Christian name, even a false one, established a new intimacy. It made her lies more heinous.

Disappointment shadowed his face as he sat back against the worn leather. "I can't help you if I don't know what trouble you flee."

"You are helping me." Charis blinked back the mist that appeared in front of her eyes. He deserved better return for his generosity than deceit.

She tried to tell herself he was a man, and, for that reason alone, she couldn't trust him. The insistence rang hollow. Her father had been a good man. Everything told her Sir Gideon Trevithick was a good man too.

She forced a stronger tone. "It's my turn for a question."

He folded his arms across his powerful chest and surveyed her from under lowered black brows. "Ask away."

TRUE CONFESSIONS

The classic novel by
***New York Times* Bestselling Author**
RACHEL GIBSON

Tabloid reporter Hope Spencer is in a rut. But when she flees her same-old LA life for the respite of Gospel, Idaho—she gets oh-so-much more than she bargained for. Sticking out like a sore thumb in her silver Porsche and designer duds, Hope isn't looking for any entanglements. But when a years-old murder mystery throws her together with Gospel's sexy sheriff Dylan Taber—she might not want to avoid this snag in her plan.

W hat in the hell is that?"
Dylan glanced across the top of the Chevy at Lewis, then turned his attention to the silver sports car driving toward him.

"He must have taken a wrong turn before he hit Sun Valley," Lewis guessed. "Must be lost."

In Gospel, where the color of a man's neck favored the color red and where pickup trucks and power rigs ruled the roads, a Porsche was about as inconspicuous as a gay rights parade marching toward the pearly gates.

"If he's lost, someone will tell him," Dylan said as

he shoved his hand into his pants pocket once more and found his keys. "Sooner or later," he added. In the resort town of Sun Valley, a Porsche wasn't that rare a sight, but in the wilderness area, it was damn unusual. A lot of the roads in Gospel weren't even paved. And some of those that weren't had potholes the size of basketballs. If that little car took a wrong turn, it was bound to lose an oil pan or an axle.

The car rolled slowly past, its tinted windows concealing whoever was inside. Dylan dropped his gaze to the iridescent vanity license plate with the seven blue letters spelling out MZBHAVN. If that wasn't bad enough, splashed across the top of the plate like a neon kick-me sign was the word "California" painted in red. Dylan hoped like hell the car pulled an illegal U and headed right back out of town.

Instead, the Porsche pulled into a space in front of the Blazer and the engine died. The driver's door swung open. One turquoise silver-toed Tony Lama hit the pavement and a slender bare arm reached out to grasp the top of the doorframe. Glimmers of light caught on a thin gold watch wrapped around a slim wrist. Then MZBHAVN stood, looking for all the world like she was stepping out of one of those women's glamour magazines that gave beauty tips.

"Holy shit," Lewis uttered.

Like her watch, sunlight shimmered like gold in her straight blond hair. From a side part, her glossy hair fell to her shoulders without so much as one unruly wave or curl. The ends so blunt they might have been cut with a carpenter's level. A pair of black cat's-eye sunglasses covered her eyes, but couldn't conceal the arch of her blond brows or her smooth, creamy complexion.

The car door shut, and Dylan watched MZBHAVN walk toward him. There was absolutely no over-looking those full lips. Her dewy red mouth drew his attenion like a bee to the brightest flower in the garden, and he wondered if she'd had fat injected into her lips.

The last time Dylan had seen his son's mother, Julie, she'd had that done, and her lips had just sort of lain there on her face when she talked. Real spooky.

Even if he hadn't seen the woman's California plates, and if she were dressed in a potato sack, he'd know she was big-city. It was all in the way she moved, straight forward, with purpose, and in a hurry. Big-city women were always in such a hurry. She looked like she belonged strolling down Rodeo Drive instead of in the Idaho wilderness. A stretchy white tank top covered the full curves of her breasts and a pair of equally tight jeans bonded to her like she was a seal-a-meal.

"Excuse me," she said as she came to stand by the hood of the Blazer. "I was hoping you might be able to help me." Her voice was as smooth as the rest of her, but impatient as hell.

"Are you lost, ma'am?" Lewis asked.

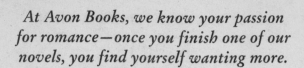